C000242636

SPANISH HOUSE SECRETS

Enjoy reading!
Susan Gray

Susan Gray

First published in Great Britain as a softback original in 2023

Copyright © Susan Gray

The moral right of this author has been asserted.

All characters and events in this publication, other than those
clearly in the public domain, are fictitious and any resemblance
to real persons, living or dead, is purely coincidental.

All rights reserved.

No part of this publication may be reproduced, stored in a retrieval system,
or transmitted, in any form or by any means, without the prior permission in
writing of the publisher, nor be otherwise circulated in any form of binding or
cover other than that in which it is published and without a similar condition
including this condition being imposed on the subsequent purchaser.

Editing, design, typesetting and publishing by UK Book Publishing

www.ukbookpublishing.com

ISBN: 978-1-915338-87-7

SPANISH HOUSE SECRETS

To Agnes, who loved her Spanish House.

CHAPTER 1

LOFTAM

ENGLAND 2019

GRACE

Grace sat in the newly finished Summer House. The warmth of the late September sun radiating through her old bones. This will be my sanctuary, my escape room, she thought – a place where I can relax and let all the cares of life drift away. A place where I can remember, reflect, recall, and relive...what? My life of course...my experiences...my discoveries. The Summer House – doesn't it sound grand – was a replacement for a tumbledown, rotting old shed which had long since passed its usefulness. It contained old garden equipment, unused plant pots and other broken items, all discarded and stored away. Isn't that a bit like life? Grace mused... experiences, discoveries –discarded and stored away in case they became useful again one day?

Suddenly, she heard the faintest bars of a melody, a tune drifting through an open window. It awakened a memory. I know that tune, Grace thought, it's 'Fur Elise' by Beethoven. She had not heard it in years, but immediately she was transported back to her piano practice days when she was a girl. Grace was not particularly musically minded, but her parents desired for her to be a pianist of sorts – to be able to play a tune when they entertained guests or 'company' as the guests were usually called. 'Fur Elise' was one of her party pieces...one of the few she could play from memory. Piano tuition proved a long-drawn-out process, but she managed to scrape through the required exams to achieve a set of certificates, which ended up being stored in the piano stool with the broken hinge. I wish I still owned a piano, she thought – a casualty of downsizing. I wonder how far I could get with that melody now, she asked herself, and started to finger the opening notes on the glass coffee table.

She really should get up and sort some lunch but the warmth of the sun and the comfort of hearing that melody again rendered her immobile. The Summer House – now that awakened another memory. There was a summerhouse before...yes, when she'd been a child. Not a modern structure like this one. It was hidden away at the top of the garden in the house her parents bought when she was five years old. It was a wooden structure with a door and three windows – real glass then, not this Plexiglas stuff. It was a magical place for a child...one day it was a house, to play at being a grown up...another day a shop, serving imaginary customers...sometimes a hospital caring for sick dolls or teddies. I wonder what its purpose was when it was built?

CHAPTER 1

Another memory filters in... yes, the hiding place! One day a coin dropped out of her cash machine and rolled into a corner. Trying to retrieve it ...the coin lodged in a gap in a floorboard. She pushed the board and it loosened. It was a short piece, sawn off then replaced. Her coin dropped down into an empty space... but something else was hidden there... a small, dusty, wooden box! Grace smiled... I thought I'd found treasure that day! I wonder who it belonged to and why was it hidden?

***

LOFTAM

ENGLAND 1921

SIMON

Simon was making his way downstairs when he heard the familiar notes rising-up the stairway 'Fur Elise'... was it the only tune in his sister's repertoire? It was obviously easy to learn – not that he would know, piano playing was not his forte. He recalled his father's rationale... 'Piano playing is for girls,' he declared. 'A trumpet, boy, you must learn to play the trumpet.' So, Simon did, but really it was not the most convenient instrument to play – you needed a band or an orchestra to perform with. As he walked into the drawing room his sister was in full flow.

"Can't you play any other tunes, sis?" he teased. "It's a bit repetitive." But tall, slim Serena was lost in her music

3

and his comments fell on deaf ears. His two siblings were both academically gifted and received plaudits from the family all the time. He was not without brains, far from it, but he was not a pianist like Serena or a bookworm and academic like William ... he was just loveable, likeable Simon, full of mystery with a glint in his eye. He loved the girls – no one in particular – but his mother called him a 'ladies' man'. His father said it would be his downfall, but he just laughed it off. Life was for living and Simon was determined to live it. At twenty years old his life was ahead of him – he wanted to travel... see the world... have some fun, that was his philosophy. Now things were settling down after the Great War, he might soon be able to do that.

Simon 'slipped into' the family firm after leaving school. It was not expected that he would go to university – he was needed in the firm. Sadly, some staff did not return after the war, so he ended up in charge of men's clothing.

"I know nothing about men's clothing," he howled at his father, on his first day.

"You're a man and you wear clothes –don't you?" his father replied.

So, one week after leaving boarding school, Simon became an expert in men's tailoring. He smiled a lot, talked a lot, and charmed a lot, and loveable, likeable Simon made it work... and sales boomed. He learned how to measure waists, necks, inside legs, arms and shoulders, record lots of numbers, give interesting comments on styles and fabrics – and became an overnight success. Sales in Guilder's Men's Outfitters went from strength to strength, and Simon, who was always a snappy dresser, soon gained his father's approval as he patted him on the back and sang his praises.

But after three years in men's tailoring, Simon was bored... very bored. His ambition was to travel... but it was a dream, how would he finance himself? However, the answer to that question came in the form of some unexpected news and it gave Simon a way out of becoming 'The Golden Boy of Guilder's'...

***

LOFTAM

ENGLAND 1926

OLIVIA

Olivia sat, brushing her golden, wavy hair. Each stroke seemed to brighten the sheen that glowed in the sunlight. This was part of her daily routine. Almost thirty now, but she was maturing into a beautiful woman. Nature had been kind to her – she had inherited the best of the physical traits from both her parents and could carry herself with charm and poise into whatever social setting she was called upon to attend. Her eyes caught the reflection behind her – a large double bed draped with a bedspread and eiderdown in a deep pink shade. The room was bright and benefited from two windows – one tall and thin with metal frames in a zig zag pattern – so clear, chic, and modern. The other window was wide and overlooked the rear garden. Her home – a Spanish House, in the north of England.

"It's a place we can raise a family, Livvy," her husband remarked when he showed her the plans. "It's not too big – we'll only need a daily to come in and do what's what – people don't have live-in staff anymore."

It was such a contrast to the family home she knew. It was a novel idea to only have two bedrooms. She had been raised in a large Victorian house in York with three floors, an attic, and a basement. Her parents employed a cook and a housekeeper, but her home was happy – a place of security. Now she was a homemaker herself – a modern homemaker. She was going to be the perfect wife – entertaining in their modest but totally unique house... if only she could be sure of her husband's love. Twice a year, he travelled abroad on business, leaving her on her own. He showered her with love and attention, and she was head over heels in love with him, but in the shadows, the dark recesses of her mind there was always a nagging doubt. No – she was being ridiculous.

'I will not be an overwrought wife,' she declared to herself. She walked over to the deep pink bed, pulled back the eiderdown and bedspread, and slid into the crisp, cool sheets to spend another night in her lonely bed.

***

CHAPTER 1

MADRID

SPAIN 1921

ELISE

Elise was sitting in a side ward in a hospital in Madrid. She hated the antiseptic smell and the groaning, clanking sounds. She was holding her aunt's hand. She looked so peaceful, lying in the hospital bed... but she was unconscious. Her other arm was in a plaster and there were superficial cuts and scratches on her usually flawless face. Eugenie was a beautiful woman. Elise was not sure of her exact age, but she guessed she would be in her early forties. She looked up at the clock – its persistent tick was another annoying sound invading her ears. It was nearly midnight. The staff had allowed her to stay – they were unsure if Eugenie would survive the night – they suspected internal injuries and a clot on the brain. Oh, thought Elise, how did a visit that began so normally... turn into this nightmare?

It had been the usual rush to leave the house yesterday morning...gosh was it only yesterday, she thought. Eugenie always forgot something at the last minute, and they only just caught the ten o'clock train and in less than an hour they were in Madrid. The trip to Madrid was a regular event. Every month Eugenie attended business meetings and Elise travelled into the city with her and spent the day shopping. Eugenie always stayed overnight in her hotel apartment, but Elise travelled back to their home in Toledo late in the afternoon.

'You go and enjoy yourself, Elise,' she would say, 'buy yourself a treat and have some lunch, while I attend my laborious meetings. I'll be home tomorrow afternoon,' the older woman insisted.

However, Eugenie failed to return home the following afternoon, so Elise ate alone. She tried to stay calm, convincing herself there would be a perfectly simple explanation for her aunt's delay. Eugenie was not a blood relative. She was an aunt through marriage – her uncle's wife. Uncle Juan was her guardian but had died two years ago – a victim of the Spanish flu. Elise loved Eugenie – she'd been like a mother to her, since her own parents died many years ago.

The clock continued to tick, and Eugenie did not move. Elise replayed the events that had brought her to this hospital. The Guardia Civil officer had knocked on the door in the early evening. An accident had occurred – a train derailment on Eugenie's afternoon train back to Toledo. There were many injured and some fatalities. As her 'next of kin' Elise was taken by car to the hospital. How can I be her 'next of kin'? Elise wondered. Surely, she has other relatives. But no-one else came to the hospital so she sat... and waited... and kept vigil in the long hours of the night at her aunt's bedside.

CHAPTER 2

1921

LOFTAM ENGLAND

SIMON

I t was a bright, cool morning in late September. Simon closed the front door of his home The Gables and headed off down the hill to the family Firm – Guilder's Men's Outfitters. As usual he walked from the leafy outskirts of the small market town in the north of England. It took him about thirty minutes, but he enjoyed that time of the day. Simon had lived all his twenty, soon to be twenty-one, years in Loftam. His brother and sister were much older than him, and his parents Robert and Gertie were 'getting on a bit' to put it kindly. He was a 'late baby'. Simon smiled to himself remembering the day he had heard his mother refer to him in that way. He was a young boy at the time and when he entered the drawing room his mother, a rather buxom lady, was entertaining some friends. 'This is my youngest son Simon,' she said introducing him, with pride. 'He was my late baby, but he's brought me great joy.' Simon pondered this phrase wondering what it meant, until a few days later when he was out walking with his older sister Serena. She asked him to hurry up and not trail behind.

He replied, "It's alright, I can be slow, because Mother said I was a late baby."

Serena burst out laughing, hugged her young brother and ruffled his dark hair. "Oh, don't be silly, Simon, she only meant you were born when she was older." She took him by the hand and explained to him ladies usually stopped having babies when they reached their forties, but he was born when their mother was nearly forty-five, so was referred to as a 'late baby'.

Simon did a calculation. His mother must be in her mid-sixties now. This week, Simon would turn twenty-one. His coming of age – whatever that was supposed to mean. The age you grow up and start acting like a man, his father would probably say. Well, plenty of time for that. Life tended to go on as normal at The Gables. His father's business kept them in a comfortable style of living – the only one Simon knew. When others struggled during the war years, things hardly changed for the Guilder family. In fact, the only real changes Simon observed when he came home from boarding school were the shrinking staff. As a youngster he remembered several staff bobbing around the house doing all sorts of no doubt essential tasks, but now there was only Mildred, a delightful lady –almost part of the family. She did not live on the premises. but attended to all the household chores and prepared the evening meal – or dinner, as

Mother insisted on calling it. When Mother hosted her dinner parties Mildred would do extra hours and her niece would help to wait on the table – to give the right impression...it was always to give the right impression.

It was a happy home and Simon loved returning during his boarding school vacations – some of his friends at school dreaded the holidays. Simon was fortunate. His family doted on him... well, apart from William. He was down the hill now. Loftam was starting to wake up to a new day. He was on the last stretch – through the park, past the bandstand and out onto the High Street. Yes, his home was a happy place, but he could recall one holiday, when he detected a strange atmosphere in the house. On that occasion, Serena, who was his anchor, disappeared to stay with an aged aunt in the country. He had no idea this aunt existed – she was probably a second cousin, twice removed sort of an aunt. Serena was a big miss that holiday – she always fussed over him. At the same time, his brother William was in a foul mood. William the 'know it all' was a pompous sort of chap, the sort everyone looked up to. He was clever and being years and years older than Simon, or so it seemed to a young boy, he was the one who must be obeyed. 'Fetch this, fetch that, do this, do that' was about all the conversation he recalled having with his big brother most of his life. Simon shook his head at his remembrances... that holiday William was even more aloof, sullen, and distant. Next holiday, Serena was back home, so normal times returned.

Well, here he was –Guilder's Men's Outfitters – a double-fronted, quite imposing shop in a commanding position on the High Street. He opened the door and disappeared into the back shop to prepare for the new working day.

***

That evening he walked home at a much slower pace than the one he had adopted in the early morning. He removed his coat and hat and popped into the drawing room to say hello to his mother. "Has it been a good day?" his mother would always ask, and he would answer he'd spoken to Mr So-and-So and they were asking after her. It was the kind of town where most people knew the family, so there was always a snippet or two of town news to be shared. His mother, a matronly soul with her grey hair styled in a bun at the base of her neck, was reclining in front of a cosy coal fire. She looked up at him as he gave her a peck on the cheek.

"Dinner will be at seven o'clock," she announced. It was usually the same time each evening, so he could never understand why she made a specific announcement. Mildred would leave the food keeping warm when she left at half past six. However, tonight Mother continued, "William, Emily, and Felix are coming for dinner tomorrow night. A special occasion to celebrate, Simon... it's your coming of age – so please try to be hospitable towards them, you know how it pleases me to see all the family together," she pleaded with him.

"Of course, Mother," he replied, in his usual nonchalant tone.

"Do you have any other plans to celebrate?" she continued.

"Yes, my dear mother, I'm going to go into town, get very drunk and have my wicked way with a gorgeous girl," he teased.

"Simon Guilder, don't you dare," she retaliated, trying to sound outraged.

Oh dear, thought Simon as he left the room and climbed the stairs two at a time – an evening of brotherly cheer to look forward to...not his idea of a special birthday treat.

The relationship between the two brothers was frosty to say the least. In fact, they didn't really know each other – there was a twelve-year age gap between them. Yes, they were raised in the same house, but William attended university after boarding school. He married Emily the year before war broke out. After his war service, spent in this country, behind a desk, apparently due to some ankle injury, he returned to work as a solicitor practising in the city, about fifteen miles from Loftam. Emily was from a good family, and being an only child, she inherited the family house when her parents died, along with considerable savings. So, William landed on his feet, so to speak.

Their son, Felix, was five years old now. Simon loved his nephew, and they enjoyed building models together. Gertie absolutely adored her only grandchild and gave an endless commentary about him showing potential for this or that. Serena also made a fuss over Felix, she loved children – strange, Simon mused... I wonder why Serena has never married. She was ten years his senior – a plain woman, with pale skin who was always adorned in drab colours. Her hair was worn in a severe bun, but she was good fun and loved a laugh. I guess it was something to do with all the eligible young men dying in the war – but sometimes he observed a sadness in Serena and these days she was the one who ran the household as Mother's memory was not what it used to be. He was shaken from his reverie by his sister's voice.

"Simon, you didn't pick up your post," she called upstairs.

"What's that, sis?" he asked, leaning over the banister rail.

"You must have walked right past it," she admonished him. Quite frankly, Simon didn't bother to look on the silver letter tray on the hall table. He rarely received post, but Serena always made a big thing about writing and receiving letters – 'you have to write them to receive them' she used to say. Simon did not write letters.

"Coming," he shouted and sauntered down the stairs to find a large cream-coloured envelope addressed to him lying on the tray. I bet that's raised Serena's eyebrows every time she's passed the hall table today, smiled Simon, pocketing it and dodging a questioning Serena coming out of the kitchen. He was going in search of something to satisfy his hunger pangs, as he calculated it was about an hour to go until dinner.

"Good evening, Master Simon," said Mildred, their daily help, "you'll be looking for some fruit I guess."

"Yes... any chance of those delectable cookies you made yesterday, dear Mildred?" he asked.

"Go on," she beamed, opening the tin, "there's enough of them to satisfy your appetite!"

"Thank you, dear Mildred," he cooed, placing a kiss on her cheek. He helped himself to a couple of biscuits and some fruit and left the kitchen, almost bumping into a hovering Serena standing outside the kitchen door. Bet she wishes she could see through paper, grinned Simon as he turned to run up the stairs two at a time, to his bedroom.

Back in the privacy of his room he stared at the envelope – no clues except it was typewritten and firmly sealed. He sat in the chair by the window and put on the lamp. Carefully he opened the envelope and took out a sheet of stiff writing paper headed *Hodgson, Smith and White Solicitors*, Grey Street, Newcastle upon Tyne. His curiosity was bubbling inside of him, and he quickly scanned the contents. He was being informed that Mr Frederick Hodgson of the above establishment was in possession of *'some facts of a delicate nature'* to bring to his attention. He had taken the liberty of making an appointment for Mr Simon Guilder to attend his office on Friday morning at 10 am. Should this be inconvenient, he needed to contact his secretary on the above telephone number to rearrange a more suitable time.

Simon let out a long, low whistle then ate his apple. Well, well... he thought to himself, this is a surprise – what can it be about? He mused on the words *'some facts of a delicate nature'* – that could mean anything. Strange how you always thought the worst receiving a summons such as this, but he truly was perplexed. He'd never heard of *Hodgson, Smith and White*, but then all the firm's business affairs were conducted by a solicitor in Loftam. He knew it was not the firm that William worked for –

they were called *Archibald, Simpson and Jones*. William was not named yet – probably still too young.

Now, Simon considered, rubbing his chin, and dusting down the cookie crumbs, do I or do I not divulge the contents of this letter to Mother and Father? Or do I leave it until after the appointment – when I might have more information? Perhaps it was something he would not want to share – no, better to keep it quiet for now- especially with the professional conflict there might be with William. What about Serena? – they were so close, and she was already curious about the letter. No, thought Simon, I'll keep it to myself for now and palm Serena off with something I am sure I can dream up.

Dinner that evening was a normal affair, and he couldn't wait for it to come to an end. He was hoping to avoid Father tonight as he had an inkling he might want to have a little 'man to man' talk, with this important birthday looming tomorrow. Father never really talked to him about 'life matters', but Serena was always on hand to tell him things and the ones she failed to mention were well and truly discussed in the school dormitory – so he doubted his father could add much to his twenty-one-year-old son's life knowledge.

However, his father started droning on about some tradesperson asking far too much for a consignment of cloth.

"I need to have your opinion, Simon, first thing in the morning in my office, I'll give you a call when I'm free."

Simon nodded and then realised he would have to clear his way for this appointment on Friday morning. Perhaps he would mention it to Father, after the cloth discussion tomorrow, that way he would not have to fabricate an excuse. Now, he thought, rising from the table – how to keep out of Serena's way?

As it happened, it wasn't too hard to achieve. After dinner, they sat in the drawing room, drinking their tea. Serena was giving a recital – thankfully, not 'Fur Elise' tonight, thought Simon. She was an excellent pianist, and it really was not a chore to listen to her playing; also, it avoided any kind of conversation. Suddenly, Mother made a strange noise. Robert dashed over to where she was sitting beside the fire. She was having one of her 'turns'. Serena was flapping about with the smelling salts, and it was decided to get her to bed. Unfortunately, she did not respond, so Robert telephoned the doctor who arrived about an hour later. He gave her some medicine and said she needed bed rest. So, Simon retired early, his mind racing with all kinds of thoughts about his mother's health and his appointment with the solicitor.

When he arrived at the store the next morning – he made a telephone call to *Hodgson, Smith and White* confirming his attendance for the Friday appointment. At half past nine, Gwen, Robert's secretary, informed him his father would see him now. Simon shook his head at the formality of it all. He climbed the stairs in the centre of the shop, turned right along the mezzanine level and knocked on the frosted glass, half-panel door, labelled 'Manager Mr Robert Guilder'.

"Hello, Father," said Simon.

Robert moved around the side of his desk and greeted his youngest son with a strong handshake.

"Simon, dear boy," he declared in his deep voice. "Congratulations on your twenty-first birthday, take a seat... I'll be with you in a few moments."

Simon sat and looked around the office. This room had remained unchanged for as long as Simon could remember. He recalled visiting the store with his mother as a young boy. Climbing the grand staircase and entering Father's office was a daunting experience, with dark wooden fixtures towering above his small frame. All the staff used to make a fuss over him – an older man, long since retired, kept a tin of black bullets under the counter. He produced the tin and with a twinkle in his eye said, "Now, young master, a special treat for you today." Then offered him a sticky sweet, which he seemed to suck for ages. Sometimes he would come to the store with Serena, and they would wait until he heard the squeak of the door at the end of the balcony and his father would emerge tall and erect, smartly dressed and neatly groomed. He would survey both sides of the shop floor from his elevated position, before reaching into his buttoned waistcoat and pulling out his pocket watch on a chain, he would check the time and say, "Come," in a commanding voice. Then with a wave of his hand, they were beckoned into the office –the same office in which Simon now sat.

The office was cluttered, to say the least. The desk filled most of the room but around the walls were large, dark wood cupboards, filled with ledgers kept in an orderly fashion by his faithful secretary Gwen. I guess if I asked what sort of suit Mr Smith ordered ten years ago, she could produce a ledger and find the entry. Simon sighed, inwardly – was this what life held for him? Was this how to run a successful business?

There was a large arched window overlooking the rear of the premises and on the walls some framed artists' impressions of various styles of men's suits. The room was light and airy due to the size of the window. One of the windowpanes was open – a quirk of his father's – fresh air whatever the temperature – and today it was cool. A small fireplace was just visible beneath a mantel shelf, littered with carved wooden animals. He smiled at how scary those animals had seemed to him all those years ago, but they soon become a distraction in ensuing years, when he could play with them while the grown-ups talked.

"Now, my boy," boomed his father, pulling Simon from his reminiscences. "About this matter I referred to last evening." He then proceeded to 'discuss', although to Simon he just outlined the decision he'd already made. Simon doubted if it would have made any difference to the decision if he'd interjected with a suggestion. Fifteen minutes later, the 'discussion' concluded, signalled by his father consulting that same pocket watch.

"So that's agreed then, we'll proceed as discussed," he said, rising to his feet.

Simon had almost reached the door, when he remembered his appointment on Friday morning. His father listened intently, while Simon gave an account of the letter he had received the previous day.

"Which solicitor?" his father inquired.

Simon told him and Robert Guilder stroked his beard. For just a second, Simon thought he detected a look of panic in his father's eyes – or did he just imagine it?

19

"Yes, yes… you must keep the appointment. Mr Thorn can attend to your duties for the morning. I expect you will be back for the store opening in the afternoon." With that Simon was dismissed and he made his way downstairs to the shop floor.

After Simon left the office, Robert Guilder sat down heavily on his chair. He stared into the blotter on his large green leather-topped desk. Oh dear, he thought, something must have happened …this was too soon, far too soon – surely another ten or even twenty years yet. I should not have been alive to witness this summons. Suddenly, he felt the desire to be outside the office walls. I'm an old man, he thought, ready to retire –why can't I live out my days in peace?

He got up and went over to the coat stand, put on his hat and coat, picked up his walking cane and left the office. As he descended the stairs, he looked around to locate Simon, who was finishing an order in the ledger. Simon looked up and was surprised to see his father dressed for outside so soon after he had left him – he was unaware of any outside business his father needed to fulfil that morning. Robert caught Simon's eye, as he paused at the bottom of the staircase – Simon hurried over to him.

He looked pale and concerned as he spoke quietly. "Don't mention what you told me earlier to your mother, Simon," he intimated, then he opened the shop door. The clang of the bell sounded as he stepped out onto the High Street – a fine figure of a man for all his sixty-one years.

***

Serena was feeling weary. Mother was most definitely not well. Her 'turn' last evening was not like any she'd experienced before. She was trying to put the finishing touches to Simon's birthday cake but could not concentrate. She was expecting the doctor to call on his morning rounds later. Mildred was making some tea.

"Come and have a cuppa, Serena. Your mother will pull through. Shame she's going to miss Master Simon's birthday meal. Do you want me to take her a cup of tea?"

"No," replied Serena, "I'll take it after I've finished mine; she didn't drink the one I took up at breakfast time."

Serena took her cup and went to sit in the morning room, next door to the kitchen. She loved this little room... it was comfortable with a cosy fire, not too big, all that was needed during the day. The coal fire in the drawing room was not lit until after lunch, so this was the warm spot in a morning. She glanced out of the window into the back garden – this was a lovely house. They were blessed with a garden front and back. Most houses in the town had a yard and outhouses at the back. The Gables was a house of character. The kitchen, morning room, drawing room and dining room all radiated off a large hallway, with stairs leading to two floors of bedrooms and a large bathroom. Bill, the handyman, tended to the garden throughout the spring through to autumn. They were always neat and tidy, but he was quite slow and arthritic these days.

Her mind drifted back to her mother. She knew she was five years older than her father and always struck a matronly figure next to his more youthful one. Gertie was in her thirties when she married Robert, and William and Serena soon completed their family, until Simon arrived unexpectedly.

The front door knocker sounded, and Serena jumped up, almost spilling her tea. "That will be the doctor," she called through to Mildred and went to answer the door.

Dr Morton had been the family doctor for about fifteen years now and was familiar with Gertie Guilder's 'turns'. They usually passed after a few days in bed and a further few days resting with her feet up and a blanket over her knees, downstairs. But, after examining his patient that morning he indicated to Serena he needed a word before departing. They stepped into the cold drawing room.

"I think your mother is much worse this time, Serena," he said with a grave look on his face. "I must speak to your father as soon as possible. I will need to carry out some tests."

Serena felt herself starting to shake and grabbed the back of the chair to steady herself.

"Oh dear, I'll get him to call you... he'll be in at lunchtime," she replied, turning to look at the grandfather clock that stood in the hallway, just visible through the open door of the drawing room.

"Please do," smiled the doctor. "Try not to worry, my dear," he said, patting her arm. "I'll see myself out." With that he was gone.

Serena climbed the carpeted stairs to the large first-floor bedroom, which her parents occupied. She entered. It was decorated in heavy shades of green and brown. Gertie lay in the bed, her long, grey hair parted and plaited by Serena earlier that morning. She went over to her and kissed her wrinkled, paper-thin brow. Gertie opened her eyes and smiled weakly at her daughter... there was a faraway look in her eyes. A realisation things were not normal suddenly hit Serena. What will we do without her? She questioned herself. Her mind started racing, thinking of all the basic adjustments to their daily lives that would be needed if mother's illness were to be prolonged. She heard the front door open and realised it was her father home for lunch – he seemed early today. She went downstairs to give him the doctor's message.

***

When Robert Guilder had left the High Street two hours earlier, he walked over to the park. He found a bench near to the bandstand and sat down. Loftam...his home for most of his life. He was born in Newcastle, but as a young man he spotted a business opportunity in this market town...men's tailoring. He was in his mid-twenties and with some help from his parents, he acquired a small shop off the High Street. Late Victorian Britain and the gentlemen had an eye for dressing smartly in this up-and-coming market town fifteen miles from the city. The railway link was good, but soon he was so busy he needed to hire a room, so he could stay over during the week and return to his parents' home in the city, at a weekend.

The widow, in whose house he rented a room, was an amiable lady called Mrs Green. She had one daughter a few years older than Robert. He soon discovered that Gertrude Green possessed a great sense of humour and a bubbly personality. A year later, Gertrude and the lodger were betrothed. Around the same time some premises became vacant on the High Street and having by now gained a good reputation, Robert moved from his side street shop to become the proprietor of a High Street store and so Guilder's Men's Outfitters was launched.

Robert and Gertie continued to live with her mother after their marriage, but after baby William was born, they decided to look for their own home. So, with a healthy business, a lot of encouragement and financial help from Robert's parents and Gertie's mother, they became the proud owners of a three-storeyed house – The Gables, in a residential area of the town.

Robert sighed as he thought back to those heady days – lots of hard work, but with a loving and supportive wife they had raised their two children – Serena was born when William was two years old. They took their place in the Loftam social scene. Gertie was a born leader and seemed to know just who they needed to befriend...and he trusted her judgement implicitly.

A tear came to his eye, and he blinked it away. I think I will walk up the hill in time for lunch, he thought. He knew he would be early, but he just needed to clear his head and could not face returning to his office yet. As he walked, he rehearsed the possibilities of Simon's looming appointment, but he knew deep down in his heart... the time had come for Simon to know the truth about his parents.

***

Later that afternoon Robert spoke to Dr Morton, who told him the news he was dreading... Gertie, his rock, was dying. He would carry out some tests, but it would only be a matter of time. There was nothing to be done, other than to make her final weeks, or months, as comfortable as possible. Considering this news, Simon's twenty-first birthday was a very subdued event. William, his wife Emily, and son Felix came for dinner – a lovely meal was served with a birthday cake to follow – but without Gertie's presence the proceedings seemed dull.

CHAPTER 3

1921

On Friday morning, Simon left home early. He took a crowded, early morning train into the city and arrived with plenty of time to spare. He reflected on the news the family had received... it was a devastating blow. His father had not returned to the office the other day after leaving so suddenly. Serena had telephoned the store to say Dr Morton needed their father to speak with him and would Simon make sure that all the day's business was finalised before he returned home. Later that evening, after dinner, his father asked Emily to keep Felix busy while he went into the drawing room with his three children. The news from the doctor was grim. Gertie had been ill, unknown to the family, for some weeks. Her condition was terminal, and the best prognosis was three to six months.

The prospect of watching his mother die without there being any treatment, seemed so cruel to Simon. It was the closest he'd come to facing death. All his grandparents were dead before he was born and although he'd been a teenager during the war, death did not come calling at their door. Relatives of friends had died, but no-one close. Robert was an only child and Gertie's brother had died in infancy. Robert and Gertie's cousins were not close enough for Simon to recall. After hearing the news, they took turns to visit Mother in her bedroom – she grabbed Simon's hand and wished him a 'happy birthday'... he fought hard to hold back the tears.

Simon checked the time, on his new watch – a present from his parents. He knew that whatever 'the delicate nature' of this appointment turned out to be... it would go on hold, until after the inevitable happened. Five minutes before the appointment time Simon found himself standing at the door of *Hodgson, Smith and White Solicitors*. A feeling of trepidation started to descend. He gave an audible sigh and went inside.

He was shown into a room, not dissimilar to his father's office. He sat at a desk opposite an elderly, bespectacled Mr Hodgson. For a moment, he felt like a naughty schoolboy, waiting to hear his punishment. Mr Hodgson looked stern and sorted the papers in front of him then gave a little cough.

The next thirty minutes changed Simon Guilder's life. When he had entered that office, he was a confident young man, on the threshold of a life with modest prospects. When he departed that office, he was not only uncertain of his identity, but in possession of an unexpected means, whereby he was to become a very wealthy young man.

As he made his way back to the station, he went into a tearoom to have some much-needed refreshment. After placing his order, he removed his hat and coat. He stared at the tablecloth and tried to digest and mentally absorb what the elderly Mr Hodgson relayed to him. Apparently, his mother – that was his biological mother – had met with an untimely death as a victim of a rail accident. She was a passenger on a train, which had collided with a goods train. She had survived the accident, but never regained consciousness and died from internal injuries three months later. Simon remembered staring at the old man in total disbelief as he shuffled his papers and added, "That would be three weeks ago, Mr Guilder. Senora Dominguez died the first week in September."

The solicitor added that he, Mr Simon Guilder, as her only son, was the main beneficiary in this lady's will. A substantial legacy was left in trust, until he attained twenty-one years of age. The solicitor coughed at this point, consulted his papers again then looked directly at Simon saying, "As you have just attained that age, you are being informed in person, Mr Guilder."

Mr Hodgson then informed Simon he possessed no further details of this matter, other than to say a firm of solicitors in Madrid, Spain would be handling the estate of this lady. He was then given the address of the solicitor in Madrid, along with a letter of verification from *Hodgson, Smith and White,* to vouch for his identity. The matter was now in Simon's hands; Mr Hodgson was to have no further role to play, having fulfilled his small obligations. He advised Simon to contact this firm in Spain promptly and suggested he visited Madrid in person, after making initial contact by letter.

Simon drank his tea and ate his scone, more like a robot than a human. His mother was not his mother. He was just getting his head round the fact that his mother was dying, but now he'd learned she was not his mother after all – not biologically anyway. That raised another question – who was his father? No-one in the family had ever given the faintest hint, that he was anyone other than Robert and Gertie Guilder's son. Yes, he knew there was a gap in the ages of himself and his siblings, but he always accepted that he was a 'late baby' for his loving parents. His mind continued to unravel facts – so, that meant that William and Serena were not his brother and sister, not blood relatives anyway. That explains, mused Simon, why William and I are so different.

But then there was this other fact – a legacy, and not just a legacy, but a substantial legacy...oh dear, this was all too much for Simon to take in. Also, there was the location – Madrid. What did all this have to do with the capital of Spain? He finished his refreshments, settled his tab and checking his watch realised the lunchtime train back to Loftam was due in ten minutes. He grabbed his coat and hat and hurried to the station.

As he departed the station in Loftam and made his way to the High Street, he came to a decision. This information was private. He would share it with no-one, except his father, but in the light of recent events, he would leave it to his father to see if he approached him. His father's distress at the news of his mother's – no, Gertie's – impending death, was all too apparent and Simon doubted if his father would raise the subject, at the present time. No, thought Simon, as he opened the door of Guilder's Men's Outfitter's – I must put this revelation to the back of my mind, for the foreseeable future. However, he knew he must contact this address in Madrid and acknowledge receipt of the information, begging their understanding, regarding the delay, in making his personal visit to their establishment.

***

FOUR MONTHS LATER
FEBRUARY 1922

Olivia glanced across the carriage at her grandmother. She was a sprightly woman for nearly seventy. They were travelling north from York to a market town called Loftam. They would change trains in Newcastle. Their journey would take about two hours, but they should arrive with plenty of time to find a tearoom, to have a bite of lunch, before going to the church.

Her grandmother had asked Olivia at the weekend, if she would accompany her to an old friend's funeral. Olivia knew that her grandmother and Gertie were close friends years ago and had kept up a regular correspondence after Jane, her grandmother, moved to Yorkshire. She was not aware that they had met in recent years, but the shock of hearing about her death was enough to urge Jane into action –she wanted to attend her friend's funeral but needed a companion to help her. Olivia was only too willing to oblige – two days away from her part-time position at the local library was not too difficult to arrange.

So, here they were travelling north through pleasant scenery on this cold but bright February morning. They only needed a small overnight bag each, as they were invited to stay the night, at Gertie's home after the funeral. They were to be the guests of Mr Robert Guilder and his family.

As if reading her mind, her grandmother spoke while staring out of the carriage window. "Gertie's daughter Serena said it would be no trouble to accommodate us. They don't have many relatives – she doubted if any would make the journey, so that means there is a guest room for us – if you don't mind sharing with your old grandmother." She smiled and went back to her former reverie.

Of course, Olivia did not mind – she really didn't think of her grandmother as being old. She lived with them in the family home on the outskirts of York. The house was large enough for Olivia and her parents, especially since her brother Fred moved out, when he had married a few years ago. They all got along amiably. She had vague memories of her grandfather and guessed Jane must have come to live with them soon after his death.

"Did Gertie have any other children besides Serena?" Olivia asked, realising she needed to acquaint herself with a few facts, before accepting this family's kind hospitality.

"Oh, yes...two sons," Jane replied. "One a few years older than Serena, the other is much younger."

**

31

Simon finished dressing and descended the stairs to the drawing room. The family were all present plus the minister and some friends of his parents, who until recently were regular attendees at his mother's dinner parties. Everyone was dressed in black with mournful expressions on their faces to match. This was Simon's first funeral experience, and he really did not know what to expect. Serena gave him a brief outline of what would happen, so he would stay close to her... in case he did something wrong.

Sadness had pervaded the atmosphere in the Guilder household over the last few months. Gertie, as he now referred to her in his own mind, was a model patient – or so Serena said. She became weaker by the day and eventually seemed to sleep most of the time. Each evening, when he came back from the firm, Simon went to sit with her – to give Serena a bit of a break.

At first, he chatted away to her, telling her bits and pieces of town news, then he used to read to her, but soon her drugged state rendered that unnecessary, so he just held her hand and rambled on about anything. He was not sure she heard much of what he said but he felt he 'did his bit'.

Christmas and New Year came and went. William, Emily, and Felix stayed over for a few days to spend as much time as possible as a family. The weeks passed by without any major incident, until last Sunday morning when his father tapped on his bedroom door. Simon knew what he would say as soon as he came in.

"Mother passed away peacefully during the night, Simon. I have already telephoned William – he will be arriving later. Please offer to help him with the arrangements."

So, his 'mother' was dead. He'd loved her and now she was no longer here. A gaping hole was left in his life.

Three hours later they were back at The Gables. The service and the burial proved sombre. Gertie was a 'big' Methodist all her life and attended church regularly, until the last few months. Looking back, Simon realised she'd gradually gone 'downhill', but at the time he was unaware of anything different. Simon hoped he did not have to attend another funeral in a hurry – it wasn't a pleasant experience.

He went through to the kitchen, as he was feeling peckish. Mildred and her niece were bustling around, preparing a buffet lunch for the guests but Simon was promptly shown the door, as he tried to help himself to some of the delicious food. "You'll have to wait like everyone else," chided Mildred with a grin.

So, he left the kitchen and went into the drawing room to make polite conversation with people he didn't know. Apparently, they were to have two guests staying overnight – an old friend of Gertie's from Yorkshire and her granddaughter.

***

Olivia often wondered how it would be to meet 'the man of her dreams'. She was such a romantic and loved to read novels and poetry – probably the reason why she became a librarian's assistant – such was her love for literature. It was not expected for a young lady of Olivia's social standing to earn her own living, but since the Great War and the liberty of women, things were really changing. She didn't go seeking for a position – the position found her. She spent most of her free time in an afternoon in the city library in York. She loved books – their feel, their smell, their ability to transport you to another world. One day about a year ago, she had been in the library sitting reading, when she noticed a commotion taking place near the librarian's desk. One of the librarians, an older lady, whom she'd conversed with on several occasions, was taken ill.

She went over to see if she could be of assistance and was asked if she could put a pile of newly returned books back on the shelves. She obliged and the next day when she arrived at the library, she was approached by the senior librarian who asked if she would consider helping while the other lady was indisposed. She responded positively and six weeks later she was offered a paid, part-time position, as the former librarian was unable to return to her duties. She loved her role. It combined her love of literature with the luxury of earning her own money. The money was not really needed, as she received an allowance from her father, but she decided it would be good to build up her own little pot of savings, for the future. She enjoyed being fashionable, and it was good to be able to treat herself now and again without feeling guilty.

She often reflected, in the many novels she'd read, how two would-be lovers caught each other's eye across a crowded room, or a dinner table. But for Olivia, it was across an open grave. Hardly a romantic setting. She did not recall their eyes meeting either. But she noticed him. He was tall, slim, dark haired – neat hair, small moustache – very handsome. A dapper young man and she was smitten instantly. She did not know who he was, but she suspected he was a close relative of the deceased, because of his position to the open grave. She held the advantage of being able to gaze at him without anyone noticing. She took in the details of his appearance – very smartly dressed and yes, an air of boyishness about him, yet he was a man, an attractive man – in his early twenties she guessed. During the fifteen minutes, while the interment took place, on that bitterly cold, but sunny February day – Olivia knew she'd met her Mr Right.

Olivia and Jane were offered transport back to The Gables by Serena, who came over to them in the cemetery. Once in the house they were shown to their room by a lovely lady called Emily.

"Are you related to the family?" asked Jane.

"Yes," replied Emily, "I'm William's wife, Emily."

She pointed out the bathroom and explained refreshments would be served in the dining room shortly. Afterwards, Olivia accompanied her grandmother into the cosy drawing room. It was a comfortable, welcoming house. She soon made the acquaintance of Serena. She was a thoughtful hostess and made her guests feel at home in no time. Olivia took in the surroundings – not lavish but good quality furnishings, a roaring fire adding to the welcoming atmosphere. The widower, Robert, made a point of welcoming them. He'd met Jane before, many years ago, and talked fondly of his departed wife.

It was quite some time, or so it seemed to Olivia, before she was properly introduced to the handsome young man she had spied at the graveside. She felt her heart fluttering as he came over to where she was sitting beside her grandmother. "Hello," he announced, introducing himself, "I'm Simon." His voice was manly, not boyish. His eyes lit up as he spoke. "You must be Mother's friend Jane from Yorkshire – and who have we here?" he asked, looking directly into Olivia's eyes.

Jane smiled. "This is my granddaughter Olivia – she has travelled with me as my companion."

Simon bent over and shook hands with both. "Thank you so much for making the journey on such a cold day. We do appreciate it. I gather you are staying over tonight, so I'll see you later," he added, then moved on to converse with other guests.

"What a charming young man," noted Jane.

Later that evening, after the other guests had departed, the Guilder family, Jane and Olivia enjoyed a splendid meal in the dining room. The conversation over the meal was cordial – Jane took delight in relaying her friendship with Gertie, how they had met in the chapel choir and remained firm friends when her family moved to Yorkshire, because of her father's work. They corresponded regularly and attended each other's weddings. After the meal, they enjoyed a cup of tea around the fire in the drawing room and Jane asked Gertie's sons about their occupations.

"Oh," she commented, "it's so good to put faces to names after all these years. Gertie often used to tell me about the pranks you got up to when you were young, Simon."

Simon raised his eyebrows and gave a playful grin. "Did she, indeed. All good, I hope."

Olivia smiled... She found this young man delightful.

At the end of the evening Olivia and her grandmother retired to the guest room – quite exhausted from the day's events. As she slid between the sheets in the comfortable bed, and listened to her grandmother's snores, Olivia felt alive and awake. Somewhere in this house lay a young man who seemed to have stolen her heart, but how could she ever befriend him? Tomorrow she would leave this house and their paths would probably never cross again. She lay awake for what seemed like hours, then she drifted into a lovely sleep... dreaming of Simon Guilder.

***

As he lay down to sleep Simon went through the events of the funeral day. It was all a bit of a haze. Yes, he was there physically, but mentally he was miles away. He remembered the heart wrenching moment when the coffin was lowered into the ground...the finality of it all was so poignant. Then returning to the house having to make small talk with the many guests who attended the 'do'. Thankfully, his ability to converse easily, helped. Most people he recognised by sight. Robert and Gertie were well known in Loftam, and the service was well attended, but the number returning to the house was select. He mentally scanned the guests in the drawing room and came to an abrupt halt in front of a charming young lady – she was the one bright light in an otherwise doleful day. His mind lingered on that moment when he had looked directly into her eyes as he introduced himself. She intrigued him. Mmm... he thought, worth a second look. Then he turned over and went to sleep.

The next morning, without warning, it descended – the realisation that today he could put off no longer what he knew he must do. It was early, so he sat on the edge of the bed and started to think. Since that morning in early October, when he had visited the solicitor's office in Newcastle, he knew this day would dawn. He looked back on that day as his 'bombshell'. He'd been suffering a kind of 'shell shock' ever since. He'd heard of many men who had returned from the Front, after the war with 'shell shock'. He was not trivialising the dreadful state of health many men were still suffering, but in his very sheltered life this was Simon's form of 'shell shock'.

Coupled with the events of Mother's illness he found himself putting his life into 'boxes'. Box one was his home life and all the changes that ensued. Box two was his work life, which became more demanding as his father was often missing, spending time at home with his dying wife. Simon was being thrust into management whether he wanted it or not. But box number three... was the unknown future. He rarely investigated this box, having decided that day in October to keep the matter private. He sent a letter of acknowledgement to the address in Madrid, along with an explanation of why he would be detained for the foreseeable future. A prompt reply returned, which he somehow managed to intercept before Serena or his father could catch sight of it. The letter explained there was no hurry for him to visit – it would be several months before the properties and the financial investments could be assessed. So, if he were able to make contact in person in about six months, details should be clearer.

By Simon's reckoning six months would be up in April – two months away. Oh, dear the enormity of it all hit him afresh. Where to begin? He was clueless at this point, having shelved any decisions until after Mother's death. He went over to his desk and pulled out the letter from Madrid. He'd read it many times before, but he reread it. It referred to the estate of Senora Eugenie Cristina Dominguez –deceased. This lady – his real mother... sounded very foreign, Spanish he guessed. He felt ignorant and bewildered – who could blame him? The furthest he'd ever travelled was to London with his father, not long before he started working at the firm, during his final holiday from school. The idea of travelling didn't bother him... in fact it excited him. He read further down the letter and was impacted by the phrase 'properties and financial investments' – this was mind-blowing. It was obviously more than just a few hundred pounds.

The previous afternoon, after most of the guests departed from the funeral 'do', the local solicitor, a family friend, remained. Father called William, Serena, Simon, Emily, and Mildred to accompany him into the dining room. There then followed the reading of the last will and testament of Gertrude Guilder. Simon was bemused. He'd never given any thought to his 'mother' having left anything – he assumed what was his mother's, was his father's, and vice versa. But apparently, Gertie possessed a savings account of her own – an inheritance from her mother and she wanted it to go to her three children in equal amounts. There was a small monetary gift for Mildred. Serena and Emily were to receive named jewellery items.

Apart from his modest remuneration from the firm, which was more than adequate, Simon never gave much thought to finance. Oh, he really must grow up and quickly. He'd been left money in two wills now. His little bank account would be bulging! Apparently, the bequests from Mrs Guilder would be available within a few days and the solicitor would await instruction from each benefactor, where to deposit the specified amounts. With that the local solicitor, who was also a client of Guilder's Men's Outfitters, took his leave and the family returned to the drawing room to entertain their two guests.

Simon dressed and breakfasted alone. He wanted to get an early start at the firm to make up for yesterday's closure. He was just putting on his coat and hat when Jane and her granddaughter descended the stairs. Robert appeared from the drawing room and greeted the guests.

"Good morning," Simon acknowledged them. "I trust you both slept well. Please excuse my early departure. I hope you have a safe journey," he added by way of explanation. "Thanks again for taking the trouble to travel from Yorkshire." He shook hands with both. For the briefest of moments, when he shook Olivia's hand and looked into her eyes, he experienced a fluttering sensation.

"I hope we will have the opportunity to meet again," he added, more by way of departure than anything else. Robert followed Simon to the door.

"I'll be in the office for a couple of hours later. I need to speak with you, Simon."

Simon nodded and was soon on his way. As he made his regular trek down the hill that February morning, his mind drifted to the young lady whose hand he had shaken... he knew Jane's granddaughter was someone he wanted to meet again.

Three hours later Simon received another bombshell. His morning was busy. He was aware of his father's arrival at the store – Robert's attendance at the office had been spasmodic over the last few weeks, but Simon guessed he would be returning in his full capacity as manager, very shortly. I guess he will be scrutinising my part in the handling of the last few weeks, he told himself. Personally, he thought he'd done a decent job, mainly down to the efficiency of Gwen – who was an accomplished secretary to his father and knew the business side of things inside out. She'd taken over the role from her father, a few years ago, and was making her mark as a woman in a very male-dominated environment.

At eleven o'clock he heard his father's footsteps on the mezzanine landing above. He gave the little obligatory cough, signalling his presence. Simon glanced upstairs. His father lifted his eyes to indicate Simon was required upstairs. He passed his customer over to the ever-attentive Mr Thorn, ascended the stairs, and followed his father into the office. Gwen was filing some ledgers. He heard his father dismiss her before he added, "We are not under any circumstances, to be disturbed."

Oh, crumbs, thought Simon, that sounds ominous.

Looking back on the conversation that morning, Simon would always remember it as the second instalment of his journey into manhood. He grew up, right there in his father's office on that February morning in 1922. It was preceded by the first instalment – four months earlier in a similar, solicitor's office in Newcastle. Once again, he went in not much more than a boy but emerged a man.

CHAPTER 4

Robert Guilder had also woken early the morning after the funeral... even earlier than Simon. In fact, he'd hardly slept. He put on his dressing gown and slippers and drew back the curtains – it was still dark, and it was cold, but somehow it didn't matter- it matched his mood, his life. For nights he'd slept alone in this bedroom. His Gertie was gone – she'd been his rock and oh, how he loved her, respected her, and depended on her. He knew that today, he would impart some information which would be painful and embarrassing, but at least Gertie was not here to witness it – spared by her untimely death. Gertie enjoyed a good life and they'd made a great partnership –she was blessed with insight, integrity, understanding and the ability to resolve problems in a straightforward, sensible way. Oh, how he'd given her problems...he didn't deserve her.

Gertie had shown these amazing characteristics when they first started 'stepping out' together. He was the lodger in her mother's house, but their attraction to one another was hard to deny and after a brief courtship they married. She was the one who sourced the business premises, which now housed Guilder's Men's Outfitter's

– he was too busy seeing to the day-to-day work in the little shop off the High Street. She was the one with the vision. She was the one who saw the future of men's tailoring in this small market town – he would have been content to stay put in the back street, but Gertie saw the bigger picture.

Not long after William was born, Gertie was the one who suggested they should buy a house. Robert was alarmed at the idea of buying a house, as well as new business premises. But Gertie was acquainted with the bank manager, so armed with the glowing business accounts, they soon secured a loan, sufficient to make the deposit payment and furnish the house he was now sitting in. That was nearly thirty-five years ago. Yes, they worked hard, but they had made their mark on the town and it was Gertie's influence which made the right connections. They soon found their place in the social scene of the town. Gertie wasn't a social climber – she just liked people and they liked her in return. She never 'put up' with anyone because of what they could offer – no, she was genuine through and through, she was astute. Serena followed William and completed their little family. Gertie's mother and his parents had all died when the children were small, so they became a neat little unit and apart from Gertie's dinner parties they kept themselves to themselves.

Robert shivered and put his head in his hands. He started to sob. He was grieving – not having shed a tear since her passing. The tears flowed and flowed. After a while he wiped his eyes – he must brace himself for what was to come. He looked out of the window – he could just detect the changing colours in the morning sky, heralding the awakening of the new day.

As he gazed at the sky, he saw her face, her mesmerising eyes, her dark hair, her slim, graceful figure, her long slender fingers and the dainty features of her flawless face. He remembered how his heart jumped into a gear he'd never experienced before. A wave of desire engulfed him. He was on a path leading to an inevitable outcome. And that was it...his big mistake. He was captivated by her beauty, driven by the longing coursing through him... being sensible never entered his mind. He knew it was infatuation. He pursued her with flirtatious comments and a passion he could not believe himself capable of...his thirst was unquenchable... until the moment he possessed her.

It was the closing months of 1899. The old queen was still hanging on – but Victorian Britain was good to Robert. He accepted an invitation to a trade fair to be held in London. He was not one for business events, but his friend Monty Chapman prevailed upon him to attend and said they could stay with his sister at her home in London, situated near to the venue where the trade fair was being held. Gertie encouraged him to make the trip.

"You need to socialise more with your colleagues in the trade, Robert," was her response. William was at boarding school and Serena was attending an excellent girl's school in Newcastle.

So, Robert made the journey south on a Monday morning in early December. It was to be a four-day exhibition and they would return on Friday. It was to be a week engraved in Robert Guilder's memory. Monty

Chapman's sister Flo and husband were very hospitable. Their family of four were in their late teens and early twenties and were still living at home. The house was buzzing with young life. Lots of comings and goings, laughter and chattering, music, and fun. Robert was soon infected with the light-hearted, feel-good atmosphere pervading the house. It was a large house, beautifully furnished – there seemed to be no shortage of money in this family.

His first sight of Eugenie took his breath away. She was a friend of one of the daughters, from Spain, and was spending time enjoying the 'London scene'. Eugenie, oh, how that name would haunt him for the rest of his life.

Looking back, he could hardly remember the sequence of events, but the attraction was mutual. She was twenty years old, almost half his age, at thirty-nine. But age didn't matter – she captivated him. He was a smartly dressed man, good looking he supposed, and he was mature – maybe that was what appealed to her? After three evenings of lively banter, lots of laughter, music, and some alcohol, he found himself outside her bedroom door, by subtle invitation on her part. He chided himself – he should have known better, should have resisted...why, oh why, did he succumb? He never thought there would be consequences. She'd been in London for nearly three months, enjoying the London life. I guess I am just one of the many gentlemen she has been involved with during her stay, he thought, as she invited him into her room.

What followed was so different from his intimacy with Gertie. Maybe, it was Eugenie's Spanish blood coursing through her veins, urging him on, which led to the heights of passion he'd never experienced or even dreamt about. He could never recall how long he spent with her, but the house was still and silent when he eventually crept back to his own room.

The next day he did not see Eugenie at breakfast and after bidding his hostess farewell, Monty and he left for the station and took the train back north. That, he thought, was that. One very enjoyable episode. A one-night fling. Goodness, he knew men who engaged in those pleasures, weekly. No-one saw him, and no-one was even aware of the attraction between them... as far as he knew. Gertie was the love of his life, and he was so happy to be back in her bed. Theirs was a steadfast love. She was his comfort, and he certainly enjoyed a life of satisfaction on that score.

However, that was not 'it'. One morning about three months after his London encounter, he received a letter addressed to Mr R. Guilder – Private, in his office post tray. The letter was from Monty Chapman's sister Flo. She was straight and to the point. Their daughter's friend, Eugenie, was expecting a baby and she was in no doubt whatsoever... Robert was the father, as she had been with no-one else. Monty's sister was obviously a broadminded lady. She suggested he meet her when she visited her brother at Easter, next month. She then gave her address saying she looked forward to hearing from him.

Panic! Shock! Disbelief! Regret! Robert rocketed through a mountain range of emotions – but the bottom line was ... a baby, his baby. His indiscretion was uncovered. One small lapse in his otherwise ordered life. Just one lapse, one mistake... but he kept coming back to the one fact he could not avoid. This girl was going to have a baby...his baby. He was responsible and he must face his responsibilities. He went around in a state of shock for days.

Financial support – that is what the girl would need. However, to give her money, he would have to confess to Gertie, because she handled all the accounts; he would not dream of taking money from the firm – he was just too honest. How could he tell her without losing her love? They'd never held secrets ...until now.

He met Flo in a tearoom in Newcastle, the day after the Easter holiday. She was returning to London the following day. He thought long and hard about his response – but he'd failed to pluck up the courage to tell Gertie. He decided he would make a one-off payment to see to the girl's immediate needs. Flo was pleasant and put him at ease immediately – it occurred to Robert; Flo had dealt with this kind of situation before – she was not fazed in the slightest. She informed him Eugenie was well and thriving – there did not seem to be any likelihood of her miscarrying. The baby was due in September, and she was coming over to London in July, to stay with Flo for the confinement. She added that her two sons were going to be abroad in the summer, so there would be plenty of room in the house. She assured him that her own doctor was very discreet in these matters. Yes, thought Robert... Flo has encountered this kind of predicament before! He remembered his jaw dropping, at the matter-of-fact way Flo talked about it. He cleared his throat and asked – "And then what will happen?"

"Well, Eugenie doesn't want to keep the baby, so it will be found a good home, unless you have any suggestions?" she said, smiling.

Robert almost choked on his cup of tea, but replied, "No, but I will make a payment to her, to cover the expenses of the birth...plus a little extra."

Flo said that would be acceptable, then stood indicating their discussion was at an end. "I'll be in touch via your office," she added and after shaking hands, she departed. Robert felt he'd negotiated a business deal.

Making his way back to the station that day, he was flabbergasted something so life changing was arranged over a cup of tea. He was going to have another son or daughter...how could he let his child, his own flesh and blood be handed to strangers? How could Eugenie part with her baby? Then he realised he'd omitted to ask Flo about the girl's prospects – did she have family? Had they turned her out without any money and told her to get rid of the child? In five months' time he would have to make this payment. Gertie would have to be told.

**

In the July of that first year of the twentieth century, Robert and Gertie Guilder left Loftam. Gertie was travelling to London to a private clinic for treatment, rest, and recuperation. Ten weeks later, Robert, Gertie and their new baby son returned. Oh, what joy! What a celebration! What a fuss!

Gertie Guilder in that changing point in her womanhood had conceived, and under the strict and watchful eye of Dr Proctor in a private nursing home in London, an uncomplicated birth and confinement took place. Robert travelled to London as soon as he received the telegram. Three weeks afterwards, he travelled to London again. This time Gertie and their new baby, Simon, accompanied him on the journey home. This was the version of events any interested folk in Loftam were told.

Robert never met Eugenie again in person. They communicated many times by letter, and he knew she had married an older, wealthy gentleman a few years later. To his knowledge, Senor and Senora Dominguez remained childless. He knew Simon was to be a beneficiary in her will, but he always assumed that he would be dead long before Eugenie died – so Simon would never need to know the events surrounding his birth – unless he needed to see his birth certificate.

Robert realised it was sunrise – he could hear the rest of the household coming to life, so he dressed and descended the stairs for breakfast with his two guests, Jane and her granddaughter. He spoke briefly to Simon as he left for the firm.

Later as Robert walked down to the store, he felt into his jacket pocket to make sure the document in the leather-bound folder was secure – he'd retrieved it from a box on top of the wardrobe earlier. Once again, he recalled his love, his rock, his problem solver ...his Gertie. When he had confessed his sin to Gertie, a week after meeting Flo, she sat quietly for a few minutes. Then she smiled and threw her arms around him.

"We're going to have another child, Robert," she whispered into his ear.

He gazed at her in amazement asking, "What do you mean?" His voice was barely audible.

She then told him of her longing for another child over the last few years, but now nature showed her that was not to be.

"I can easily mask a pregnancy," she declared excitedly, patting her plump middle-aged figure.

"Loose clothes work wonders, and an unplanned baby can often arrive at my stage of life," she added.

Robert was delighted to see Gertie so enthusiastic at the prospect of a new baby.

So, plans were made. The only person in on the secret was Flo. She was more than willing to organise a 'nursing home' in the form of a rented apartment, just around the corner from where she lived. Gertie enjoyed her two months' 'rest and recuperation' taking in the sights of London, window shopping, buying baby clothes and dining in various tearooms.

On the 27th of September, Gertie received a call from Flo. She packed her bags and moved into one of the many guest rooms in Flo's large house. Later that day a healthy, baby boy was kissed by his beautiful, young Spanish mother, then taken down to the guest room, and placed into the arms of a beaming Gertie – his new mother. The next day, the excited father arrived. Eugenie by this time had relocated to the 'nursing home' around the corner. Robert and Gertie did not have any more connection with Flo, after they left London, but she was given a substantial cheque to cover the incurred expenses.

***

LOFTAM ENGLAND
1922

As Simon sat nervously on the other side of the desk, he watched his father go over to the office safe and pull out a leather-bound folder. Strange, thought Simon, I have been in that safe many times and never noticed that folder. His father sat down, adjusted his jacket, and gave his little cough. He put his hand on the folder and slid it across the desk to Simon.

"In there," he said, "is your birth certificate. I surmise, by now, you know that your mother – your biological mother – was a Spanish lady called Eugenie Silvestre. She later became Senora Eugenie Dominguez after her marriage."

Simon noticed how pale and aged his father looked. He watched as Simon opened the folder and pulled out the certificate. He looked at the document – he had never seen a birth certificate before. He read the name of his mother. Then the name of his father... Robert Guilder.

Robert continued, "I, however, am still your father, which is why you were not adopted."

The implications of what his father intimated, slowly started to dawn on Simon. An awkward silence ensued. Then Robert cleared his throat.

"I met Eugenie when I was on a business trip in London. Our liaison was brief – you were born in London the following year. It was decided that Gertie and I would raise you as our own child. Only Eugenie, Gertie, the lady with whom Eugenie stayed and I, knew about this." Robert stood, indicating the end of the conversation. He walked around the desk and shook Simon's hand firmly.

"Know this young man, you were a longed-for child by Gertie, and you were very, very much loved by both of us. I lost touch with Eugenie many years ago, but I knew you were a beneficiary in her will. I expect you will be travelling to Spain soon, to find out what you have inherited."

Simon picked up the folder and left the office.

Robert sighed and buried his head in his hands. It was over – at least the first part. Now Simon and he would have to explain to William and Serena...if that is what Simon wanted. It was out of his hands now. Again, he thanked God that Gertie did not live to see this day.

***

Simon made his way back downstairs to the shop floor. He couldn't concentrate and attended to his work in a perfunctory manner. Later that afternoon he returned home. His father had left the store much earlier. The house seemed so strange. There was no mother to pop in and see, sitting in front of the cosy fire. He looked around the room – not lavish but comfortable, tasteful but bought to last.

"Good," said his father's voice behind him – it made Simon jump. His father seemed to have aged so much over the last week. "I hoped to catch you, before you went upstairs. Do you want to tell your brother and sister what I divulged earlier? They are going to have to know sooner or later – so perhaps telling them now, would be for the best." He looked questioningly at Simon, who was still reeling from the shock – but what was the point in keeping quiet? He needed to travel to Spain soon, so that required an explanation. He looked around the room, searching for an answer.

"Yes, Father, I suppose we'd better tell them," he replied.

***

Baby Simon's arrival was such a surprise to the Guilder children. Serena went into raptures of delight. At ten years old, she could be a little mother to her new baby brother. William was disgusted – what an embarrassment for a teenage boy to endure. They were totally opposing reactions. All they knew was that mother had gone to stay in a clinic in London, for medical reasons.

As youngsters they were none the wiser. Robert and Gertie thought it best not to inform them about the baby in case anything unforeseen happened. So, when Robert returned two days after the birth, he sat them down and told them the news. Serena shrieked with delight and William got up to leave the room. "At least I'm away at school most of the time," he retorted. Serena glowered at him. There was no love lost between them.

***

The next evening William arrived in time for dinner. Robert requested Emily did not accompany him as it was a family matter. William assumed it was an issue to do with his father's business so was totally unprepared for what Robert was about to disclose.

After a dinner accompanied by small talk and matters relating to a headstone for the grave and a suitable inscription, the family retired to the drawing room. Serena served a hot beverage and then Robert cleared his throat, a signal Simon now knew heralded some uncomfortable words were about to be spoken.

"What I have to say now is not easy for me," he pronounced. His face was ashen.

"Yesterday, I gave Simon his birth certificate." William and Serena looked on non-plussed.

"Simon now knows that his birth mother was not my dear Gertie, but a Spanish lady called Eugenie. I am, however, his father." He then looked at Simon and gave a nod.

Simon took up the refrain. "Four months ago, I was informed that my birth mother was a victim in a rail crash, and I was subsequently an heir to her estate."

William prickled and sat up straight in the armchair. Serena gawped at Simon who continued.

"I am required to visit the solicitor handling her estate in Madrid, as soon as possible. That has not been the case until now. So, in the next few weeks I will fulfil this appointment – then I will know more about this strange situation."

The atmosphere was tense. William could not help himself. It was like a cork erupting from a bottle of champagne – he exploded with venom in his voice. "Strange situation be damned," he growled. "Father had a fling with a Spanish floozy and got caught out." He stood and pounded across the floor to the window.

Serena was mortified, never before had words like this been spoken in their home.

"Please, William," she begged, but he was on a roll and ignored her.

"Where did you meet this bit on the side, Father? For how long did you enjoy these illicit pleasures? How did you dupe my poor mother to take on your bastard?" The volume of his voice increased.

Robert just sat there as if all resistance had deserted him.

Then William turned on Simon. "And you, baby brother, haven't you done well?" He paused and let out a scornful laugh. "Haven't you landed on your feet, inheriting – dear knows – how many saucy pesetas. Well, I hope you enjoy spending them, and when you do – remember their lustful origins." Then he stormed out of the room. A few minutes later the front door banged shut.

What seemed like an age passed. Then, slowly, tears began to trickle down Robert's face, but still no-one spoke. Eventually Serena got up and walked over to her father and looking adoringly at him, gave him a hug and said with feeling, "I love you, Father, that was a very brave thing for you to say."

Robert dried his eyes and stood. "I think I'll retire now," he announced and left the room. He looked stooped and beaten, crushed, and defeated.

After a while, Simon spoke to his sister. His elbows were resting on the arms of the chair, his fingers together pointing upwards, as if in prayer. "Did you have any idea, sis?" he asked.

Serena shook her head. "None whatsoever, but she doted on you, Simon, as if you were her own flesh and blood." She smiled at him pleadingly, almost begging him to believe it. "You completed the family, she adored you – as I did and still do."

Simon got out of his seat. He hugged her, then whispered in her ear, "Please will you help me, Serena, to organise this visit to Madrid?"

She nodded. And Serena kept her promise. She enjoyed having a 'project' to complete.

***

So, 'Operation Madrid' went into action over the next few weeks. Serena knew various people in the town, who travelled abroad frequently. They gave her a wealth of information to make travel arrangements for her brother's European adventure. She helped him with his passport application, currency, rail tickets, hotel accommodation and clothing. Simon was clueless about where to start, but in a few short weeks Serena had gobbled up the problem and talked him through every stage of the expected journey.

He would travel to London and stay overnight. Then travel down to the English Channel and take a steamship to France. From there it was onward to Paris. After another night's accommodation, he would board a final train, crossing over the border into Spain and onto his destination... Madrid.

Simon communicated with the solicitor in Madrid, informing him of his arrival date and asked if he could recommend a suitable establishment for him to stay and how long it would take to complete their business. A week later he received a reply, giving him the address of a nearby hotel, adding he'd taken the liberty of booking a room for one week, which would give Simon plenty of time to view his properties and make further arrangements. Two days before his departure, Simon sat with his head in his hands... what lies ahead of me? He asked himself with trepidation.

It was six weeks since the outraged encounter with William and nobody in the family had heard from him. The whole incident was not referred to again. Robert resumed his normal duties at the office. Simon was kept busy at work training a new employee, who would help Mr Thorn while he was away for an estimated three weeks. The staff in the store were excited and full of questions when they heard about Simon's holiday. He had often talked of his desire to travel and now was as good a time as any.

Serena welcomed 'Project Madrid' to keep her occupied alongside the household duties, but she was going to miss Simon terribly. "Send me lots of postcards," she requested.

Simon would feel lost, without Serena at his side, organising him – but now he needed to stand on his own feet.

The morning of his departure, Robert and Serena accompanied Simon on the early morning train to Newcastle and saw him seated in his carriage on his train to London. They hugged and kissed him until finally he boarded. He gazed after them as they waved him out of sight.

CHAPTER 5

APRIL 1922

The morning of Simon's departure Serena felt bereft. She lay in bed asking – what am I going to do with the rest of my life? The sun was already shining brightly on that April morning. Her 'baby', as she thought of Simon lovingly, was going to pastures new. He probably won't need me anymore. There'd always been someone to need her – Simon, Mother and now it would be Father. Serena had accepted her role in life to be the daughter of the household, who stayed at home in a caring capacity until she married...but it looked as if that boat had sailed without her – she was thirty-two and seemed destined to become the 'maiden aunt' in their family.

After they left the station that morning, her father suggested they look around Newcastle and have some lunch before returning to Loftam. Serena loved 'window shopping' – she was a regular visitor to the city, having been a daily traveller in her school days. But since Mother's illness, she'd only visited to sort Simon's travel arrangements. Robert and Serena noticed the abundance of women's clothing being displayed in the shop windows – they ventured inside some of the shops and viewed the products. Serena was in her element – Robert smiled, pleased to see his daughter enjoying herself.

"Look at this, Father," she kept saying, dragging Robert off in different directions, until he was almost dizzy. Serena become excited and as she tucked her arm into her father's on their way to lunch, she announced, "Father, I think it's time 'Guilder's Men's Outfitters' became 'Guilder's Outfitters'."

Robert followed her line of thought and patted her hand. "My dear, I think you are right, I was thinking along similar lines. I see a business opportunity for Loftam."

As they ate their lunch, Serena and Robert talked about introducing ready-made women's clothing into the store. When they left the station in Loftam, Serena almost bounced her way back up the hill to The Gables. She was so full of ideas and Robert encouraged her. He knew Simon's departure, following so closely after her mother's death, would be unsettling for Serena...perhaps this idea could help his daughter deal with the changing circumstances. That evening father and daughter talked at length.

"You've got your mother's gift for vision in the business world," Robert remarked, as he climbed the stairs to bed.

The next morning Serena stretched and got out of bed. She'd lain awake and planned into the early hours of the morning – yes, she thought, my new project... 'Serena's Fashions'. She laughed to herself, where did that bright idea come from? Suddenly, there was a purpose in life again and she was going to visit Olivia in York.

After the funeral, Olivia had written on behalf of her grandmother to thank Serena, Robert, and Simon for their kind hospitality. She asked Serena if she would like to spend a few days in York as her guest. Serena jumped at the idea but explained it would be a few weeks before she would be free to accept Olivia's kind offer. Yesterday, she mentioned the invitation to Robert.

"Of course, you must go, my dear," he encouraged her. "It's been a demanding time for you. A holiday and young company will be a treat – don't worry about me, I'll be fine."

Serena really did worry about her father these days. He was not the same man he'd been only six months ago – before Mother's illness, her death, the revelations about Simon's birth, and that dreadful outburst from William. He needed 'looking after' but it would only be for a few days and Mildred would be around each day, she thought. So, that morning she sent a letter to Olivia, saying she would love to visit and was available next week, if that was convenient.

***

One week later Olivia was standing on the platform awaiting the arrival of the train from Newcastle. The two young women had only met briefly at the funeral, but they seemed to 'hit it off' immediately. Serena was a few years older than Olivia, but somehow the age gap was irrelevant. As soon as they met, they were chattering away like old school friends.

Leaving the station, they took a taxi to Olivia's home on the outskirts of York. When they arrived, Serena looked up at the imposing Victorian house, sitting alongside similar properties on the crescent-shaped road. It was an old house, but on entering the hallway, Serena was suitably impressed with the standard of furnishings. Soon she was unpacking her bag in a delightful room overlooking the rear of the house. Olivia informed her that she would have her position in the town library in the mornings but would be free each day by lunchtime and they could spend the rest of the day sightseeing or shopping. It was Serena's first visit to York, so she was excited at the prospect of seeing this beautiful old city. They enjoyed a walk and found many topics of conversation.

That evening Serena met Olivia's parents and her grandmother Jane.

"How's that young brother of yours?" asked Jane. "My, he's got a glint in his eye, I imagine he'll break some young girl's heart before he settles down," she commented, chuckling.

Olivia felt herself blushing, as she remembered the dashing young man at the funeral – she'd often thought about him during the intervening weeks.

"Well, I wouldn't know about that, but he's on holiday in Spain at present," replied Serena.

The next two days passed in a whirl for Serena. They visited historical sights and enjoyed a boat trip down the river. I must do this kind of thing more often, thought Serena. On one of the evenings Olivia's brother Fred, his wife Betty and daughter Ann, joined them for dinner. Fred was a schoolteacher. They were such a happy family – carefree and jovial, with no hint of any tensions Serena could detect.

On the final day, Olivia suggested a shopping trip. As they made their way around the shops admiring the fashions, Serena started to share her vision for the expansion of Guilder's into ladies' fashions. Olivia was very stylish and since having her own income, she'd become quite a serious dresser and was up to date with the latest fashion trends. Serena asked her advice regarding a new dress and promptly made a purchase – the first item she'd bought ready-made. Previously, her clothes were made by her mother's dressmaker. Serena listened as Olivia talked about the latest styles and about a recent visit she'd made to London. The two young women shared a love of fashion and Serena promised to keep Olivia informed of the progress of ladies' fashions at Guilder's.

To round off their afternoon, they went for tea in a smart new tearoom. While they were chatting, Olivia asked Serena about Simon's holiday. Serena didn't mention anything about Simon's inheritance, only his ambition to travel. But as she talked about Simon, Serena sensed Olivia was more than interested in her brother's whereabouts... she was interested in him.

Olivia then asked Serena if she'd been romantically involved with anyone. Suddenly, from nowhere, tears sprang to Serena's eyes.

"Oh, I'm so sorry Serena, I didn't mean to upset you," she apologised.

Serena dabbed her eyes and stared out of the window.

"I could never be involved with a man... not now," she whispered.

As she gazed out of the tearoom window, the haunting events of her teenage years hit her like waves crashing against rocks on the seashore. She was transported back to that night many years ago, when she was undressing in her bedroom. Her parents were downstairs, and her young brother was fast asleep on the floor above. The door opened, and William, her brother, had entered uninvited. He was wearing only his dressing gown. What happened next would be imprinted on her mind forever. Over the ensuing years, during his school vacations, William frequently visited her, after hours... 'our little secret', he called it. She'd wanted to scream but was struck dumb. So stood there and obeyed.

She blinked, realising Olivia was talking to her. "Oh, sorry," she replied, "I was miles away."

Olivia guessed Serena was recalling a sadness in her past and quickly made some reference to the food. The subject was forgotten, and they resumed their afternoon tea.

The next day Olivia bade farewell to her friend on the station platform. They'd formed such a bond during those few days in York. As they hugged goodbye, Olivia whispered in Serena's ear, "If it would help to talk... about your sadness, Serena, I'm a good listener." Then as she squeezed her hand tears started to well up in Serena's eyes again, and she quickly boarded the train without comment.

On the journey home she revisited the dark secret she carried as a burden. Her older brother's abuse had continued for years. It got to the point where she just expected his arrival. She was so relieved he was away studying most of the time. Finally, it ended, when Mother collided with William as he was leaving her room. That was his last nocturnal visit, and she was so thankful. Never again did she have to suffer the degradation. The following day she was taken to visit a friend of her mother's called Aunt Agatha, not a blood relative, but a dear old lady. Mother took her on the bus – she lived out in the country. She told Serena to pack a bag, as Aunt Agatha needed some help for a couple of weeks while convalescing. She lived in a delightful place and Serena really enjoyed herself. The only disappointment was not seeing Simon that holiday – he'd only just become a boarder and she missed him. However, it did help her to forget about William ...well, almost forget.

All that was history now, but it left Serena with an uneasy feeling where men were concerned. It also undermined her confidence talking to men in general. She'd once been invited to go to a dance hall with a charming young man, the son of one of Mother's friends. She'd met him several times before. He was about her age, and they enjoyed a pleasant evening together, but she dreaded he would want to kiss her. In the end he just shook her hand – she felt rather foolish afterwards.

But it was an area in which Serena felt vulnerable and awkward. If only her mother had talked to her about what had happened, but it was a taboo subject – almost as if she, Serena, was as much to blame as William.

Now, in her thirties she doubted she would ever marry. She was not naïve – she'd learned plenty about physical relationships from friends at school. She realised things could have been a great deal worse with William ... his little ritual with her seemed to have satisfied him. But he disgusted her. How Emily could have married him, she did not know ... her brother William's behaviour had scarred her for life.

*****

SPAIN

APRIL 1922

Simon enjoyed every stage of his journey to Spain. He'd visited London before, but walking around after his arrival, he managed to revisit some of the sights his father had omitted years before. It was springtime and nature was waking up after the long winter sleep. Trees in bud, some in blossom, seemed to paint a delightful picture. He walked for miles, and it was only when hunger pangs gripped him, that he realised the time and went to find somewhere to eat. Back in his hotel room he checked his tickets for tomorrow's leg of the journey. Strange, he thought, as he lay in bed that night – too excited to sleep – London is the place of my birth.

Next day, after a train journey to the south coast, he crossed the channel in a steam ship. A further train journey brought him to Paris where he stayed overnight.

Paris in the springtime – he fell in love with the city and promised himself he would return when time allowed. The final stage of his journey took him over the border into Spain. He was fascinated by the changing landscape and architecture – so different now from England. Once in Spain, the style of the buildings charmed him, and the temperature surprised him – he felt completely overdressed and realised his overcoat would be surplus to requirements while he was in this country.

It was early evening when he arrived and stepped outside the station. The scene before him was chaotic. In all his imaginings of what Madrid would be like, he did not expect this – it was teeming with life. Cars, bikes, trams, buses, an occasional horse and carriage – all seemed to go their own way – he was amazed how they avoided colliding!

He looked in his pocket for the address of the hotel – Hotel Palace in the Centro District. He found a taxicab and was soon entering the foyer of an elaborate hotel. The fittings, furnishings and décor were opulent. Simon was stunned by it all. He felt he needed to pinch himself to see if it was real and not just a dream. The cost to stay here will be extortionate, he feared as he approached the front desk. He spoke to the receptionist in English and was rewarded with a blank stare. After showing his passport and gesticulating, he was eventually given a key, and going by the three raised digits he assumed his room was on the third floor. His bedroom was fabulous, including the luxury of a private bathroom! He flopped onto the bed...Simon Guilder, where have you landed? He chuckled to himself.

After a sumptuous dining experience ordered with 'sign language' and lots of pointing, he stepped outside into the slightly cooler evening air. He walked nearby the hotel to try to get a feel for the place – the city was alive and vibrant. This is the start of the rest of my life, he thought. Loftam is a dim and distant memory. I have seven days to explore – after my appointment tomorrow.

The new day dawned...after a sound sleep and a hearty breakfast, Simon felt fresh and ready to begin his adventure in this amazing city. He was already feeling a complete idiot as far as the language was concerned – he'd totally overlooked what a barrier it would be to communicate. Even his competent sister had failed to prepare him. If only everyone spoke English, he wished, as he stepped out of the lift on his way to his appointment. He'd written the name of the solicitor's office on some paper before leaving his room, so when he handed it to the concierge, he was taken to the door and clearly indicated, in broken English, the location. It was just around the corner.

At five minutes to ten, he was stood outside the building which housed the offices of Senor Miguel Perez. His office was situated on the second floor. The building was elegant and was positioned in a busy square. Now... how am I going to understand what this gentleman has to say to me? He pondered. He was shown into an office – typical of any solicitor's office in Europe. Senor Perez was about his father's age, with thick, grey, wavy hair and a large moustache. He stood to shake hands, said something in Spanish, and beckoned a young man to step forward.

"Hello Mr Guilder, I'm Carlos, your interpreter, and this is my uncle."

Simon was so relieved... at last someone could speak English! As Simon and Carlos shook hands that morning, neither of them could have envisioned that this was the beginning of a lifelong friendship.

Enjoying his first 'siesta' – a totally new experience – he reflected on what he had learned that morning. His head was buzzing at the enormity of it all. Carlos was about two years older than Simon and spoke three languages: Spanish, French, and English – fluently. His uncle spoke little English and so, much to Simon's relief, through the interpretation of Carlos, the full extent of Simon's substantial legacy was unveiled. He returned to his hotel room, ordering a room service lunch at the desk. This time he wasn't concerned in the slightest how he was going to meet his hotel costs... because he was a very wealthy young man.

Senora Eugenie Cristina Dominguez had died in September the previous year –she was forty-two years old and a widow. She had lived in Toledo forty miles from Madrid and was returning to her home when a rail accident occurred. Her husband Juan was much older, and he had died two years earlier during the Spanish flu epidemic. The couple were childless. Juan was an astute businessman and Eugenie became a very wealthy lady on his death.

"She visited me earlier that day," Senor Pérez announced, and Carlos interpreted. "Oh, the tragedy... such an elegant lady... to think I was one of the last people she spoke to that day." The old solicitor was obviously upset and sought a glass of water before he continued, and Carlos interpreted.

"Senor Guilder... as Eugenie's only blood relative you are the major beneficiary. A small legacy is left to a Senorita Elise Dominguez, her husband's niece. The estate comprises six properties – a house in Toledo, where Eugenie lived for many years; a residence on the Mediterranean near Barcelona; a hotel here in Madrid, which contains on one floor a private apartment which Eugenie used when visiting the city. The office buildings in which we are sitting also belongs to her estate and two other apartment buildings on the outskirts of Madrid." The solicitor paused and sipped his water. "These are rented out and overseen by the watchful eye of a manager, who attends to the leases and day-to-day maintenance. In addition to these properties there are considerable investments and shareholdings in a variety of banks, a shipping company and two manufacturing plants." Senor Perez paused and looked at Simon over the top of his glasses. In broken English he exclaimed... "You ... very, rich young man!" Then he grinned.

Bombshell number three was all Simon could think. He just sat there flabbergasted and bewildered. At this point, Carlos took control of the proceedings. He explained that he was on holiday and was willing to take Simon to view the properties over the next week. His uncle could put him in touch with an advisor, who could help with the management of the companies and investments. Simon was only too happy to have someone guide him through this maze. Carlos picked up a bundle of papers. "I have helped my uncle to prepare these documents in English – they will need to be read carefully and signed to transfer the ownership of the properties and financial holdings into your name, Mr Guilder." He then gave them to Simon. "I suggest you scrutinise them carefully this afternoon, then return tomorrow to sign them in the presence of Senor Perez."

Simon left the solicitor's office, after making an appointment for the following morning.

Simon fell asleep. His head was spinning. When he woke up, he realised he'd slept for nearly two hours. Goodness, he thought, a sleep in the afternoon...he was soon to learn the pleasure of siesta time. He took a bath and dressed. Tonight, Carlos was taking him out for dinner. He was looking forward to meeting the young man again.

Having eaten a satisfying meal, Carlos leaned back in his chair. He was about six feet in height with a tanned complexion and brown eyes. His hair was dark like Simon's, but he sported a neatly trimmed beard. The two young men dispensed with formality when they met in the hotel foyer.

"So, Simon...I understand this legacy has come as a surprise," he commented.

Simon laid his napkin on the table and looked over at his companion and raised his eyebrows.

"I'll say! Six months ago, I thought my mother was an older English lady. Then I received this news out of the blue...I was shocked to say the least, but it's only two months since I learned the circumstances of my birth, after Gertie, my father's wife, passed away."

Carlos watched Simon carefully.

"How do you feel now you know the size of your inheritance?" Carlos enquired.

Simon sighed. "Shocked; bewildered; overawed. I'm a shop assistant in a small family firm...what do I know about stocks, shares, financial holdings and property management? It's daunting and such a responsibility...I don't know where to begin. I guess I need advice," replied Simon.

Carlos looked thoughtful. "My advice is to view the properties, while you are here. Secure a manger to oversee your assets and do nothing in a hurry. My uncle will help you. But you are young – so we will 'live a little' also, while you are in my country," he suggested, smiling.

The next few days passed in a flurry of activity, which invaded Simon's senses from all angles. Carlos proved an excellent host. Simon enjoyed eating and drinking in the many outside cafes that lined the streets and surrounded the plazas. He listened to excellent guitar players, watched flamenco dancers playing their castanets. He tasted coffee for the first time from a coffee roaster on the side of the pavement. He walked through bustling markets and bought gifts for Serena, Father and Felix. He admired new styles of architecture, attended a bullfight and an opera. He was reeling from the thrill of it all. He felt he had lived a lifetime in a few days.

Once all the documents were signed, Simon was informed about an advisor who spoke English, although not as fluently as Carlos. Alberto, the advisor, possessed an accountancy and banking background and was highly recommended by Senor Perez. The solicitor suggested they interviewed him together and if Simon thought him suitable, Senor Perez advised offering him an attractive salary, to retain his services. After interviewing him, Simon decided to employ him, and Alberto soon set about the task of transferring the management of the assets to a company in Simon's name. Simon decided to name his company 'Silvestre Holdings', using his mother's maiden name, from the time he was born.

Viewing the properties in the city he realised they needed careful management and oversight. There was always maintenance work to be carried out. The tenants in the apartments were mostly long-term, but leases needed to be renewed and occasionally new tenants found. The hotel was already an efficient business venture, having been established five years previously. The staff were stable and hard working. The office premises were insular units and were let to reliable firms. As there was a vacant office in the same building as the solicitor, this was utilised for Alberto, as Simon owned the building anyway.

One week in Spain was proving insufficient. The properties outside Madrid were still to be visited. The hotel was in central Madrid and close to the office building. Entering Eugenie's private apartment Simon felt instantly at home.

"Carlos, I've decided to stay at least another week. I'm going to check out of the hotel and take up residence here," he announced. He felt much more relaxed in the apartment. He enjoyed being in a place used by his mother. Next, he sent a postcard to Serena explaining he would be away for much longer, as there was still business needing attention...he would purchase his return tickets when he was ready.

Carlos, who was still on holiday, accompanied Simon to Barcelona. He was so grateful to have an interpreter on hand. The trip by rail was fascinating. The house in Barcelona was delightful, and Carlos suggested it was probably used as a summer residence to escape the heat in the city. The house stood in its own grounds, not far from the beach and only a short bus journey into the city. Arrangements were made in advance for the caretaker to show them the property. Simon felt he would need to spend time staying in this house, before deciding what to do with it. He still couldn't get his head around the fact that someone would need more than one house.

Returning to Madrid, Simon took time to relax and reflect. One property remained to be viewed. Access to the house in Toledo was not straightforward, as it was occupied by Senorita Dominguez, the other beneficiary in his mother's will. Senor Perez had been unable to contact her, but was investigating the whereabouts of the housekeeper, so would get back to him in a few days regarding the viewing.

Over the next two days with no appointments, Simon slept, walked, relaxed, and tried to assess the implications of his newfound wealth. Spain ... it was a country only mentioned briefly in his school geography and history lessons. Now at twenty-one years of age he was absorbing the information that he was half-Spanish by birth and owned substantial properties in this country, along with enough financial assets to keep him in a wealthy style of living for the rest of his life. What was now slowly dawning on Simon, was that part of his life was now in

Spain. Initially, he thought this trip would sort out the financial details of his legacy and then he would be back home in Loftam, working in Guilder's Men's Outfitters. That was now unlikely. At the very least he would need to split his time between Spain and England. Really, deep down, Simon knew that the life offered to him in Madrid was far more appealing than his life in Loftam, as a department manager in a men's outfitters. It was a dilemma, and not one to which he could see an easy solution. It would take a great deal of time to sort himself.

Two days later he met up with Carlos again. He was becoming a firm friend – not too overpowering – but they certainly shared an affinity. Meeting with Carlos seemed to ease the seriousness of this legacy situation. They spent time talking over some of the thoughts Simon considered over the last two days. Simon learned that Carlos did not work for his uncle. He was a lecturer in languages at the local university – hence his extended vacation. He had been invited to act as an interpreter, as his uncle's English was limited. The two young men chatted and laughed – they shared a mischievous sense of humour and complemented each other. Their friendship provided a 'valve' for Simon to let off steam and be a young man. He hoped they could remain friends after the duties of this week.

"Next time you visit Madrid, Simon, we will meet some ladies...how does that sound?" Carlos remarked grinning.

Simon raised his eyebrows and nodded.

Simon's stay in Madrid was drawing to its conclusion, but the house in Toledo was yet to be viewed. Later that day Senor Perez received news about the Toledo house. Apparently, Senorita Dominguez was staying with a friend in France and the housekeeper was unsure when she was returning, but she could easily prepare the house for an overnight stay for the English gentleman and provide meals. Simon only expected to visit for a few hours, but as the housekeeper was willing, Simon asked Senor Perez to confirm his arrival. He asked for two rooms to be prepared, as Carlos would accompany him. The following day Simon and Carlos travelled to Toledo. On the journey Simon was struck by the fact that less than a year ago his mother – his real mother – had made this journey, only for her life to be cut short so tragically.

If the house in Barcelona was delightful nothing could have prepared Simon for his first sight of Casa Galiana. He was completely blown away. If anyone had told Simon previously, he could fall in love with a house – he would have laughed at them. However, that's what happened. It was stood in its own grounds with a sweeping drive. Simon and Carlos walked up to the front door. Simon just stood and looked at the sight before him.

"Wow!" was all he could say.

"My word," added Carlos, "a sight to behold."

Simon later learned that the house was built in a 'hacienda' style with whitewashed walls and shutters. It had arches and balconies so unlike anything he'd ever seen. Before knocking on the door, he just stood and declared, "My Spanish house... I will never part with this house."

The housekeeper, a lady called Isabella, was quite taken with the arrival of the 'Caballero Ingles' – the

English gentleman – and proceeded to treat him as if he were royalty. She invited them in and showed them to their rooms. Amazingly, this house had only two bedrooms, and a bathroom on the first floor and a lounge, dining room, kitchen, and cloakroom on the ground floor.

Simon sat down on the bed and looked around him. Obviously, a ladies' bedroom –pale pink drapes, and floral wallpaper. A French door led out onto a balcony overlooking the rear of the house. Simon opened the balcony door and stepped outside. The view was breathtaking. From its elevated position it looked down over the town below. He went back inside, and his eyes alighted on a dressing table with frilled covers and a glass top. Scattered on the top were brushes and combs and a mirror, reminding him of his mother's dressing table at home.

He went over and sat on the stool in front of the dressing table. He noticed a small square box with a lid and opened it. It was lined with green baize material and was a jewellery box. Inside were an assortment of earrings, brooches, and rings. There was a small handle on the side of a raised part of the box. He turned the tiny handle and instantly a familiar tune started to play... 'Fur Elise' – the tune Serena played so often. He closed the box. Then his eyes alighted on a small double photograph frame. On one side of the frame was a smart young soldier in uniform. On the other side, a strikingly, beautiful girl. Who was she? He wondered. Who was he?

On returning downstairs, Isabella invited Simon and Carlos to take a hot drink and delicious pastries, served in the kitchen. Following this she showed them the rest of the house. Simon was fascinated with the details of the design. The staircase was a central feature with a small archway, child sized, underneath it, stretching from the front door to the kitchen entrance... it served no purpose, just a quirky characteristic. The dining room contained alcoves and built-in cupboards. The lounge was L-shape with double French doors leading onto the spacious garden.

However, the feature that caught Simon's attention in this room was the beautiful marble fireplace and above it an artist's portrait. The portrait displayed a beautiful woman, about thirty years old in a sitting position. She was slim, holding herself erect. Her hand was resting on the arm of the chair, her fingers were long and slender, her face was flawless and her features dainty. Her dark hair was swept upwards into a style, no doubt typical of the day. But it was the eyes that pulled Simon in.... his eyes. He felt a shiver run down his spine. His birth mother...she was elegant.

"Hello, Mother," he whispered, "I'll look after your house – I love it." He did not realise Carlos was standing behind him.

"Your mother was beautiful, Simon, I can see the likeness," he said, staring at the portrait.

Early in the evening Simon and Carlos enjoyed a delicious meal, courtesy of Isabella. Then they went for a stroll around the town. Simon noted its charm, compared to the busyness of Madrid...I could live here, he thought. Settling to sleep in the Spanish house, Simon felt 'at peace'.

***

LOFTAM ENGLAND

2019

Grace closed the door and headed off on her afternoon walk. She always aimed to walk for at least thirty minutes a day unless it was pouring with rain or too wintry. Although approaching seventy, she was still quite agile. She did not mind the days when she walked by herself – she could lose herself in memories. She'd become rather reflective these days. Hearing the piano piece 'Fur Elise' had stirred up memories of her childhood home. Without doing it consciously, her walk that day took her down the road where she used to live as a child. She'd not strayed far in her lifetime, having lived within a half a mile radius all her days – apart from being at college.

As she walked past some of the houses, she remembered people who lived there – mostly long since dead. New, younger families were making their own mark on these houses now. A couple of houses she remembered visiting frequently – school friends lived in them – I wonder what happened to them.

Then she stopped. There it was... 'The Spanish House'. Of course, it was never called that – but that's what it looked like. As if someone had picked it up in Spain and planted it in this town of Loftam. There were no houses like it nearby – it was unique.

Grace's eyes scanned the house. Whitewashed walls, shuttered windows, balconies, and arches. A sweeping drive. High hedges surrounded it still – it was like that when she was a child – her dad had had quite a task keeping it trimmed. The garden was spacious. She recalled the games she played there as a child in that garden and summerhouse.

Then she looked above the front door – there was a Juliet balcony and behind the window was a bathroom ...at least that's what it was when she lived there. Is it still a bathroom? she mused. Grace knew it used to be a bathroom...a bathroom with a secret.

CHAPTER 6

1922

ENGLAND

O n her return from York Serena started to investigate the proposed ladies' fashions at Guilder's. She walked the streets of Loftam and realised that apart from two long established dressmakers, in side street premises, there was no competition for what she had in mind. She sent for catalogues from various companies who were advertising in the national newspapers. She was amazed at how much was already available by mail order. She knew she needed to make a small investment to see how much interest they could generate. After writing letters and placing orders, she was able to purchase a selection of ladies' ware – Mother's inheritance came in useful. She corresponded weekly with Olivia, giving her an update. Olivia was able to give Serena some addresses of wholesale firms, whereby Serena could buy products and sell them at a profitable price. Olivia acquired this information by visiting stores in York, that she frequented to make her own purchases. Serena was delighted to receive these and even more excited when one of the wholesalers invited her to visit their factory and showroom on the outskirts of York.

Olivia agreed to accompany Serena on this visit. So, two weeks after saying goodbye to her friend, Serena was travelling back to York, but this time on a business trip. The two-day visit was successful and, acting on Olivia's advice, Serena placed a substantial order; her father having now given her access to funds. The two young women were so full of ideas.

"Olivia, you must come and stay in Loftam and help me to set up a display in our store's window. We also need to clear the stockroom in readiness for my new customers!"

Olivia was as excited as Serena.

"How's Simon?" Olivia asked, hoping she would meet him again when she visited Loftam.

"Oh, he's still away...we have no idea when he will be returning from his travels," she replied.

Olivia was disappointed, but hopefully she would be visiting Loftam again in the future.

It was a step into the unknown, but as Serena observed the ladies' shops in York, she picked up lots of ideas. She noticed these shops were totally separate from men's shops. She came to a decision... she needed her own premises. However, there was an urgency to 'get started', as stock was beginning to pile up in one of the spare rooms at The Gables and she needed to generate some income.

Serena and Olivia were like two sides of the same coin. What one saw as a problem, the other saw as an opportunity. When Olivia arrived in Loftam the following week, the two young women were in raptures bouncing ideas off each other. The plan was to use a window display in the Guilder's store to invite ladies to book an appointment to visit an upstairs room. This room was previously a storeroom, but with some sorting out and long needed decoration, it was a reasonably sized room, in which to display some products. A curtained off fitting room gave the ladies an opportunity to try on a 'would be purchase'. What was holding Serena back? Nothing. So, with her father's blessing and some dubious comments from Mr Thorn, one side of the double fronted window display was given over to Ladies' fashions – a large board within the display inviting ladies to come in and book an appointment.

Sadly, during all this excitement, Olivia knew she would have to return to York. The evening before her return the two young women were making their way up the hill from the store.

Olivia stopped and turned to face her friend. "Serena, it makes me so happy to see your cloud has lifted."

Serena was puzzled at first, then Olivia continued.

"I realise I hit a very raw nerve that day in the tearoom in York. You seemed to be so affected by some experience in your past which has been eating away at you, perhaps without you realising it –am I correct?"

Serena flung her arms around Olivia and started to cry. Through her sobs she started to confide in her friend. She told her of the dark secret she'd harboured since her teenage years.

"It's years since it ended, Olivia, and this is the first time I have ever spoken about it. I must really trust you to unburden myself in this way." The remainder of the walk was a revelation to Serena – she shed the daunting cloak of disgust and hate hanging over her for so long, all in one conversation.

"Thank you, I feel so much better now," she admitted to Olivia. "I feel I can put it behind me and step out into my future."

Olivia was unsure she'd done anything, but her observation provided the catalyst required to help Serena verbalise her secret –once out in the open, it brought her freedom. Serena felt she'd turned a page – a new chapter was about to begin.

***

Simon was never sure when his double-sided life began. He never set out to be secretive, but he just knew on that beautiful day in May, when he returned to Newcastle station, the Spanish side of his life must remain largely secret. Before taking the train to Loftam he needed to make some arrangements. So, he made his way to the premises of *Hodgson, Smith and White* where he had first learned of his legacy last autumn. The events of those months were mind blowing. His intention was to make an appointment with Mr Hodgson, but the lady behind the desk informed him Mr Hodgson was no longer with them, having retired due to ill health. His clients were being handled by another solicitor, new to the firm, called

Mr Adams. This information suited Simon, as he had found Mr Hodgson rather imposing. He made a future appointment with Mr Adams then took the train home to Loftam.

In the bubble that was Simon Guilder's world, he expected a welcoming homecoming – a celebration meal and Serena jumping about eager to hear all his news. Instead, he entered an almost empty house –no father, no Serena, no cosy fire in the drawing room – only Mildred, in the kitchen finishing off the cold buffet for tonight's evening meal.

"Oh, Mr Simon, it's so good to see you, sit down – you seem to have been away for ages. I'll get you a cuppa," she said.

"Where is everybody?" Simon asked, grabbing a biscuit.

"Serena's at the store, busy with her new venture, but I'll not steal her thunder – she'll be wanting to tell you all about it. Serena and Olivia have been in ecstasy – they've been like two busy bees – she only went home today."

Simon stopped munching his biscuit and asked, "Olivia?" sounding very puzzled.

Mildred replied, "Oh, you must remember her, Mr Simon – she stayed over after the funeral with her grandmother. She lives in York."

Olivia...Olivia... thought Simon, trying to sift through the many, many, people he'd met in recent weeks, and then... there she was in his mind's eye ...an attractive young lady, someone he thought was worth a second meeting, something about her eyes intrigued him, as he recalled.

"Well, that's me done. I'll be off now," Mildred called, retrieving her coat and hat from the hall. Mildred's words pulled Simon back from his faraway thoughts.

"Your bed is newly made up and I opened the window to let some air in this morning. Cheerio, Mr Simon...it's so good to have you home," she called, walking out the back door.

Simon climbed the stairs to his room. The sun was still shining, and the garden was bursting with life, as he looked out of the window. Everything was normal for Loftam...but in the six weeks since he had gone off to Spain, Simon knew life would never be 'normal' for him again. This is where I take off 'Spanish Simon' and put on 'English Simon', he thought. Then he went to take a bath and change for dinner.

That was how Simon's secret Spanish life started. He was never deceitful – just careful with the truth. He sat for a while after returning from the bathroom. He was trying to decide how much to impart to his father and sister. In the end there were no problems with that decision. When Robert, Serena and Simon sat down to dinner the questions started to come thick and fast. 'Tell us this, tell us that'; but very quickly Simon realised Serena was distracted and bursting to tell him something. So, the questioning turned around.

"Right, big sis," said Simon "What have you been doing? Mildred says you've been a busy bee while I've been away – so tell me."

It was just the opening Serena needed and it all tumbled out. Her excitement was infectious, and Simon found himself being caught up in the drama unfolding.

The 'first performance' was to be in two days' time and Serena was so glad Simon was back home to see it. So, without really trying, Simon, managed to keep things to himself as far as Spain was concerned. He returned to the store and resumed his duties but informed his father he would need to have an occasional morning off to attend to his Spanish business, which was being handled by a solicitor in Newcastle. His father seemed to accept this without any further questions. Robert retained the services of the young man who had stepped in to help when Simon was away, and he was now a permanent member of staff and proving himself to be very efficient.

A few days later, Simon kept his appointment with Mr Adams, the solicitor in Newcastle. He reflected... the family know enough, but really, they know little. This was the way he intended to keep it. Mr Adams was a discreet young man and Simon felt instantly at ease. He informed him he'd recently inherited some properties and financial holdings in Spain and set up a company called Silvestre Holdings. His involvement in this company was not to be shared with anyone in this country. In Loftam he was Simon Guilder, a manager in Guilder's Men's Outfitters. In Madrid he was a wealthy businessman, sole owner of Silvestre Holdings.

He, Mr Adams, would receive mail addressed to Mr Simon Guilder. He was authorised to open it unless it was marked 'personal'. Simon would make a weekly visit to see Mr Adams and the contents of the mailings would be discussed then. He was given Simon's store telephone number, to be used only in an emergency. The two men shook hands and Mr Adams' new client took his leave. Simon smiled to himself as he left those offices –a different young man to the one who had entered them last October.

Two weeks after Simon's return, Robert, Simon and Serena were just finishing breakfast when the post arrived. As usual, there were letters for Serena. She opened one of the letters and whooped for joy. Simon looked bemused as he munched his toast.

"Olivia's coming up for a week," she announced with glee.

Olivia's name had been mentioned many times since Simon came home. He was pleased his sister had made a friend. He sensed long ago a sadness and void in her life, and it seemed to have vapourised with the birth of Serena's fashion idea, but Simon suspected it was also something to do with this new friendship.

"Do you remember Olivia?" Serena asked, remembering her friend's interest in Simon.

"Yes, yes, I do," replied Simon.

Serena was so pleased –her brother needed a woman in his life, and she was keen to do a bit of 'match-making'. What can I do to bring these two together, she pondered – my dear brother and my dear friend.

On Monday the following week, Simon was going into Newcastle to visit Mr Adams.

"What time is your friend arriving?" he asked Serena.

When she told him, Simon indicated he would meet her and escort her back to Loftam, as he was in town on business. A small coincidence, perhaps, thought Simon as he waited on the platform for the York train. It was more than a friendly gesture on Simon's behalf – the more he thought about the elegant young lady from York – the more interested he was to meet her again. This was coupled with the many favourable comments his sister had passed on about her, since he returned home.

Suddenly, there she was, stepping from the carriage. Elegant, poised, petite...and beautiful. His heart did a little flip. He lifted his hand and waved. As she approached him, he noticed how chic and stylish she looked in her modern coat, hat and dainty shoes.

"Olivia, how delightful to meet you again," Simon greeted her, unsure whether to hug her, shake her hand or kiss into the air on both cheeks, like the Spaniards did. She smiled and lifted two bags, one in each hand, which Simon took and he continued, "It's about thirty minutes until the next train –shall we go for a cup of tea?"

Minutes later, they were sitting in the station café, Simon having ordered a pot of tea. Later, when he tried to recall their first encounter, he could hardly remember what they talked about, but he could remember being utterly captivated by this charming, young woman and the flutters gave way to stirrings, deep down in his inner being.

***

For Olivia, that visit to Loftam changed her life. Over the next week, she fell head over heels in love with Simon Guilder. She'd been dreaming about him ever since she had met him four months earlier at his mother's funeral, but she doubted if their paths would ever cross again. Over the weeks since her friendship with Serena began, she gradually built a picture of Simon in her mind – little details Serena gave – his preferences for this, dislikes for that. His quirky sense of humour and the way he loved to tease. His way of saying things, even his mannerisms were all catalogued in Olivia's mind – Serena talked a great deal about her young brother. It was all incidental on Serena's part at the beginning, but after she sensed the nugget of interest, that day in York, she let them fall like gold dust and Olivia picked them up.

Dinner that first evening was a joyful experience. The three young people chatted and laughed, and Robert realised he was enjoying himself for the first time in months. It was hard to believe Simon and Olivia had only spoken briefly before that day, but Robert sensed an affinity between them and smiled a blessing upon them. Oh, the vibrancy of youth, he thought to himself.

After dinner Serena was keen to show Olivia some new dresses which had arrived that morning. They disappeared upstairs, leaving Robert and Simon alone.

"What a charming young woman," remarked Robert.

"Yes, indeed," replied Simon. "Good for Serena to have a new friend and she seems knowledgeable about ladies' fashions."

They were interrupted in their conversation by a flurry of activity as the two young women bounded down the stairs. Serena opened the drawing room door.

"Gentlemen, a fashion show with our very own Olivia Brown."

Olivia stepped into the room. Simon gasped. Before him stood... the most beautiful girl he'd ever seen. Olivia was dressed in a floor-length, smartly draped silver evening gown, with a plunging neckline – it hugged her shapely figure. On her head was a silver band complete with a single feather which added an air of sophistication to the outfit; her shoes were heeled. Simon started to clap, Robert joined in, and a confident Olivia paraded across the drawing room floor, turning, and pausing for full effect.

"Splendid," exclaimed Simon.

"Beautiful," echoed Robert.

"Elegant," answered Simon.

"Perfection," continued Robert.

Olivia suddenly became embarrassed and dropped her eyes. Serena took up the refrain. "This supplier specialises in formal dresses, the quality is excellent, but I doubt if the ladies of Loftam are ready for this kind of occasion wear."

Olivia lifted her eyes and met Simon's gaze... he was enchanted.

"Oh, I'm sure Loftam ladies will celebrate this new style, especially when modelled by Olivia – go for it, Serena," he declared. "And thank you, Olivia, for modelling the gown so perfectly."

With that, the moment passed, and the ladies left the room. But an impression had been made, and it was etched on Simon's mind. Later that night Simon reflected on the swathe of beauty he'd witnessed that evening... something was happening to him... he decided to act.

***

The following morning Simon breakfasted alone and left the house before Robert, Serena and Olivia appeared. He was early, but his mind was so full; he needed to walk down to the High Street, to sort himself, before the demands of the day started. The previous evening Simon's senses had been awakened. The sight of Olivia, dressed in that gown, enhanced his dream-filled sleep... in which he reached out, took her hand, touched her skin, and kissed her lips. The sound of her voice still resonated in his ears. Oh, what's going on? He asked himself, on that perfect summer's day. He'd escorted many young women to concerts and dances since leaving school...and kissed a few, but he'd never experienced feelings like this before.

Another thought had crossed Simon's mind earlier that morning, which caused him to take a detour on his way to work. He checked his watch – plenty of time. It occurred to him, after last night's 'fashion show'... if Serena was going to make a success of this fashion business, she was going to need her own premises. The present arrangement of secreting a customer to an upstairs room to view garments in a cramped setting, did not make good business sense. He walked the length of the High Street twice – there were not many people about to distract him. He spotted two potential properties, both offering a similar size and advantageous positions. He knew he must act quickly on two scores. One, these days an empty property on the High Street did not linger long – businesses were 'taking off' in these post-war days and these would be snapped up quickly. Secondly, Olivia's influence was vital. In the few short hours he had spent in Olivia's company last evening, he observed how much

Serena listened to her friend. Olivia, he felt sure, was more of a risk taker, than his sister. Of course, he smiled to himself, it would not be that much of a risk... I would be her landlord!

Simon's knowledge about buying property was non-existent. I need to learn what to do, he told himself, so he made a note of the agent handling the sales. Later that morning he asked his father what he thought. Robert was interested in Simon's proposal and endorsed the idea of a separate location for the ladies' fashions. He possessed limited knowledge of buying properties but outlined the basic principles as he understood them. That afternoon Simon made two appointments for the following day. Later, when the Guilders and their guest were relaxing after dinner, Simon told them of his idea. As expected, Serena was cautious, full of what-ifs.

Olivia listened carefully, and it was some time before she spoke. "I think your suggestion is sensible, Simon. Ladies need to feel free to browse, try on garments – perhaps go away and think about a purchase before returning. The arrangement at present does not allow that freedom and may hinder some ladies. Stepping into a men's shop could be a restriction to many."

Serena listened to her friend then replied, "Yes, I realise that. We'll see what the properties have to offer."

Robert retired early and the ladies continued to chat, but Simon lingered as he wanted to ask Olivia a question. As they were leaving the drawing room to go upstairs Simon turned to Olivia.

"May I ask if you like orchestral music, Olivia?"

She felt herself blushing, but replied, "Yes, Simon... I do."

Simon continued, "That's good. There's a symphonic orchestra playing at the theatre in Newcastle on Thursday night, I wondered if you would like to go?"

Olivia looked from Simon to Serena.

"You two go," smiled Serena, happy for her friend.

The next afternoon the three young people viewed the two potential properties. Simon wanted his father to join them, but Robert declined. It was strange viewing an empty space and trying to visualise the furnishings and layout. Afterwards they went to a tearoom on the High Street to discuss their feelings and findings. They were unanimous in their decision.

Then Serena started to speak. "But Simon, what about the cost?"

Simon lifted his hand to silence her. "I'm doing the buying," he replied with a definite tone.

Serena and Olivia stared at each other in amazement. The next morning, Simon made an offer on the property, which was accepted, then he went into Newcastle to see Mr Adams and arrange the funds – his first purchase since becoming a man of means.

The conversation over dinner was very lively. After Robert retired, Serena cleared the dining room table and produced paper and pencils. They all sketched their ideas and then perused the results. Two hours later they were looking at a design layout which picked the best from each plan.

"Now," added Simon, "you need a name."

"Oh, that's easy," commented Serena, remembering her brainwave from a few weeks ago. "It's Serena's Fashions."

They all applauded.

The week was flying by, and Olivia was so looking forward to the concert that evening. After breakfast as Simon got up to leave the table, he bent over Olivia as she was still sitting. She felt her heart skip a beat at his closeness.

He whispered in her ear, "Shall we go into town early and have dinner before the concert?"

Olivia felt herself blushing at the intimacy of the moment, but answered, "Oh, yes... I'd like that."

As he lifted her chair, she thanked him, and he winked at her with a mischievous grin on his face, causing her insides to turn into jelly.

Olivia took extra care with her choice of dress and make-up, that evening. She was so excited. They took an early train into town. Simon had arranged a pre-concert dinner in a popular restaurant, close to the theatre. They made an elegant couple as they were shown to their table and turned a few heads. Over their meal, they conversed easily; Simon was very attentive, and they enjoyed a bottle of wine with their food. Olivia asked Simon about his holiday in Spain. He went into detail about the city of Madrid. He talked about the atmosphere, the architecture, sights, people, language and food. Olivia listened with enthusiasm. Simon's face lit up as he described his journey.

"I love travel," he added, "but I must be boring you with all this detail."

"Not at all," added Olivia, "but can I ask why you chose Madrid?"

It was one of those pivotal moments for Simon. He could have divulged the full extent of his connection with Madrid, but for some reason he refrained from doing so. He cleared his throat and added, "I was left some money in a will and needed to travel there to sort the details." Then, he looked at his watch and indicated it was time to go to the theatre.

Unbeknown to Simon and Olivia, someone was watching them in the restaurant, with great interest.

"My, my," thought William, "My little brother has acquired himself a lady friend – and an attractive young lady - I wonder who she is?"

William was more than curious. He was envious. His wife, Emily, was not at all glamorous. She was rather staid in her choice of dress. She was a 'suitable match' to quote his mother, at least financially, hence the reason they had married. She made him a good wife – friendly, a good homemaker and a loving mother to their son Felix, but she bored William. She was a dutiful wife, and many men would have been happy with that aspect. However, William wanted more excitement, more passion and recently he'd taken to finding an extra dimension elsewhere, on the recommendation of one of his clients. He was careful – it was not a frequent pastime, but it added a bit of spice to his otherwise dull solicitor's life.

Tonight, he was dining with two colleagues and then he would make his way across town to his comfortable home where his willing wife would be waiting for him. Oh... for some excitement tonight, he sighed. Why does my little brother have the glamorous girl and probably, by now, plenty of money to spend on her? If only William knew the full extent of his brother's wealth, his envy would have doubled.

***

The concert was enjoyable. It was such a balmy summer's evening. Simon suggested a walk before they went for the train. It seemed so natural, walking together, to hold hands. They walked through a park and sat down on a bench. They found so many things to talk about and laugh about. As they talked, Simon's arm moved around Olivia's shoulder. There was a pause in the conversation and Simon looked down into Olivia's green eyes – the eyes which had first caught his attention the day after the funeral. He reached out and tilted her chin towards him and gave her a gentle kiss. Embarrassment caused them to pull apart, but then Simon picked up her hand, brushed it to his lips and gazing into her eyes said, "Olivia, you are beautiful. Can I kiss you again?"

"Oh, Simon," was all she could say, as his lips found her lips again.

This time the kiss was lingering. They remained that way, neither of them wanting to break the idyllic moment. Eventually, Simon knew they would have to leave to catch the train. It was a night to remember for Simon and Olivia...and William.

The last two days of Olivia's visit flew by. The official notification arrived, saying Simon's offer on the shop was acceptable. Serena and Olivia were bursting with excitement. Olivia said she would investigate the display requirements from her contacts, when she returned to York.

Simon and Olivia had spent no time alone since the night of the concert, but he insisted on accompanying her to the station in Newcastle. Serena intended going, but she was sensitive to the growing feeling between her brother and her friend and invented an appointment she needed to keep.

So, Simon and Olivia spent precious time together, as they took the train from Loftam to Newcastle. They parted with a long lingering kiss and Simon made sure to obtain Olivia's address and details of where she worked. He indicated that he'd often thought about visiting York and gave her a wink accompanied by that mischievous grin.

Finally, they embraced for the last time, before she stepped onto the train. He looked again into her beguiling eyes and said, "I think I might be falling for you, Livvy."

Her reply was interrupted by the train's whistle, but he managed to hear her say: "I think I've already fallen, Simon."

CHAPTER 7

ENGLAND
SUMMER 1922

S imon knew the touch paper was lit as he made his way back to Loftam. When would he see Olivia again? It might be weeks before she visited Serena. She was in his mind all the time. The next few weeks proved hectic. The legal side of the shop purchase moved along, very slowly, too slowly for Simon, but his father assured him that these things took time, and he must exercise patience. Eventually, he was given a date in August for the completion. Serena used the intervening weeks to order fixtures and fittings and organise tradesmen to attend to decorating and carpentry jobs as soon as they got the keys. She then hired the services of a signwriter to paint Serena's Fashions in gold lettering above the window. Finally, she went to the printer's to order an amount of advertising leaflets and to the local newspaper to prepare an advert to be featured as soon as the premises were ready. Simon was amazed at his sister's business head and her efficiency. She confided in Simon that it was Olivia who had talked her through most of it, but putting it into action was her doing.

Meanwhile, Simon's desire to meet Olivia again gained momentum. One morning as he was dressing, he decided he could wait no longer. On impulse, he informed his father at breakfast he would be missing from the store that day. By now, Robert was getting used to Simon's absences. He asked no questions realising Simon probably didn't need to work at Guilder's anymore; he suspected his youngest son was a wealthy man. But it was Simon's private business, and he was happy for him. He would accept whatever time Simon could give to Guilder's – he would make no demands. He admired the way Simon showed maturity keeping the source and extent of his inheritance to himself – it held the potential to damage his own reputation in the town and Simon was circumspect in that regard.

Simon's plan that day was to make a surprise visit to York. The journey took less than two hours and, on his arrival, after a quick refreshment, he went in search of a jeweller's shop. He found more than one, but making his choice stepped inside to the sound of a jingling bell. The shop was small with a faint, musty smell. It contained several display cabinets. He was busy perusing the jewellery when an elderly man appeared and asked if he could be of assistance. Simon asked if he could see a pearl necklace. Ever since the night of the impromptu fashion show, Simon had longed to see a single, dainty strand of pearls around Olivia's slender neck. He was shown several necklaces in varying lengths, single and multiple strings, but he knew what he wanted and quickly made his decision. They were quite expensive, but it was the first time he'd purchased an item of jewellery, so he was naïve as to the pricing. He was just about to leave the shop – the pearls having been placed in a padded box and neatly wrapped – when he noticed some attractive brooches. Serena, he thought – a gift to signify the opening of her store. It was difficult choosing, but he eventually selected something small with emeralds. Both purchases wrapped and paid for, he left the shop but not before inquiring the way to the city library.

The library was only two streets away and checking his watch realised Olivia should be free in thirty minutes. He knew it was a bit of a gamble...would she be at the library today? If not, then he'd made a wasted trip! He'd learned from Serena that Olivia worked mornings only and was free in an afternoon. Occasionally she did a full day's work in return for a full day off. It was a risk – but she was worth it.

It was two weeks since Olivia's return and they'd exchanged five letters during that time. They never seemed to run out of things to write about, but it was Olivia's tangible presence which prompted his visit today...he wanted to kiss her again. Hoping she would be free to spend the afternoon with him, he waited outside, pacing up and down. He was like 'a cat on hot bricks', so decided to go inside. It was quiet and cool compared to outside. Simon was surprised at the size of the building and realised it would be very possible to miss Olivia as she left. His eyes scanned the ground floor for a glimpse of her, but tall bookcases made it impossible. Eventually, he went over to the desk and asked a rather stern gentleman if Miss Brown was at work today. He viewed Simon suspiciously over the top of his half-rimmed spectacles and without speaking nodded to the side. Simon turned and almost bumped into Olivia as she walked towards him, her eyes wide with apprehension.

"What are you doing here?" she whispered.

"I've come to see you," Simon replied, smiling.

A rather loud cough sounded from the gentleman at the desk. Olivia's finger went to her lips, then she mouthed, "See you outside at twelve."

Simon took the cue and left the building.

At twelve o 'clock she descended the steps of the city library and ran into Simon's arms. They kissed and hugged.

"I'm so thrilled to see you," she exclaimed. "Why are you here?"

Simon held both of her hands. "I was longing to see you again... so came on impulse."

Olivia's heart was racing.

It was a beautiful summer's day in July. They walked along, hand in hand, not really going anywhere in particular, just so delighted to be in each other's company and spend a few precious hours together. They wandered along the riverbank and found a quiet place to sit. Simon put his arm around Olivia's shoulder and pulled her close. They kissed.

"Oh, Livvy, that feels so good – I can't stop thinking about you. Now... I've got something for you," he added. He reached into his pocket and handed Olivia her present.

Carefully, she opened the box. Her eyes lit up. "Oh, Simon, they're beautiful, thank you so much," she said.

She was wearing a pretty, open necked blouse and as he fastened the clasp on the pearls, he kissed the back of her neck.

"You are very special to me, Livvy," he whispered in her ear.

"That's the second time you've shortened my name," she replied, smiling.

"I hope you don't mind – it just suits you – my 'pet name' for you." He gazed into her eyes and caressed her cheek. Then, lifting her chin, he kissed her again adoringly.

He could have called her whatever he wanted, she wouldn't have cared, she just wanted these hours to last forever.

Sadly, they knew their romantic interlude was nearing an end. Simon suggested they go for some refreshment, and Olivia took him to the same tearooms she had visited with Serena. Over tea Simon asked Olivia about her family, her schooling, her work, her friendships and they chatted about the store opening. Finally, with lots of promises to write, they parted, Simon to the station and Olivia to take the bus home. It had been an impromptu day and seemed to lay a foundation for their relationship.

The following week on a Sunday afternoon Simon walked into the morning room and found Serena absorbed in a page of figures.

"What are you up to this fine afternoon, sis?" he asked. "It's a beautiful day out there... why don't we go for a walk?" He looked at her pleadingly.

"Oh, Simon, I'm far too busy sorting all these figures."

"Nonsense," he added. "Come with me and we'll sort them together." She didn't need a second bidding and soon they were walking along towards a wooded area behind The Gables.

"Remember when we used to play here?" asked Simon.

"Of course," she replied, smiling at the memories.

"I loved to play hide and seek and climb trees to fool you, so you wouldn't find me," he recalled. They laughed at their reminiscences.

"It was always you and me, I don't recall William ever playing games with us," he remarked.

A look of sadness clouded Serena's face at the mention of William's name. Simon enquired if William had made any contact while he was away. Serena shook her head and commented that she doubted if he would unless something unusual happened.

They chatted happily after that – the moment forgotten. Simon asked Serena about the figures she was working on earlier.

"I'm trying to get an idea of my financial outlay, Simon. I need to employ an assistant to help serve the customers and a young girl to run errands. Then stock will need replenishing on a regular basis. I'm so inexperienced and we haven't discussed what the rent will be. How much I will need to pay you and how often?" she asked, anxiety creeping into her voice. She looked so serious. He decided to tease her and suggested a particular amount to be paid into his bank account on the last day of each calendar month. She stopped and her jaw dropped.

"Oh, Simon, I would have to sell a lot of stock to cover all that," she added despondently.

She looked near to tears, but he could tell her mind was working overtime, trying to calculate sales and profits.

He started to laugh and called, "Catch me," then ran off to the top of a grassy mound. Of course, she couldn't catch him, but he flopped down on the grass and started to suck a piece of long grass. She caught up and sat down beside him.

"I am so unfit," she declared.

He put his arm around her and looked very solemn. She scanned his face searching for the reason in his changed expression. After a few minutes he spoke. "Serena, the premises at 21, The High Street, Loftam, will be transferred to your name next week on the 2nd of August."

She just stared at him, her six-foot baby brother.

"What do you mean?" she stuttered.

"I was informed on Friday that the sale will be completed on 1st August, and I have instructed my solicitor to have your name put on the deeds. So, my big sis, you can take rent off your list of outgoings – you will be the owner, but you'll need to put aside a regular amount for maintenance."

With that he pulled her to her feet. She thanked him and hugged him around his chest, the highest point she could reach. Strangely for Serena, she did not query the gift. They made their way back to The Gables. Simon had decided the previous week he would make a gift of the premises to Serena – he already possessed enough property in his portfolio. He would keep a close eye on her accounts, but he was sure she'd developed, and perhaps inherited, a keen business mentality from both her parents. He had told his father of his intentions the previous evening. Robert did not doubt Simon's ability to make such a generous offer and thought it was a splendid idea.

The 2nd of August arrived, and Simon and Serena went into Newcastle to the solicitor's office to sign the relevant documents and receive the keys. Serena was beside herself with glee as they returned to Loftam later that morning. They went straight to the shop and Simon handed the keys to Serena along with a little package.

"What's this?" she enquired.

"Just a little present to remind you of this significant day," he replied.

She opened the door and once inside opened the package. She pinned the little brooch onto her white blouse.

"Oh, Simon," she declared, "it's delightful, I'll wear it every day. Thank you so much for all you have done for me."

A team of willing helpers and tradespeople worked hard over the next week, deliveries arrived, and all Serena's careful plans were put into action. The opening date of the twelfth of August was agreed, and the leaflet and adverts duly printed. A special invitation made its way to York. Upon its receipt Olivia jumped for joy and replied to Serena the same day, having secured a few days' holiday.

It was a hive of activity as stock from The Gables and Guilder's Outfitters was transferred to complete the picture. The newly acquired 'dummy models' arrived for the window display and Serena and her new assistant Marjorie had great fun dressing them. The night before the opening Simon stood on the platform to meet the York train. The two sweethearts embraced, so pleased to be in each other's arms again.

"I've missed you, Livvy," Simon remarked, kissing Olivia lovingly.

Opening day at Serena's Fashions dawned wet and dull. Not a good omen, thought Serena, but she quickly put aside any doubts and proceeded to beam for the rest of the day, making up for the lack of sunshine. The store was to open at 11am and the local newspaper was in attendance. Several photographs were taken of Serena, holding a bouquet of flowers with her two assistants in the front row. Simon, Father and Olivia stood behind. The weekly 'Loftam Herald' was available two days later. A large headline halfway down the front page declared:

NEW STORE OPENS, underneath was a photograph
with the caption

**'Serena Guilder opens her new store. Pictured with her
are her staff and family.'**

The excitement lasted for days, or so it seemed to Serena. Olivia stayed over the weekend and helped in the store on the first Saturday of trading. They were all exhausted by Sunday and took a well-earned day off.

Fifteen miles away on the outskirts of Newcastle, William finished his midday meal and announced to his wife Emily he was going to visit his family in Loftam.

Emily looked up surprised. "What... after all these months?" she questioned.

William didn't mention it, but Emily had spotted the photograph in the 'Loftam Herald' about the opening of Serena's shop.

"I suppose you'll be wanting to find out all about the new shop your sister has opened?" she asked, raising her eyebrows.

William realised he should have mentioned it sooner. Emily was not the fool William took her for. In fact, she was quite the opposite. She had William well and truly weighed up. She was aware of his occasional 'dalliances' with other women. She could smell the tell-tale aroma of a different perfume, and the stray blonde hairs on his clothes. She also knew there was more than a 'slight disagreement of a business nature' with his father, as he put it, shortly after Gertie's funeral. She knew no details – William didn't credit her with the sense to be informed, but in all these months he'd not been to Loftam to her knowledge – so it must have been quite a disagreement.

"I'll go with you," she announced unexpectedly.

William was angry but felt he could not refuse her. Anyway, he thought, as they made their way to the station, it's less likely there will be any reference to the unpleasantness, as he thought of it, if Emily and Felix are present.

William picked a bunch of flowers from the garden to take with them to help calm any troubled waters lying ahead. He still felt antagonism towards his young brother, it had been eating him up for six months now, but in truth he'd always been jealous of Simon. He was old enough to understand the implications of this new addition to their tight family unit when his father informed them of Simon's birth. His mother was besotted with the new baby, also his sister – it was as if he became invisible, so he hit back in ways he felt he could. He alienated himself from his father by refusing to show any interest in the firm. He hurt his mother repeatedly, by being contentious at her dinner parties and other events. Serena suffered his abuse with his selfish actions during her formative years – and the outcome? He was still eaten up with jealousy towards his family. Marriage removed him from the tight family circle he'd known, but even marriage failed to stem the desire to hurt his close relatives.

The news of the circumstances surrounding his brother's birth were hard to swallow – not so much his father's adultery – that only helped to make him despise his father; but this inheritance for Simon – that was too much for him to tolerate and so he lashed out with harsh words. Over the intervening months he had calmed, but realised he needed to be back 'in' with the family to gain his revenge. The presence of the elegant young woman standing beside Simon in the newspaper photograph, stirred his curiosity and his jealousy – maybe there was another potential family member he could hurt?

After Sunday lunch at The Gables Robert retired to his bedroom for a snooze. Serena busied herself in the kitchen, then settled in the morning room to read, leaving Simon and Olivia to themselves. They went for a walk. Olivia would be returning to York later in the day and Simon wanted to spend time alone with her – she was becoming an important part of his life, even if it was only three months since their first 'date'. They walked along to the woods behind the house. On the way he told her about the games he used to play with Serena in the woods, when he was a boy.

"She was like a little mother to me," he commented. "She was the one who played with me, took me on adventures and picnics – Mother and Father were more interested in my academic achievements, and William just didn't bother with me."

Olivia told Simon about her childhood, how she was close to her brother Fred – they were great companions growing up. Fred hadn't gone to boarding school so was always there for her. It was a sad day when he was 'called up' towards the end of the war, but thankfully he returned unscathed and went on to train as a teacher. He married his childhood sweetheart Betty, and their daughter Ann was born the following year.

"You must come and meet my family, Simon," added Olivia.

"Yes, I will... soon," replied Simon.

Shortly after returning to The Gables, there was a rattle on the front door. Simon and Olivia were sitting relaxing in the drawing room.

"I wonder who that can be?" questioned Simon, as he heard Serena go to answer the door. He also heard her startled reaction.

"Oh... it's you, come in." The door to the drawing room was flung open and in bounded a boisterous young boy.

"Uncle Simon, Uncle Simon," shrieked Felix. Simon jumped up and reached out his arms to envelop his young nephew – he twirled him round and round, then putting him down exclaimed,

"My... how you've grown, young Felix."

Behind all this a very demure Emily entered the room, having left her coat in the hallway. Simon went over and gave her a hug and a kiss.

"Emily, how lovely to see you, how are you?" he enquired. He liked Emily – she didn't deserve to be lumbered with his brother.

Ever the gentleman, he then introduced her to Olivia, who by now was standing behind Simon.

"Emily, this is my good friend Olivia, she's visiting from York."

Emily and Olivia shook hands and exchanged pleasantries. Felix distracted Simon at that point, as he heard his father descending the stairs. William was now standing in the room; he walked confidently over to Simon and clasped his hand, as if no unpleasantness hung in the air.

"Simon, it's good to see you. It's been a while – and who is this?" he asked looking directly at Olivia.

Simon was taken aback at his audacity, but quickly pulled himself together and repeated the introduction he had made earlier with Emily.

William smiled and said, "Pleased to meet you, Olivia. You look familiar – were you at Mother's funeral?"

Olivia commented that she had indeed accompanied her grandmother to Gertie's funeral.

While the introductions were being made Robert entered the room and stood surveying his family. Serena came bustling through the door carrying a vase of flowers.

"William and Emily brought these lovely flowers to congratulate me on the opening of my store," she said to no-one in particular, placing them on a small table.

To say the conversation that followed was stiff, would be putting it mildly... Olivia picked up on the taut atmosphere immediately. Thankfully, Felix's presence helped to dispel any potential awkwardness. William was on a two-fold mission: firstly to find out about Serena's new venture and secondly to meet this elegant young woman, whom he'd seen on Simon's arm that night in the restaurant.

"Serena," he said, smiling charmingly at his sister. "Tell me about this new store."

Serena was not one to hold grudges, so launched herself into the background details of the store's conception up to its opening. William listened with interest to the development of Serena's Fashions. William then asked if this was to be a branch of Guilder's, so Simon decided to come clean about his part in the venture.

"The venture has been funded by me, William," he announced with a bland expression.

"Oh, I see," said William thoughtfully. "Putting your inheritance to good use I suppose."

Simon did not enlighten William any further – it was none of his business if Simon gifted the store to his sister. Serena thought she was going to explode. Emily quickly took up the conversation and asked Serena questions about the current fashions. So far, Robert and William had not acknowledged one other, but Felix was making a fuss of his grandfather, which was easing the tension.

Simon then remembered the gift he had brought back from Spain, so he jumped up and said, "Felix, I've got something for you. Come with me."

Uncle and nephew left the room.

William turned to his father. "So, Father... how are you?"

Robert cleared his throat – he was too old to admonish his oldest son. "Oh, I'm pulling myself together now," he replied.

William proceeded to ask about the store and how the business was going. Serena was listening in to this conversation while Olivia and Emily were discussing skirt lengths and other fashion highlights.

Felix came bounding into the room carrying a box of toy soldiers. He went straight to his father to show him the gift Uncle Simon had brought back for him from Spain. Simon was amazed how William engaged with young Felix, and soon they were both down on the floor playing a game. Serena stood and suggested she would go and make some tea.

"I'll help," offered Simon, desperate to vacate the room. Once in the kitchen he let out a big sigh "Phew... that went better than I expected," he exclaimed. "But no word of apology from our high and mighty brother, I notice."

"I suppose the fact he made the effort to turn up after six months of silence, is something to be thankful for – good job Felix and Emily are here, otherwise – who knows?" added Serena.

The remainder of the afternoon passed peaceably. William had achieved what he set out to do.

Simon looked at his watch and realised it was time to leave for Olivia to catch her train. They could have left it until later, but Simon was tired of playing 'happy families' and thought he would rather spend extra time in the station waiting room kissing Olivia. They made their departure. Simon hoped Serena and Father would be spared any difficult conversation once they were gone.

As Simon and Olivia journeyed from Loftam to Newcastle, Simon commented, "Well Olivia, you've had the pleasure of meeting my brother."

She snuggled up to him in the carriage. "I'd never have guessed you were brothers – you are very different."

Simon decided that now was a good time to explain his birth to Olivia. "We are different, because we have different mothers."

Olivia looked aghast.

Simon continued, "I'm only telling you this in strict confidence, Olivia. No-one except Serena knows this – not even Emily. I was the product of a brief encounter on my father's behalf ...it was an isolated occurrence, and thankfully, my mother, the dear soul that she was, forgave him, and I was raised as their son. Please keep that information to yourself, my darling," he added, squeezing her hand.

She kissed him spontaneously, despite the busy carriage. She leaned in closer to him and said, "Thank you for sharing that with me, Simon." Olivia felt sharing this confidentiality was evidence of a step forward in their relationship.

As they said their 'goodbyes' on the station platform, Olivia asked Simon if he would be able to visit York to meet her parents in two weeks' time and he agreed.

***

A letter with a Spanish postmark was lying on the hall table when Simon arrived home from the firm the next day. He was alone in the house. Father was visiting Serena at the end of business that day, so Simon walked home alone. He spent his time of solitude mulling over this proposed visit to York. There was no doubt in his mind that his feelings for Olivia were overwhelming – she occupied his thoughts constantly. He longed to be with her, soaking in her tangible presence. Reading her letters brought some sense of connection... but their relationship was only in its early stages – in three months things had moved quickly. Somehow going to visit her parents seemed a big step ... one he was unsure he was ready to take just yet.

He sat down and opened his letter. It was from Carlos. It was a very cheery letter and Simon felt the comradeship that had developed between the two young men back in the spring, jump out of the pages. He was full of news, places he'd been, people he'd met, but he was travelling to London in two weeks' time and wondered if Simon could meet him. Apparently, Carlos was obsessed with motor cars, and knew about a racing track in England called Brooklands. There was an event taking place there at the end of August and he would like to visit with Simon, if it could be arranged. He would book a hotel for them both for a long weekend.

Since his visit to Madrid Simon had also developed an interest in motor cars – they fascinated him. This was a great opportunity to find out more about this new aspect of life which was developing quickly. He often dreamed about driving a motor car. He imagined it would be an exhilarating experience. He also liked the idea of spending time with Carlos again.

Suddenly, it dawned on him... it was the same weekend that Olivia had mentioned visiting York to meet her parents. Could he get out of it? It was only a suggestion. It would 'put off' meeting Olivia's parents a bit longer. Decision made, he climbed the stairs two at a time and wrote two letters – one to Carlos accepting his invitation, the other to Olivia, explaining how sorry he was but his friend Carlos from Spain was going to be in London the last weekend in August and he was invited to spend a few days with him. He sealed both letters and posted them the next day. A few days later he received two replies. Carlos was delighted. Olivia was disappointed. Spanish Simon and English Simon – two sides of the one coin.

Olivia was more than disappointed – she was devastated – she thought a weekend for Simon to meet her parents would set their relationship on a forward course. However, she replied saying she hoped he would enjoy his weekend with his friend and looked forward to hearing about it. She was sure there would be opportunities in the future for Simon to visit her home.

The extended weekend in London was just up Simon's alley. He had a fantastic experience. Carlos knew how to show Simon a 'good time'. The two young men partied, laughed, drank, and had tremendous fun. The motoring event lived up to Simon's expectations and each evening they found new places to dine and drink. They went dancing and visited nightclubs. Two young men out on the town. Simon enjoyed smoking cigars and drinking cocktails – two things totally unimaginable back home in Loftam.

On the last evening they were enjoying cocktails in a nightclub and Carlos went to the bar. Simon pondered... if Father and Serena could see me now. Suddenly, Olivia came into his mind. He realised he'd not given her one thought all evening – he felt guilty...was this evidence he wasn't ready for a permanent relationship? He'd been carried along on the crest of a wave hurtling its way to the seashore and for the first time since meeting Olivia, he began to have doubts. He shrugged his thoughts off as Carlos returned from the bar with an attractive young lady in tow.

"Do you mind?" Carlos asked Simon.

Simon was nonplussed at first and thought Carlos wanted the girl to join them for a drink, but after a while Simon began to feel awkward... three was most definitely a crowd, so he politely took his leave, saying he would see Carlos at breakfast.

The next morning, Simon realised that Carlos had spent the whole night in the company of the young lady and thanked his friend for being so understanding. It was the end of the 'boys' weekend'. They enjoyed a walk and a fine lunch before parting. Simon indicated to Carlos that he might be returning to Madrid soon and hoped they could meet up again. The idea of visiting Spain again wasn't imminent, but once spoken it gained momentum.

CHAPTER 8

SPAIN 1922

Elise Dominguez stepped out of the taxi, paid the driver, and stood staring at the house – Casa Galiana. She shivered, despite the warmth of the September day. It was fifteen months since she had left this house...the night the Guardia Civil knocked on the door when Eugenie failed to return home. Slowly she made her way up the sweeping drive. This house never ceased to impress her. It had been her home, on and off, for years – but would it continue to be her home now Eugenie was no longer here? She knocked on the door and after a short wait the door was flung open as Isabella, the housekeeper, answered.

"Senorita Elise, how good to see you," she declared excitably, kissing the young woman and taking her bag. A little dog rushed out of the door making such a fuss.

"Pepe, I've missed you so much," shrieked Elise, bending down to pat Pepe, Eugenie's dog – a King Charles spaniel. She was promptly welcomed with affectionate licks.

Isabella was talking at high speed as she led Elise into the house and through the French windows, leading to the back garden where refreshments were waiting. Elise enjoyed her glass of home-made lemonade and listened to the elderly lady, who hardly stopped for breath. So much had happened she said, and Elise smiled. She could feel her eyelids starting to droop – her journey had begun early that morning. Most of the commentary was irrelevant and washed over Elise until Isabella referred to the visit of two young men...who had stayed overnight.

"Who were they?" asked Elise, very puzzled.

"One man was Spanish, the other English. Senor Perez, the solicitor, told me to offer them accommodation and food."

Elise was totally perplexed at this, and Isabella continued. "The Englishman is the new owner of this house, Senorita."

Elise gasped and covered her mouth, as Isabella stood up and went bustling off into the kitchen. Elise let out a big sigh. 'The new owner of this house,' she said out aloud. 'How can that be?' She rubbed her forehead wearily. I suppose I should have expected this, she thought to herself as Isabella returned carrying a box full of correspondence.

She handed Elise a piece of paper on which was written the name and address of a solicitor in Madrid, Elise recognised the name – it was the solicitor who had organised Eugenie's graveside funeral.

"You must contact Senor Pérez, the solicitor, on your return," announced Isabella. "In there are all the letters since you left," said the housekeeper indicating the overflowing box. "Your friend told me to keep them and not send them to you, because you were ill."

How thoughtful of her friend Francoise. When Eugenie died, she came to be with her in Madrid and after the funeral insisted Elise returned to France with her to take time to rest. Francoise contacted Isabella to pack a trunk with Elise's belongings and send it to Francoise's home – she was unsure how long her friend would be away.

Elise was almost asleep. Stifling a yawn she announced, "Isabella, I need to rest, I think I'll go to my room and sleep for a while... I'll be back shortly."

"Yes, yes, Senorita... you go and rest while I prepare dinner," she agreed.

Elise climbed the stairs wearily and flopped down on the bed; within minutes she was asleep. It was dark when she woke. She went downstairs and hungrily ate the delicious food Isabella put before her. As she was finishing Isabella indicated she was leaving – she lived a few streets away.

"I'll see you tomorrow, Senorita – don't forget to lock the doors, and let Pepe out into the garden. Adios."

Elise was wide awake now. She let Pepe into the garden, then checked the doors and windows and gave the little dog some food. She wandered into the lounge, stopping to stare at Eugenie's portrait hanging above the marble fireplace. The portrait was so lifelike...it was hard to believe this handsome woman was gone, taken in the prime of her life. A lump formed in Elise's' throat.

"Who have you left this house to, Eugenie?" she questioned the portrait. She looked around the tastefully furnished room, then her gaze rested on the piano.

'I haven't played in months,' she declared out aloud. She walked over to the piano and opening the lid, sat down and began to play. Her fingers danced over the ivories...she played from memory and as she did, something released inside her... a peace enveloped her. Music always soothed Elise. Eugenie, although a pianist herself, loved to hear Elise play. Most of their evenings were spent in this room with Elise playing, and always Eugenie asked her to play 'Fur Elise' by Beethoven – it was her favourite. On one occasion she brought Elise a gift from Madrid – a square musical jewellery box, with a tiny wind-up handle – it played 'Fur Elise'. 'For you my dear,' she had said, giving the musical box to Elise. And now that little box was sat on her dressing table upstairs.

She stopped playing and shut the lid. A calmness surrounded her – something she had not felt in months. She went to the kitchen and made herself a bedtime drink – a habit she had acquired while staying with Francoise. She returned to the lounge, Pepe following at her heels. She sat down in one of the elegant chairs beside the fireplace and curled her feet underneath her. She let out a sigh... home...it was good to be back. She could have returned after Christmas, but she had stayed away deliberately...why? Because there was no-one to return to...no mother, no father, no aunt, no uncle, no sweetheart...only sad, sad memories. In the space of seven years, Elise had been a chief mourner at four gravesides, and she was only twenty-one years old. After Eugenie's passing, Francoise insisted she needed time to grieve properly. So, Elise stayed with her friend in France.

"It's just us now, Pepe," she said, bending to stroke the little dog. "Here we are in a stranger's house and for how much longer?" The dog thumped his tail as if in answer. She glanced at the box of letters – tomorrow... I will open them tomorrow, she promised herself, finished her drink, put out the lights and went to her bedroom. Pepe followed.

As she sat brushing out her long, dark hair before undressing, she glanced down at the double photograph frame. Herself, wearing a wistful smile and Phillipe... she ran her fingers over his face – he was so handsome, her soldier. He was Francoise' brother. She had first met him when she was fifteen, when she stayed with Francoise and her family during the vacation from the convent boarding school she attended. Francoise was also a boarder. She and Phillipe were attracted to each other immediately. They exchanged letters for more than three years. During the Easter vacation of 1918, Phillipe asked her to marry him. She was young and an orphan since her parents had died just before the Great War. Her father had died from pneumonia and her mother from cancer. After her parents' death Eugenie's husband, Juan, became her guardian.

That Easter, Phillipe told Elise he'd received orders to return to the Front – it was too much to resist...the passion, the urgency of youth, the brevity of wartime life. So, she gave herself to him, willingly – he placed no demands upon her. Their parting was full of unfulfilled promises. By the summer she knew she was carrying Phillipe's child. She was staying with Eugenie and Juan that vacation. She confided in them. They were understanding and urged her to write to Phillipe and tell him. However, before she had a chance to write the letter, she heard from Francoise that Phillipe was a casualty of war... killed in action. She was unable to travel to France for his funeral. She did not tell her friend about the baby. Phillipe never knew he was to become a father. She opened the back of the frame and took out the photograph, kissed his handsome face, then, ripping it into pieces, dropped them into her bin. 'I must move on – I can't let the past affect my future anymore,' she admitted to herself. Climbing into bed, with Pepe at her feet, she turned out the lamp.

Elise awoke early, roused by Pepe's whining. She quickly dressed and took the little dog for a walk. It was a cool, crisp, autumn morning. Casa Galiana was situated on a hillside above the town of Toledo – an area where the rich people built their grand houses, away from the hustle and bustle of the town. Today, she thought as she walked along, I must tackle that box of letters and telephone the solicitor to make an appointment. She felt rejuvenated...she was ready to move on.

Eugenie's accident and subsequent death was the catalyst that had stirred the memories of those sad years. For weeks when she was a guest at Francoise's home in France, she hardly registered the date. She joined in the family life in her friend's home, but her behaviour was robotic – as if she were viewing herself from afar. Francoise recognised her friend's need for recuperation. She didn't press her to come to any decisions and wrapped her in a cocoon of love and patience. Had she been a nurse, Francoise would have called it a 'nervous breakdown', but no medical advice was sought. She lovingly protected her friend and slowly watched her emerge from her dark tunnel of grief.

Isabella was busy in the kitchen when Elise returned from her walk. "Ah," she said, "that's good, I've found it tiring taking Pepe out each morning. Sometimes my little grandson comes to take him out when he is off school." Then she added: "Your trunk has arrived from France, Senorita."

Elise walked through to the hallway. Her eyes fell on her trusty trunk – it had been a companion of sorts for years. Packing and unpacking her trunk was a part of Elise's life. This time it had been with her in France. She opened it up and relieved it of its contents bit by bit. How long before I am packing you again, she wondered, as she finally pulled it along to its storage place. Entering the kitchen, she ravenously ate some tasty bread from the bakery which Isabella had collected on her way to Casa Galiana.

"I'm hungry," she remarked, as Isabella cut two more slices.

"Eat up," encouraged the older lady eyeing her. "You could do with fattening up."

Elise looked down at her petite, slim figure. Yes, she thought, I have lost weight, but I seem to have found my appetite again.

After taking a bath, Elise went into the lounge and began playing the piano again. I know I am putting off the two tasks ahead of me today, she thought, but the soothing effect of the music last night might help me again. She was aware of Isabella standing in the doorway, so she stopped playing and turned.

"That's beautiful, Senorita, my grandson would love to learn to play like that."

Elise was thoughtful for a moment then replied, "Would you like me to teach him, Isabella?"

"Oh Senorita, would you? My son will pay for the lessons."

"Oh, don't worry about that, we'll arrange a time and see how he progresses," added Elise. Perhaps using her musical gift would help to give her life a focus... she was clutching at straws, but teaching the piano appealed to her.

Without further distractions Elise telephoned the solicitor's office and made an appointment for the end of the week. Now she thought...the box. Two hours passed, but finally she came to the last letter. It wasn't the daunting task she had envisaged, and she felt a sense of achievement. She sorted the letters into different piles. Letters of condolence; official letters, addressed to Eugenie; letters from the solicitor requesting her to contact him. One letter dated about six months ago was different. It was to inform her of the visit of a Mr Simon Guilder to view Casa Galiana. This sounded like the Englishman Isabella had mentioned. But who was he? And what was his connection to Eugenie?

***

At the end of the week Elise travelled to Madrid by train. It was a journey she'd made many times. When she was born her parents lived in a small village north of Madrid. Juan, her uncle, was older than her father and she thought of him like a grandfather. The two brothers were opposites. Her father, a quiet, reticent man, owned a cobbler's shop, and they lived in the apartment above it. Juan, her uncle, was an outgoing man with an endearing manner. He had been a salesman in his younger days but with a keen eye for business soon made his fortune. Uncle Juan was always generous towards his brother and offered to pay for Elise to attend a convent school west of Madrid. When her parents died, within a few months of each other, Uncle Juan became her guardian. She was an only child and her parents' assets amounted to little – only just covering their debts. It was during this time Elise first visited Casa Galiana and she continued to stay there in her school vacations unless she was invited to stay with Francoise.

The train travelled through small villages and countryside. Elise sat back and let her mind wander... somewhere out there, she thought, my son is eating, drinking, playing, living his life. Her baby would be three years old now...does he have Phillipe's eyes? Does he resemble me in any way? It was a door she rarely opened – no good could emerge from dwelling on those kinds of questions. Her aunt and uncle were so caring and understanding towards her. They accepted her explanation of her predicament without question, and insisted she waited until after the baby was born, to make any decisions about her future, but Elise was adamant... she wanted to give her baby up for adoption. When the Great War came to an end, her Uncle Juan contracted Spanish flu. He tragically died just weeks before her healthy baby boy was born. Within hours of the birth at

Casa Galiana, she held her son, kissed him lovingly, then handed him to the nurse. Eugenie arranged for the baby to be adopted. Elise did not want to know any details; her decision was final.

Elise was early for her appointment. She went into a café for some refreshment. She looked around her. Everyone seemed to be with somebody. Oh, she felt so alone. What was she going to do with the rest of her life? I have no skills. Then she reflected...no, I do have skills... I can sing, play the piano and speak three languages. At the convent school there were nuns from England, France, and Spain. The students received language tuition in all these languages, and she spoke all three fluently. Can I use any of these skills to earn my living, she pondered?

A short time later she was sitting in an office facing the solicitor, Senor Pérez. The moment felt ominous...her future was about to be defined. The elderly gentleman greeted her and enquired about her health.

"I'm well now, thank you," she replied.

Senor Perez then went on to explain the contents of Senora Eugenie Dominguez's will. All of Eugenie's properties – he listed them – were left to her son Mr Simon Guilder, an Englishman, along with some substantial financial holdings – he did not elaborate on these. He then looked over his glasses.

"Senorita, the Trust Fund your uncle Juan Dominguez set up for you, is to continue for your lifetime under the terms of Senora Dominguez's will – and alongside that an inheritance of 10,000 pesetas is left to you." He paused then added, "You are a young lady with a secure financial future. Your finances are held by the Banco de Espana. I will give you the details of your accounts and suggest you visit their branch here in Madrid very soon, to understand what is involved."

Elise sat very still. She was thunderstruck. Eugenie's will meant she would retain her Trust Fund and an inheritance! She had expected the solicitor to inform her when she needed to vacate her home. She had questions but could not articulate them. As if he sensed her bewilderment, he continued, "The house you call home in Toledo, now belongs to the English gentleman, but he assures me he has no immediate plans for the property and specifically indicated that you should continue to live at Casa Galiana in the short term." He rummaged through some papers. "The housekeeper's services are being retained by Mr Guilder. I am hoping that he will be visiting again soon, as there are many details to finalise."

Suddenly, Elise found her voice.

"Did you say the English gentleman was Eugenie's son?"

"Yes," replied Senor Perez. "He was raised by his father in England and did not know of his mother's identity until her death."

Elise just sat and stared, but the solicitor stood – obviously deciding their meeting was over. He handed Elise an envelope. "In here are the details of the bank accounts – any other queries, please get in touch." They shook hands and she left the office.

Outside it was a beautiful day. Elise walked and found herself a seat in a park. The autumn colours were striking. How caring of Eugenie to make sure her Trust Fund continued. She would visit the bank another day, she decided, and wandered on until she found a café she'd visited before, where she enjoyed some lunch. To end her visit she went to the graveyard. It took her some time but eventually she found Eugenie's grave. Someone, probably the solicitor, had arranged for Eugenie's name to be added underneath her uncle's. They were a strange couple – almost mis-matched. Elise shook her head at Eugenie's age. She was twenty-five years younger than Juan. She did not know how long they were married. I wonder why she married a much older man, she mused, and why was she separated from her son? Questions, questions, questions... probably I will never know the answers, she thought, as she made her way back to the station.

As the train journeyed to Toledo, she reflected on what the solicitor had told her. She was oblivious to the wealth of her aunt and uncle – no wonder Eugenie needed to spend two days a month in Madrid attending to business. She gave no outward signs of wealth and lived quite modestly. She continued to muse... a house in Barcelona – she'd never heard that mentioned before. So, Eugenie was a mother... another well-kept secret and not Juan's child. He must have been born before Eugenie married Juan. It suddenly dawned on Elise why Eugenie was so understanding when she had told her about her own pregnancy ... she understood because she must have experienced the same predicament herself. The train arrived at her destination. I wonder what this Englishman is like. He is certainly a very wealthy man judging by what the solicitor conveyed. She suddenly felt contented, as she left the station to walk up the hill to Casa Galiana. At least I can continue to live in this beautiful Spanish house until this Mr Guilder decides otherwise, she thought.

CHAPTER 9

LOFTAM, ENGLAND
1922

Autumn has most definitely arrived, sighed Simon, as he made his way up the hill after another busy day...in fact a busy week. Since returning from his weekend in London with Carlos, he had found himself involved in numerous business meetings at the firm. His father was including him in the day-to-day management of the store. Maybe this was to keep his mind firmly focussed on Guilder's Outfitters. More time was spent in the office than on the shop floor these days and today he was informed he was to take his father's place at a trade fair in Leeds the following week. He began to ponder the possibility of meeting up with Olivia in Leeds. The idea started to grow on him. He'd received two letters from Olivia since declining the invitation to meet her parents and he had not replied. What must she be thinking, he mused? I'll write to her tonight to ask if she can meet me in Leeds, on Friday.

When he arrived home, he noticed a letter addressed to him with the word 'private' in the corner. It was from Mr Adams. The solicitor was requesting him to visit his office in Newcastle at his earliest convenience. Simon decided to visit on Monday, so sat down and penned a letter to that effect. While he was busy, he wrote to Olivia, apologising profusely for not having been in touch and giving a brief update on how busy life at Guilder's was becoming. He mentioned his visit to Leeds and asked if she might be able to meet him on Friday. He added a few lines about how much he was missing her and for the first time in their correspondence he signed off... 'I can't wait to hold you in my arms again, Love Simon'. Until now his letters were signed 'your friend, Simon'. It was a subtle change, but one he felt ready to make.

On Monday he went to the firm on the morning and then excused himself to keep his appointment with Mr Adams. The appointment lasted about an hour. The communication from Alberto in Madrid left Simon in no doubt that his presence in Spain was required imminently. Alberto had written to him 'care of' Mr Adams as arranged. There were loose ends to tie up from Senora Dominguez's estate, but – and this came as a total surprise to Simon – there were board meetings that he needed to attend in person. Simon was young with no experience of the business world other than Guilder's. Apparently, he could only be absent from these meetings on a few occasions, so his attendance was required most of the time. Mr Adams was diligent in acquiring the necessary information and he concluded that Simon would need to be physically present in Madrid at least twice a year, for about a month on each occasion. His manager in Madrid made this tentative suggestion but he needed to see Simon by November, as there were three important meetings. What, thought Simon, is the point of my being there when the proceedings will be conducted in Spanish! So, leaving Mr Adams' office he realised the need to make plans to be in Madrid for the month of November, plus travelling time. He telephoned Serena at her shop to ask the whereabouts of the agent who had booked his trip in the spring. She was surprised to hear that he needed to visit again so soon but gave him the details of the travel agent.

Later that evening he told his father about his proposed trip. Until now he was vague about his assets in Spain, and he saw no need to enhance this arrangement. 'Board meetings' he decided would be his explanation and amazingly it satisfied both Serena and his father, but Olivia might not be so easy to convince.

A letter was waiting from Olivia when he returned home that evening saying she could meet him in Leeds station underneath the clock at 1pm. He replied to her the next day. The following Wednesday he attended the Trade fair and stayed at a nearby hotel for two nights. He was bored at the Trade fair and was looking forward to meeting Olivia on Friday. He arrived first, excitement bubbling within at the anticipation of seeing her again. He checked his watch and looking up saw her leaving the platform and walking towards him. When he saw her, he felt a stirring deep within him. He opened his arms and enveloped her in a loving embrace, then lifting her chin he kissed her affectionately. "Mm that feels good," he added, placing his arm around her. It was a few weeks since they'd met, and there was so much to chat about. Conversation was never a problem between the pair. They talked on many topics. Olivia was well read, so any topic from history, geography, science, and current affairs brought an observation and an opinion. Simon noticed they were often on the same wavelength and could guess what each other's reactions would be. They walked and talked, ate a delicious lunch and shared a bottle of wine.

As they were finishing their lunch Simon asked, "When's your birthday Livvy and I have no idea how old you are?"

Olivia noticed the mischievous glint in Simon's eyes. She sat back and smiled.

"My birthday is October 21st, Simon, and I think I'm older than you...I will be twenty-five at the end of the month," she added, looking at him questioningly.

"Oh, that's good," he teased, "I need someone older and wiser to keep me in check." She promptly gave him a kick under the table, and they both started laughing. "I was twenty-two at the end of September," he added.

Olivia already knew Simon's age and birthdate from Serena and wondered how he would react to her being older than him. They chatted about birthdays, then Olivia asked Simon about his trip to London. She was keen to hear about his friend Carlos. Without trying he found himself being 'vague' again. "Carlos is a university tutor and an interpreter. I met him when he interpreted for his uncle, the solicitor who handled my legacy in Spain," he commented. Well, all that was true, but he omitted the fact that Carlos was 'a man about town' who loved the nightlife, drinking and beautiful women.

"So, what did you do all weekend?" enquired Olivia.

He gave details of the visit to Brooklands and their shared love of motorcars.

"I hope to own my own motor car one day," he remarked. "Other than that, we did some sightseeing, and ate lots of delicious meals in some upmarket restaurants. It was a good weekend... we must visit London together, Livvy," he added on impulse. Olivia looked bashful and Simon suddenly realised his mistake. "Er... I mean, we could ask Serena to join us, if she could arrange a weekend away from the store." He blushed trying to get himself out of a hole.

She gazed at him across the table and smiled,

"Yes, I'd like that, Simon," she responded. The time flew by and soon it was time to leave. As they stood arm in arm, waiting in the station, Simon looked at Olivia and commented, "I've enjoyed today...I must try to arrange more business trips to this area, but I'm going to Madrid at the end of October, and I'll be away until the beginning of December." He felt guilty about telling her.

She looked up at him and searched his eyes – what was it about Spain he kept so secretive?

"Hope you enjoy it," she answered.

Then he bent down and kissed her lovingly. They parted with promises to write. Olivia took the train for York and Simon the train to Newcastle. He felt sad at the prospect of not seeing Olivia for a few weeks...he was becoming attached to her.

After another busy week helping his father, he took an afternoon off and went into Newcastle to collect his travel tickets. He found himself looking forward to his Spanish visit, especially the 'fun time' with Carlos. Remembering Olivia's birthday, he went to buy a card and a silk scarf as a present. He would parcel them up and visit the post office the next day. As he was leaving the shop he bumped into William. It was about two months since the day William had visited Loftam. It was an awkward meeting – no distractions this time. William asked if he had time to go for some refreshments. Simon wanted to decline, then thought better of it. Their conversation was general until William asked Simon directly about Olivia.

"So, are there to be 'wedding bells' soon with you and Olivia?"

Simon was taken aback. "Good grief... no, we're just friends." He added, "I'm off to Spain again next week – some loose ends to tie up."

They finished their drinks and Simon indicated he needed to go, so they parted. William reflected on Simon's comments. He was convinced Simon was being evasive about his inheritance. Once again, his brother had stirred two emotions within him –curiosity and envy.

***

SPAIN

AUTUMN 1922

At the end of October Simon found himself travelling to Spain again. This time he arranged to stay overnight in London and do the London to Madrid leg in one day. It was a long day, rising early in London and arriving at his Madrid apartment late at night, but it gave him a free day to sleep in and relax and have a walk before meeting with Alberto the next morning. The place felt different to his last visit. The beautiful feeling of spring had given way to the dullness of autumn – he found it strange, assuming Spain was always warm and sunny.

That night he ate in the hotel dining room. He was quite surprised when he realised he was receiving special attention, until he remembered he owned the place. He exited as soon as he had finished his meal, making a mental note to avoid making the mistake again. Back in the safety of his apartment he studied his surroundings. It felt sparse – probably Eugenie only slept here so needed few home comforts. He made a note of some changes he would like to make – redecorate; double bed; a kitchen so he could make himself some food; a settee and a couple of comfortable chairs – in case he wanted to entertain. He popped the list in his jacket pocket to pass to Alberto the next day. He also decided to buy a couple of pictures for the walls and perhaps a clock. If he was going to be spending two months of the year living here, he may as well make it feel homely.

Staying in the apartment made him think about his mother. What was she like? He knew what she looked like physically, but what was she like as a person... what was the pitch of her voice? What were her likes and dislikes... her favourite foods?... did she read? ...like music? How would he ever find out? Surely, if she was only in her early forties, she must have living relatives – and they would be my relatives, he pondered. As he was mulling all this over, he remembered the house in Toledo. I wonder if the companion has returned. He could not remember her name, he felt sure he'd been told. He tried to think... the housekeeper commented this companion was Eugenie's niece. Simon stopped and realised he'd imagined the phrase 'companion' to mean an elderly lady in her sixties. But that's impossible, if she was Eugenie's niece, he thought. I need to visit the house in Toledo again...did I say this lady could stay there? I really must check this out.

Next morning, he was bombarded with a large amount of detail when he visited his manager. Slowly he began to realise that sitting on the board of major companies was not a task to be taken lightly. Simon did not have a clue and confided as much in his manager. Alberto was helpful and gave Simon the dates of the three meetings that month. He then suggested taking each one in turn, spending two days before each meeting going into the details of each company – how it was managed, what were its assets, distribution, staffing, accounts. He offered to accompany Simon to the meetings and interpret for him. Simon felt daunted by it all and for a moment wondered if it would be easier to sell these companies – but as he did, he saw the portrait of his mother in the Toledo house. I can't let her down, he thought. She gave me this legacy and I must do my best to fulfil this role.

The management of the properties was more straightforward, and Alberto gave a report on each relating mostly to maintenance and profitability. Simon was given a copy of each report and he suggested a duplicate be sent regularly to Mr Adams – involving another legal brain could absorb the detail and keep a watchful eye. That left the two houses in Toledo and Barcelona. Simon enquired about the one which seemed the most relevant – The Spanish House in Toledo... Casa Galiana. He learned that Eugenie's companion was indeed the niece of Eugenie's husband – so no relation to him. She'd recently returned from France, having been ill and was living at Casa Galiana.

"So, what exactly is the arrangement with Senorita Dominguez regarding the house?" asked Simon.

Alberto looked up at him and replied, "That is for you to decide, Senor Guilder." He rubbed his chin, "She is living there rent free, which does not make good business sense, so maybe you could come to some arrangement."

Simon stared at him. "I can't start charging her rent – it's been her home."

Alberto was determined. "But Senor – it's your property. She only lived there because of her uncle and aunt."

"Well," concluded Simon, not at all happy with the idea of charging Eugenie's niece rent, "I need to speak to this lady before I make any decision."

That evening he contacted Carlos to let him know he was in Madrid. He was delighted and they arranged to meet at the weekend. Simon spent two intense days being instructed in the business of one of his holdings by Alberto. On Friday morning they attended the meeting together. It was an overwhelming experience for Simon. He hardly understood a word other than the translation Alberto provided. One kind gentleman did speak some English and took time to explain some things in both languages. Simon thanked him immensely. Alberto suggested they go over what had taken place, on Monday, so Simon could gain a greater understanding. One meeting attended – two more to go.

On Saturday morning he met Carlos. It was cool but sunny and Carlos had a surprise for him. Once outside Carlos walked over to a brand-new, shiny motor car – Carlos owned his own car! He threw Simon a hat and scarf and they set off for a drive. Simon felt alive...the wind rushing past his face as they drove out of the city. It was a thrilling experience – the open road. He marvelled at the machine and at his friend's ability to drive it.

Later, the two young men went out for dinner then on to a jazz club. It was reminiscent of the weekend in London. The music pulsed through Simon's body, it struck a chord with him, and he longed to hear more. As they were partying Simon asked Carlos if he would help him to learn Spanish. He realised how much it hindered him not being able to speak the language. Carlos agreed and offered to give him his first lesson the next morning – if he agreed to go for another drive in the afternoon. The next day the lesson was hard, but the ride was exhilarating. Simon asked Carlos to write down some basic phrases for him to learn for when he visited the house in Toledo; he tried to memorise the phrases and practise the pronunciation. On Tuesday he took the train to Toledo. On the way he consulted the little book in which he'd written down the phrases. He was determined to learn this language in order to conduct his business.

***

CHAPTER 9

It was several weeks since Elise had visited Madrid and learned about her financial position. Her annuity from her uncle was enough to keep her living comfortably, but she knew she must consider moving out of Casa Galiana if the Englishman had other plans for the house. So, she needed to do something to supplement her income. The answer to that problem solved itself quite quickly. The trial piano lesson with Isabella's grandson was successful and a few days afterwards Isabella asked if she would consider another pupil. One month later Elise was teaching six pupils and really enjoying the experience. She visited the music store in Toledo to buy some sheet music and placed an advert in the window. She was advised by the music shop owner what to charge for the lessons. For the first time in her life Elise was earning an income and it was happening in her own lounge! Her days developed a structure. Elise suggested to Isabella she should reduce her hours. The older lady was looking weary these days, so it was decided she would work weekday mornings only and Elise would do her own food shopping and cooking. She enjoyed visiting the local shops and the market. She found cooking a challenge at first but was gradually beginning to try new recipes.

One morning in early November she was startled to hear Isabella answering the door and come dashing into the kitchen.

"Caballero Inglis, Caballero Inglis," she exclaimed.

Elise looked up to see what the older lady was so agitated about as she signalled for her to go to the door. She walked through the hallway to the front door. Before her stood a tall, dark, strikingly handsome young man ...with Eugenie's eyes. She was in no doubt as to his identity.

"Come in," she said in Spanish and Simon stepped into the hallway. He began to speak some Spanish words with a very English accent. The young man amused her so she thought she would play along for a little while to give her the chance to observe him. She could hardly make out what he was trying to say, but with the help of sign language she took his hat and coat and invited him to sit down in the lounge. She asked, in Spanish, if he would like a drink, he answered yes, so she went off in search of Isabella.

Simon took a deep breath once she left the room. Senorita Dominguez was not what he was expecting. Having realised Eugenie's niece was young he had failed to visualise her appearance, but she was beautiful. He realised she was the girl in the photograph frame in the bedroom. He guessed she was about his own age. Elise returned to the room and explained in Spanish some tea was on its way. As they waited Simon tried hard to remember the rest of his phrases and spluttered some words in his fledgling Spanish. "Oh, I give up," he added in surrender and fumbled in his pocket for his notebook. He was starting to ask the questions when he realised, he would not be able to understand the answers. He was totally out of his depth... and he felt foolish. Eugenie's niece sat and watched him with a perplexed look on her face. To hide his embarrassment, he stood up and went over to look at his mother's portrait. There was something very comforting about that portrait. He managed to say aloud in Spanish, "My mother." She was striking, perhaps not as beautiful as the girl in this room, but she was elegant, full of poise and dignity. He was startled by a voice behind him.

"Your mother was a caring, kind lady and I have much to thank her for."

Simon slowly turned and their eyes met. He blinked; she was mesmerising.

"You speak English," he declared with a look of astonishment on his face.

"Yes," she replied, dropping her eyes sheepishly, "I confess I do."

"You must think my attempts at Spanish very foolish," he continued, a smile spreading across his face.

"Not at all, Senor, I understand you are trying to learn the language of your mother's tongue."

Simon looked again at the portrait.

"I want to know what she was like...her personality, her likes and dislikes, and what motivated her." He was interrupted by the arrival of a little dog through the French windows.

"Pepe, come here," said Elise in Spanish. The moment was lost, and Elise sat down again. Isabella brought some tea and while they were drinking Simon started to ask her his questions – this time in English.

"Senorita, do you have future plans? Do you have any family living nearby?" Suddenly he stopped. "Forgive me...please don't feel obliged to answer." They were strangers, meeting for the first time; he was out of order trying to interrogate her. "The purpose of my visit today is to introduce myself. I am grateful that you are living here. It is a beautiful house, and it needs to be enjoyed. I understand it is your home. You are welcome to continue to live here."

She looked at him and smiled. He felt his heart melting under that smile...gosh she was so beautiful.

"Thank you, Senor Guilder, that is most kind of you, but you must advise me of the rental charge."

He shook his head.

"No, no, Senorita, you can live here rent free for as long as you wish. I will arrange for my manager to draw up a letter to that effect." Simon stood and thanked her for the tea, then bent to pat the little dog.

"It has been a pleasure to meet you, Senorita. I will call again next time I am in Spain and then you can tell me about my mother." He reached out to shake her hand. "Please call me Simon," he added.

"I will look forward to you visiting, Simon," she replied. "And please call me Elise."

They shook hands. Thirty minutes later Simon was on a train travelling back to Madrid. Something had happened to him, but he did not quite know what it was.

***

Throughout the remainder of his visit Simon learned some important lessons. During the working days, he came to understand how his Spanish holdings worked. He bought some large notebooks. He started to make notes about each, well at least the first three. He intended to repeat the process when he visited next spring and learned about the other holdings. He listened and learned, noted facts and figures, was guided around factories and shops, then at night he would diligently make notes about all he'd learned. He began to pick up some Spanish phrases and, on the weekends, he met up with Carlos for more Spanish lessons. Carlos suggested when Simon returned home, he would write to him weekly in Spanish, and he wanted Simon to reply to his letters, in Spanish. He gave him a Spanish-English dictionary to help with this task.

The two young men enjoyed more motoring adventures over those few weekends and on one occasion Carlos gave Simon a lesson in how to drive the motor car. It was a country road and straight. Simon was nervous and cautious but thrilled. Carlos was a patient teacher and went through all the basics with him. It made Simon even more determined to buy his own car one day.

Another lesson Simon learned was one he was not proud of. On the last Saturday evening, before he returned home, the two friends went out for dinner and on to a jazz club they'd visited before. Simon was passionate about jazz music. The beat set his pulse racing and he was drawn to the trumpet player. He watched and listened and was transfixed. This era was becoming known as the roaring twenties and the trumpet player could make his trumpet roar. He made a mental note to look out his own trumpet when he returned home. As usual on these occasions, Carlos managed to acquire some female company. This time he brought two attractive young ladies over to their table. The music roared, the drink flowed, and the feet tapped. Simon danced with one of the young ladies and found her company pleasing. Several hours later, as they left the club, Carlos invited them all back to his place for drinks. It was the turning point – he should have excused himself, but the alcohol had taken hold and well... one thing led to another. That night Simon learned new Spanish phrases – he also experienced a great deal more.

When he woke up the next morning, he felt dreadful. His female companion had vacated the bed. He was ashamed... 'I can't even remember her name,' he chastised himself. When he went through to the lounge, Carlos was up and about and perky. "Good night?" He questioned Simon with a twinkle in his eye and a grin on his face. Simon shook his head.

"I feel awful," he admitted then sank into the nearest chair. Carlos gave him a glass of water, picked up the newspaper and started commenting about some headline he was reading. It was a typical ending to a good night for Carlos – he was used to this lifestyle, but it was all new to Simon.

On his way back to his own apartment Simon resolved never to let alcohol get the better of him again. After a short walk he was back to the sanctuary of his own surroundings. We should have come back here last night, he thought, there's not a drop of alcohol in the place. It was too late, but the lesson was learned. He slept for most of the day and met with Carlos for dinner. This time they parted at the restaurant. Simon was contemplating a long two-day journey.

On the journey home he tried to study his business notebooks, but he kept nodding off to sleep. In his dreams he saw two faces merging into one – Olivia and Elise... English Simon, and Spanish Simon.

CHAPTER 10

SPAIN

1922

E lise found herself thinking about the 'Caballero Inglis' after his visit, especially when she looked at Eugenie's portrait...those eyes! She was enjoying her new role as a piano teacher and was becoming more independent, doing her own shopping and cooking. When she finished shopping, she often popped into a café and enjoyed a morning coffee and a pastry. Life took on a new rhythm. Her students arrived at intervals in the late afternoon. She had returned from France physically fit... but not mentally fit. However, these new routines were certainly helping. Only during the long nights when she was sitting in the lounge reading, did the pain of her losses return to her – but even those were diminishing.

One morning about a week after Senor Guilder's visit, she received a letter headed 'Silvestre Holdings'. It stated that the property in which she resided, Casa Galiana, was owned by the above company. The house was to be leased to her for a period of two years – rent free. At the end of two years the lease would be reviewed. The costs of any repairs, decoration and other maintenance would be covered by the above company. The lease was to run from 1st November1922. She was to sign the enclosed contract and return it to Alberto Martinez, Manager, Silvestre Holdings, in Madrid.

The enormity of this hit her. What a generous offer. She did not know the man. He did not know her. All they had in common was Eugenie...her aunt, his mother. He must trust her. She would not betray his trust. She was extremely grateful.

One evening, while she was reading, she glanced up at Eugenie's portrait. A thought occurred to her – what had happened to Eugenie's personal possessions? She was given the bag containing Eugenie's belongings at the hospital, but where were her other possessions? She realised she'd only entered Eugenie's bedroom to check the windows, in the weeks since her return. She climbed the stairs and entered the bedroom. Isabella must have dusted and cleaned the room regularly – it was airy and clean. It was a beautiful room. The drapes and bedcover were made in a restful blue and yellow print. There was a bed, a dressing table, a wardrobe and an armoire. There were four pictures on the walls. Three were landscapes and the other was a charcoal sketch of a house and garden. I wonder where that is, she mused?

She remembered her mission. The wardrobe was full of Eugenie's clothes, hats, shoes, and coats. Next, she opened the armoire. There were shelves at the top containing boxes, all neatly stacked. Underneath were drawers containing underclothing, nightwear, scarves and gloves and handbags. Everything was neat and tidy, but that was probably down to Isabella. Finally, she walked over to the dressing table. It contained the usual items for a lady –brush, comb, clothes brush, jewellery box, face cream, dusting powder and a toiletry bag with soaps, facecloths, and perfume. Again, all very neat and tidy. On the bedside tables there were framed photographs – Juan and Eugenie on their wedding day and a one of Juan on his own, looking much younger than she ever remembered him.

Over the next few evenings Elise went up to Eugenie's room and started to look through the boxes in the armoire. Some contained little souvenirs. Some diaries. Some contained letters. Another – official looking documents and finally some boxes of photographs. There were twelve boxes in total – they would take time to sort. All these things felt so personal, she felt she ought not to pry, but what else would happen to them? Senor Guilder was Eugenie's next of kin – but she could not see him spending the time to sort them. Perhaps I should do it, then I can give him anything personal when he next visits, she decided. So, she started sorting. Photographs first. So many formal, studio portraits typical of the era. Juan and Eugenie in various locations – they'd obviously travelled in the early years of their marriage. Then a set of studio portraits of a family, Eugenie's, taken over several years judging by the differences in the children from photograph to photograph. Where are these family members now, she asked herself? Suddenly, she gasped in astonishment at a photograph of a young man standing by himself, with his arm resting on a podium. "Senor Guilder," she said out loud, "I think this is your grandfather." The photograph was the image of Senor Guilder, it could have been him except for the style of clothes. The likeness was amazing. Those eyes again. She must pass these to him.

There was another pile of photographs tied together with ribbon. Juan featured in most of them – some when he was quite young and good looking. Then she saw other photographs with her mother and father and herself as a young child. She touched their faces – they were taken so tragically; her mother was less than forty years old when she died. Tears flowed as she remembered them. The photographs were numerous, but she did not recognise any more. Apart from the ones of her own family, she would give the rest to Senor Guilder – they were his family history.

It took Elise until Christmas to sort the remaining boxes – it certainly filled her evenings. She found the diaries to be little more than appointments, not personal journals as she'd hoped. Then she came to the letters. Eugenie's handwriting was very particular in style, but these were letters she'd received, so, as she scanned them, she was at a loss to understand what was being referred to in them. Several of the letters were condolence letters received after Juan's death, but they gave an insight into his character, life and the influence he had brought. Senor Guilder will find these helpful to understand the man his mother had married, she thought.

Finally, she came to the box of documents – Eugenie's birth certificate, marriage certificate and identity card.

Then a set of invoices for work carried out in a house in Barcelona. Extensive work, she gathered, looking through the invoices. Some of them were dated 1901. At the bottom of the box was a newspaper cutting. It was very creased and yellowed with age. She could only make out a few words – family, Silvestre, tragedy. What did all this mean? Why had Eugenie kept these? A mystery... thought Elise. Something else for Senor Guilder. She placed all the items that she needed to pass on, in a large envelope and put it on the dressing table. She was trying to think where she'd heard the name Silvestre recently. Then it dawned on her: it was Eugenie's maiden name. Senor Guilder had named his company after his mother using her maiden name.

Elise spent an enjoyable Christmas with Isabella and her family. Francoise wrote inviting her to go to Nice, but she declined, feeling it would bring back too many memories of last Christmas when she had felt so unwell. Early in the new year she took Eugenie's clothes to a lady who ran a second-hand clothing shop in the town. It took three visits. The clothing was of good quality and the owner was delighted. Elise asked if she was interested in handbags and shoes. Later that week she packed up these items but checked inside the handbags first to make sure they were empty. They were... all except one. Inside she found a handwritten letter with just Eugenie's name on the envelope, no address, no postmark, no date. The letter was brief. It thanked Eugenie for arranging the adoption of their precious baby boy. He was christened Andreas and he was thriving. It was signed Maria...but no surname. Elise began to shake. This must be her baby.

There was no date, but she remembered Eugenie using this bag quite recently. So, it must be referring to the adoption of her own baby...my son, she thought. Perhaps my child lives in this town? The fact that the letter was pushed into her handbag made Elise think it was handed to her in person...maybe at one of her committee meetings? I will never know. Elise started to sob. Another loss, but a one of her own making. One day I might pass him in the street...stand next to him in a shop. I will never know but it is for the best.

***

ENGLAND

WINTER 1922-1923

Christmas 1922 was a much happier event in the Guilder household than it had been the previous year, when Gertie was so ill. Serena was determined to make it a joyful occasion. She arranged cover at the store in the week leading up to Christmas, allowing her plenty of time for shopping, baking, and decorating. She was a real homemaker, and the happy atmosphere was tangible as soon as anyone stepped over the doorstep of The Gables. Serena asked Olivia to join them for a few days over Christmas. She knew if she left it to Simon, he would either forget or make excuses. After all, there was nothing 'official' between Simon and Olivia, and Olivia was Serena's friend, so she sent a note before Simon's return from Spain. She received a prompt reply and by the time Simon arrived home it was all decided. Simon was delighted – it gave him another opportunity to be in Olivia's company without any formality.

Simon went into Newcastle to meet Olivia's train. He was so excited to be seeing her again – it was a few weeks since the day in Leeds. He greeted her with open arms and a loving embrace. There was a definite connection between the pair. Christmas Eve was spent singing carols and other popular songs with Serena at the piano. Simon remembered to 'dust-off' his trumpet when he came home, finding it on the top of his wardrobe. He practised playing it a few times – usually when the house was empty to save embarrassment. He amazed himself at how easily the fingering came back to him.

Two weeks before Christmas, when Simon was in town meeting with Mr Adams, the solicitor, he had visited a musical instrument store. He was looking for some sheet music for the trumpet and was hoping to find something related to jazz, which was becoming so popular. He was delighted to find something suitable, but he was drawn to a gramophone being demonstrated by a salesman. Simon was instantly hooked and the fact that this machine could play flat discs called records intrigued him. He decided there and then to purchase one of these machines and some records – it would be delivered in time for Christmas. So, after another singsong on Christmas Day, Simon unveiled his new purchase. Everyone was delighted and to Simon's astonishment, Serena and Olivia seemed to embrace the jazz music. The next day William, Emily and Felix joined the family for lunch. The happy

Christmas atmosphere and the gramophone music helped to lighten the mood, but the climax of the day was when Simon produced his trumpet and tried to play along to the jazz music. There was much hilarity and laughter especially when he kept making mistakes.

Soon the Christmas activities ended, and it was time for Olivia to return to York. The young couple found little time to be on their own, but Olivia had enjoyed getting to know the family a bit more. When Simon took her to the station, she gave him another invitation to meet her parents. This time he felt he could not refuse, and they settled on a date at the end of January. They also talked to Serena about a possible trip to London for the three of them.

Early in January, Serena received an invitation to a Fashion Exhibition to be held in London in mid-February. She felt it would be an ideal way of keeping up to date with the latest fashions and introducing them to the ladies of Loftam. She mentioned the invitation to Simon at breakfast.

"What splendid timing," declared Simon. "We can have our trip to London to coincide with your Fashion Show."

Olivia was informed, replying she would be delighted to join them, so Serena wasted no time in booking their train tickets and accommodation.

However, Simon's weekend visit to York to meet Olivia's parents did not materialise. A severe snowstorm put an end to any travel plans that weekend. Another disappointment for Olivia – she was beginning to think it was not meant to happen. Simon telephoned her, and then wrote afterwards expressing his disappointment and they made another arrangement for early March, but the trip to London was before that date.

Meanwhile Simon was keeping up with his trumpet practice and his weekly Spanish letters from Carlos. He found it demanding but was persevering and gradually felt some words and phrases were sticking in his mind. On another visit to the music store in town, he noticed an advert for a new jazz club opening shortly. Simon quickly noted the address and dates, determined to visit sometime soon.

The morning of the journey to London dawned crisp and cold, but bright. The trio made their way south with lots of excitement and anticipation. Olivia joined the train in York. Unlike Serena, she'd visited the capital before and was looking forward to seeing the sights again. The exhibition was taking place over two days, leaving Simon to his own devices during the day. He'd already given that possibility some thought and after breakfast he left the ladies to go to their exhibition. He was interested in two things – music and cars. He found shops and showrooms for both quite easily and whiled away many hours observing and gaining information about the various models of cars available. He was determined to own a motor car soon. Finance was no problem, but he wanted to do his research and this trip to London gave him that opportunity. Back home in Loftam the research was more difficult. He even managed to have some test drives.

There were also several music stores and he managed to add to his growing record selection and sheet music collection. In the evenings, the threesome enjoyed a visit to a theatre, an orchestral recital, and a musical show. Simon was longing to visit a jazz club but doubted if the ladies would appreciate it. However, he did spot a poster for a jazz band concert, and they agreed to attend. The ladies enjoyed the concert – Simon, nevertheless, would have preferred the atmosphere of a jazz club. They spent Saturday touring the many sights of London before their return on Sunday. Everyone was exhausted but the trip was worthwhile.

Just like Christmas, the days in London gave Simon and Olivia no time to be alone together. On her return home Olivia reflected on what she knew about Simon. It was a year since they had first met. A year since she fell in love with him. She concluded Simon possessed many sides to his character. He was helpful, attentive, and caring both to his family and to her. This was in evidence over Christmas. He loved to be the life and soul of the party – she smiled at the remembrance of the hilarity when he played his trumpet. He had a great sense of humour and loved to tease playfully. He was a dutiful son and was trying hard to fill his father's shoes at Guilder's. It was a role which did not come naturally to him. He was very protective towards Serena and was giving her help and advice as her business developed. Also, there was his passion for motoring – she doubted if he was drawn to the mechanical side – just the fun of driving. But then there was the mysterious side to Simon ...Spain. No matter how many times she tried to ask him about his Spanish business involvement, he shrugged it off, telling her it was boring, and he would not bother her with any detail. She knew nothing about that side of his life – only that he had received a legacy from his Spanish mother. 'Multi-faceted' that is how she would assess Simon. Loveable and likeable but with an air of mystery.

Finally, there was her role in his life. What part did she play? She didn't know where she stood with him. At first their romance had progressed well. There was the desire to meet her, share intimate moments with her... but since his last visit to Spain she felt the 'romance element' had morphed into 'friendship'. Their times alone were limited, and his attention towards her, although always polite and caring, was not what it was a few months ago.

Maybe she was being oversensitive. She clutched the string of pearls at her neck. He bought me these, she reminded herself. She'd always been of a sensitive nature – she could detect atmospheres and coolness in people's relationships quickly. She knew she loved Simon. He had hinted he loved her in his correspondence...but not face to face. Had it been 'a spur of the moment' thing? Where was this relationship heading? Would meeting her parents make any difference? She doubted if it would.

The much-anticipated weekend visit finally arrived. Simon was going to meet her parents and the rest of her family. Olivia was hopeful this weekend visit would set their relationship on its future course. She met Simon at the station on Saturday morning. They greeted each other lovingly and walked arm in arm through the streets of York, chattering away like old friends. Olivia took Simon for lunch in an expensive restaurant and caught up on the news from Serena's store. She had decided to find out more about Simon's Spanish involvement and realised this lunch together would be their only chance. She was careful with her questioning, she needed to show she wasn't prying. She asked him about Madrid. He could talk for ages about the city, and she'd heard most of it before.

"Where do you stay?" she asked.

"Oh, in a hotel," was his reply. "It's near to my business office." He omitted to tell her that he owned the hotel and the building where the office was housed.

She asked about his friend Carlos. He told her about his car and the fun they enjoyed. He went into detail about the Spanish lessons – but made no mention of the nightclubs, the drinking, the smoking, or the women. Olivia knew he was being evasive. Eventually Olivia ended the 'Spanish Inquisition' as she thought of it. She was convinced there was a lot more to his visits than he was willing to share and decided she would probably never know, and she needed to accept the part of Simon that he was willing to share with her.

The weekend went well in both Olivia's and Simon's assessment. Simon found Olivia's parents and grandmother very welcoming. Conversation was easy and flowed well. Simon's sense of humour was evident on several occasions – oh... how she loved him. Simon accompanied Tom, Olivia's father, on walks both mornings with the two Springer Spaniels – much loved pets. Olivia's father enjoyed foxhunting – a sport Simon had no experience of –and it was suggested that next time Simon visited he might be able to accompany Tom. Olivia's mother was delighted with Simon and encouraged Olivia to invite him again soon. On Sunday lunchtime Olivia's brother Fred, wife Betty and daughter Ann joined them. Fred and Simon hit it off immediately –

they both shared a love of motor cars and talked at some length. The weekend was a brilliant success...until Olivia accompanied Simon to the station on Sunday evening.

They walked hand in hand into the station. They were early for his train and stood cuddled up close against the chill of the March evening. Simon turned and looked intently into Olivia's eyes. She started to tremble – from the cold she told herself, but she knew...

Simon decided it was time to be honest with Olivia. They kissed – it was a prolonged kiss... then he whispered in her ear: "Livvy darling, I think... I love you, but I'm not ready to make a commitment...I need time... please be patient with me. There are so many things going on in my life at present and I need some space to sort myself out. But I value our friendship." He paused and stroked her face lovingly, gazing into her eyes. "I hope you will understand what I am trying to say."

They pulled apart but continued to look deeply into each other's eyes. She felt numb but smiled. Tears trickled down her face. She hastily found her handkerchief and dabbed her eyes.

"I think I understand, Simon... I'll be waiting for you," she sobbed. Then without a backward glance she turned and ran away from him. Simon stared after her...what had he done?

Travelling north, Simon regretted his words. He didn't mean to be so blunt. He knew she was hurt. Yet, it was the truth, and surely, they needed to be honest with each other. He was only young. In the space of eighteen months, he'd gone from having his future mapped out for him, to embracing the lifestyle of a wealthy Spanish businessman. He required time and space to sort himself. He needed to find himself – his identity had changed. He was not in a mentally sound place to ask someone as dear and sweet and loving as Olivia, to marry him ...not yet anyway. In truth he didn't want to be married at this point in his life. He was only twenty-two – he needed to experience life... have fun... be carefree, not take on fresh responsibilities. He hoped Olivia would understand and if she didn't, well...it was a risk he would have to take.

Olivia cried all the way back home from the station. She hardly remembered the bus journey. What had happened? The weekend seemed to go so well. When she got back home, she ran straight upstairs to her bedroom. She threw herself on the bed and sobbed. She did not normally give in to her emotions, but Simon's parting words hit her like a hammer...they were so unexpected. She was sure he was about to propose...but instead he had asked for time. He said he 'thought he loved her' and 'valued her friendship'...what did that mean? She sensed it coming, as soon as they arrived at the station, almost as if she was able to see into his mind. There was a gentle tap on her bedroom door. Jane, her grandmother, put her head around the corner.

"Do you want to talk about it?" she asked. "I'm a good listener."

Olivia sat up and hugged her grandmother. Jane knew from that first day at Gertie's funeral her granddaughter was attracted to Simon Guilder. Between her sobs, Olivia told her what Simon had said on the platform. Jane held Olivia's hands and listened. After a while, when Olivia had calmed down, Jane put her arm around her granddaughter and spoke.

"I think honesty is an admirable quality to have in a relationship. Give him the time and space he's asked for, Olivia, stay good friends. That way, I am sure you will win him, and the wait will strengthen your relationship." She gave her granddaughter a squeeze, placed a kiss on the top of her head and left the room.

CHAPTER 11

SPAIN

SPRING 1923

Elise kept in regular contact with her good friend Francoise in France. Early in the new year she wrote and asked her if she would like to come and spend a holiday in Toledo. Francoise replied she would love to visit but it would be March before she could arrange for her mother to look after her young son. Elise felt she owed her friend so much. Francoise had taken Elise to her home in France after Eugenie had died. She stayed for nearly a year, and this was a way to repay her kindness. Once the date for Francoise's visit was settled, Elise started preparing. The weather was turning warmer and one morning when she was in the garden she went over to the summerhouse. It had been shut up for as long as Elise could remember, but she knew where the keys were. When she stepped inside, she was amazed at how sturdy it was. She looked around – it smelt musty but only needed a good clean out. There were boxes of rubbish along one wall but a few hours of sweeping, washing the floor, cleaning the windows and surfaces and it would be ready to use. It would provide a lovely shady retreat from the warm Spanish sun. She set to and started cleaning. Two days later she stood back and admired her efforts. When the doors were open it provided a beautiful view across the valley to the town below. She removed the rubbish – nothing of value. Later that day she walked into the town and visited the antique shop, where she had taken Eugenie's jewellery. She hoped she might find two comfortable chairs and a small table – her search was rewarded, and the shop owner offered to deliver them.

The day before Francoise's visit Elise took her morning drink down to the summerhouse. It looked perfect – a lovely place to relax. She looked at the windowsills, noting they were bare. She wandered through the house and looked around. She found a vase, a figurine and the little musical box Eugenie had given her – the one which played 'Fur Elise'. These items completed the refurbished summerhouse. She intended to use it now that she'd made the effort to regenerate it.

Elise met Francoise in Madrid the next day. They'd not seen each other since the previous summer. Elise was surprised at her friend's new look. Her hair was short and bobbed, and she was wearing the plain, short, straight styles that were becoming fashionable. Her outfit was completed with a neat cloche hat. Elise felt so drab and dowdy in comparison to her friend. They went for some refreshment – Elise asked about Francoise's family. She knew them all quite well having stayed with them during school vacations. Afterwards they took the train to Toledo.

On the way Francoise asked, "What happened to the apartment you stayed in when Eugenie was in hospital?"

Francoise had stayed with Elise in the apartment after the accident. Elise had felt lonely and frightened, when she was taken to the hospital to see Eugenie. She telephoned her friend the next day and Francoise came to be with her friend.

"Oh, I don't have use of the apartment anymore. All Eugenie's properties were left to her son," she replied.

Francoise stared at Elise in astonishment.

"I didn't realise Eugenie had any family," commented Francoise, perplexed. Her friend had never mentioned Eugenie's family in all the years they were friends.

"It was a surprise to me also," Elise answered. Then she told Francoise about meeting the handsome Englishman, Senor Guilder, and the kind offer of a rent-free arrangement for the house. She also mentioned that he had no knowledge of his mother until her death, as he had been raised by his father in England. Francoise was very curious about this Senor Guilder.

"That's a bit of mystery, Elise. Fancy Eugenie having a son...do you think she was married before?"

Elise shook her head. "I don't think she was, otherwise she would have stayed with the father...surely?"

Francoise raised her eyebrows and gave her friend a mischievous smile. "Is this Englishman married?" she asked. She knew how her brother Phillipe's death was such a devastating blow to Elise...she felt certain they would have married if he'd survived the war.

"I don't think so ...but I don't know," she answered.

"Elise, how old is this Senor Guilder?" Francoise continued.

"I'm not sure... about our age I guess," she replied.

"Do you think he will visit you again?" she queried.

Elise looked thoughtful. "I hope he does. I found some photographs belonging to Eugenie. I think I should give them to him. I must show you one of the photographs – I think it's Eugenie's father – Senor Guilder is his double."

After a lovely dinner, carefully thought out and prepared by Elise, the two friends sat down in the lounge. Elise lit the fire, as the March evening was chilly. Francoise looked up at Eugenie's portrait hanging over the fireplace.

"Your aunt was a beautiful woman. How old was she when she died?"

Elise replied, "Only forty-two – so young."

Francoise was trying to work out how this mystery son had arrived in Eugenie's life. "She must have been young when Senor Guilder was born."

Elise stood up, remembering the photographs she'd referred to earlier.

"She would only be about twenty, I think. It was before she married my uncle." She left the room to collect the photographs. She showed Francoise the family groups, indicating Eugenie on each of them and then showed her the one with a handsome young man, in his early twenties.

"I think this is Eugenie's father," she said, handing her the photograph.

Francoise's eyes lit up. "Oh, my Elise! If your Senor Guilder looks like this handsome man, then we need to bring you into the 1920s." She smiled at her friend and they both began to laugh.

"Yes," replied Elise, "I feel a bit old fashioned." Elise looked across at her friend. "Will you help me, Francoise. I am hopeless at buying clothes. Eugenie always took me to her dressmaker, and I just accepted what they suggested."

Francoise looked at her friend's dress and replied, "Yes, I can see that." They laughed again. "Why don't we have a shopping day and buy you some new clothes while I'm here... and a visit to a hairstylist."

Elise agreed wholeheartedly.

The following day the two young women set off for Madrid on a shopping spree. They wandered the streets and plazas admiring the various fashions – Elise was thrilled at the items she viewed and, guided by her friend, bought some dresses, a coat and two hats.

Then Francoise took her into a lingerie store. "Now, Elise, you need a complete new wardrobe." She smiled, anticipating her friend's objections.

"But why do I need such pretty undergarments?" she asked.

Francoise held up her arms in exasperation. "Elise ...luxurious undergarments make you feel special, and... you never know!"

They started to laugh. Elise purchased several items including a fine kimono-style nightdress which Francoise selected.

"Now shoes," said Francoise, looking at the 'sensible shoes' her friend was wearing.

Finally, purchases made, they went for lunch, struggling to carry all the packages. It was a splendid day and Elise could not remember feeling so happy since before Phillipe was killed.

That evening they emptied Elise's wardrobe and drawers. They examined Elise's clothing and discarded most of the items. A few items were put to one side to take to the second-hand clothing shop in the town. Then all the new clothing was tried on and finally put in the drawers and wardrobe.

Next day, Elise showed her friend around Toledo, and they went for lunch in an outside café.

"I had no idea you lived in such a lovely town," remarked Francoise.

"Well, it's a far cry from where you live in Nice," observed Elise.

Francoise lived in a beautiful detached house in Nice in France. Her husband, Pierre, had purchased it just before their marriage in 1919. He was an attractive, flamboyant young man who worked in the film industry. He swept Francoise off her feet within three months of meeting her. Elise was a bridesmaid at their wedding, along with Francoise's two younger sisters. The wedding was six months after she gave birth to Phillipe's child – an event which none of his family knew about, not even Francoise.

"How is Hugo, is he talking much?" asked Elise, remembering Francoise and Pierre's son.

"Oh," replied Francoise, "he chatters away all day – he's grown so much since you saw him."

Elise was very fond of Francoise's little boy – she had spent many long hours playing with him while she stayed in France – he will never know he has a Spanish 'cousin', she often thought to herself.

On the way back from lunch Francoise spotted a hair stylist and went in to make an appointment for Elise.

Back at Casa Galiana, Elise suggested they sit in the summerhouse. It was delightful, providing shade from the sun. Elise served coffee and homemade cakes.

"You are turning into a very efficient homemaker, Elise," Francoise noted.

"It's good to have someone to cook for," Elise replied.

As they were chatting Francoise picked up the musical box on the windowsill. She turned the handle and it played 'Fur Elise'.

"I remember this tune. You used to play it at our house ... that's when I could get you to play. You were very reluctant as I recall."

Elise smiled. "Well, I've certainly made up for it since returning here. I have a new occupation – I am a piano teacher. So far, I have six pupils, but I have two more starting next month."

Francoise was amazed. She knew her friend was an excellent pianist but had never dreamed she would use this skill as a source of income.

The following morning Elise kept her appointment at the hair stylist. Francoise instructed the stylist as to the style Elise wanted. An hour later, a completely transformed Elise emerged.

"That's fantastic, Elise. Please promise me you will continue to have your hair styled regularly and make sure the English gentleman visits you when he's in Spain."

The two friends laughed. Francoise was so relieved to see her friend taking an interest in life again. She only hoped Elise would behave happy and carefree when she met this man again and not the sullen, depressed person she'd been over the last two years. Francoise felt positive about this and trusted her intuition was correct.

All too soon the week of holiday ended. Elise accompanied her friend to the station in Madrid. The week with Francoise had been excellent and Elise felt grateful to have such a faithful friend. They parted full of promises to write regularly.

Before returning to Toledo Elise went to the offices of Silvestre Holdings. She did not expect to see the manager, but he was between appointments, so she was able to meet him in person. She asked if he could pass a message to Senor Guilder to visit her when he was in Madrid, as she wanted to pass on some personal items belonging to his mother. Alberto informed her Senor Guilder was arriving at the end of April and would be here for about a month. Next Elise revisited the stores she'd been to with Francoise and purchased two more dresses, two blouses and a skirt – now she'd begun there was no stopping her...she intended to replace her wardrobe. On impulse she bought a bottle of a new perfume called Chanel No 5. She was determined to change her image. Later that afternoon her piano students were surprised to see their 'new look' teacher.

***

The journey to Spain seemed to go quickly. It was a year since Simon had made his first visit. Each mile was a new adventure for him then. This third time it was a process of getting from one place to another. It was beautiful weather. Simon liked the springtime better than the autumn. He was trying to forget the last weekend in the autumn – he would not go down that path again, he vowed to himself. This time he was focussing on practising his Spanish – he felt he was retaining some of the phrases and looked forward to using them. His attendance was required at four board meetings. He'd already written to Alberto to ask for the same kind of inauguration into the companies involved this time. Arriving at the office the next morning Alberto gave him a property report, then outlined the timetable of meetings over the next four weeks. Each one was to have two days' preparation and a one-day review. So only Fridays and weekends to spare, thought Simon. As he was leaving, Alberto gave him the message from Senorita Dominguez.

"She has some personal items from your mother to pass on to you and would like you to visit to collect them."

Simon hadn't intended visiting Toledo this trip. He really wanted to go back to see the house in Barcelona and spend time there. He thought for a moment, then asked Alberto to let her know he would visit this Friday. That would leave him free to meet up with Carlos on the weekends although he had yet to speak to his Spanish friend. That evening he dined alone in a nearby restaurant. He used Spanish all the time and the staff seemed to understand what he wanted ...well, they brought the correct items! He gave himself a mental pat on the back. The next three days were 'business days'.

On Friday morning he left for the station to travel to Toledo. He left his coat in the apartment, expecting the grey skies would brighten. But by the time he reached the station the rain had started, and he was soaking. He arrived in Toledo a very soggy mess. Oh well, he thought, it will only be a quick visit. On his first visit he was rather peeved at the way Senorita Dominguez had fooled him into using his faltering Spanish, when all the time, she spoke perfect English – she enjoyed teasing him, clearly. Well, this time I'll show her, he smirked. His basic vocabulary for conversation starters was improving and he was feeling quite confident.

Although he was wet, he paused to look up at Casa Galiana when he arrived. What a fantastic house, he thought. Those windows...different shapes and sizes. An idea struck him. One day, he thought, I'm going to build a house just like this back home – how unique will that be? For a moment he visualised the white walls and painted shutters and balconies on a house on a road in Loftam, England – it's possible, he mused.

He knocked on the door. So much for his good intentions. He was just about to launch into his first well-rehearsed Spanish phrase when...wham! He was 'blown away'...what had the Senorita done to herself? She was stunning. She was attractive the last time – but now...

"Come in quickly out of the rain, Senor," she said.

Without speaking he obeyed. He stood in the hallway and opened his mouth, but he did not have the Spanish vocabulary for "I'm sorry I'm wet," so he said it in English instead.

"Leave your shoes here and give me your jacket. I'll put it beside the stove," she said looking him up and down, then added, "actually, I think you would be better beside the stove in the kitchen." She smiled or... was it a smirk? He was annoyed with himself... he was getting off to another awkward start with this Spanish Senorita – even if she did look gorgeous and he looked like a drowned rat.

The housekeeper was busy at the sink; she looked round at him and said something to Elise in high-speed Spanish which Simon failed to translate. Elise replied in Spanish, and he was none the wiser. The older lady walked out of the kitchen giving Simon a strange look as she passed. Oh, dear he thought... I've spoiled her day. He was starting to shiver. Elise looked at him.

"Isabella will prepare you a bath, Senor, and I will dry your clothes around the stove."

Simon was alarmed at all this fuss – he was just wet.

"No, no, I don't want to be any trouble. If I could just have a towel to dry myself that would be fine."

But before Elise could reply, Isabella shouted something from upstairs.

"Follow me," said Elise and again, like a little child, he obeyed. Upstairs on the right was the bathroom – he remembered it from his first visit. Elise pushed open the door, and Simon saw a very inviting, steaming bath.

"Take a bath, Senor, I'll wait for your clothes and take them to dry," she announced, stepping to one side.

Simon entered the bathroom, closed the door and pulled off his wet clothes with great difficulty. He noticed a pile of towels, quicky utilised one and placed his crumpled pile of clothes outside the door. Then he sank into the lovely warming bath. He soaked and felt the numbness in his body ease. As the water cooled, he washed using a very fragranced soap and climbed out of the bath. This was all very embarrassing, and Simon felt such a fool. How quickly could he make his departure – with dry clothes and the items he needed to collect? He dried himself then put a clean towel around his waist. As he unlocked the door he peeped out and was startled to see Elise standing there. She looked at him wearing only a skimpy towel – he thought he detected a softening in her gaze, not quite so stern as she was earlier.

"Senor, in the bedroom there is a sheet – see if you can make use of it then come downstairs, I have some hot soup for you."

"Thank you," was all Simon could manage – but at least he said it in Spanish. He felt a complete fool!

She retreated downstairs as Simon went into the bedroom – the one Carlos had occupied on their first visit. A beautiful room with two windows and a French door leading onto a balcony. I wonder if this was my mother's room, he thought. He quickly set about draping the white sheet around his body. After a few attempts it felt secure, he walked over to the dressing table and combed his hair. He looked in the mirror and grinned – he was such an idiot!

He made his way downstairs leaving the towels in the bathroom. He walked straight across into the lounge and stood staring at his mother's portrait, trying to boost his confidence by reminding himself he was the owner of this house. Suddenly, he heard footsteps coming along the hall. Elise stopped in the doorway as he turned around. She stopped and stared at him. Slowly she began to giggle... and then it bubbled and bubbled into a fit of uncontrollable giggling.

"Do I amuse you, Senorita?" Simon asked with a twinkle of mischief in his eye.

She reached out to hold the doorpost. In between her giggles she remarked, "Oh, Simon you do look funny – like a Roman emperor... wearing a toga."

Simon looked down at himself, saw her point then began to laugh. As he looked up their eyes met and that was the moment a spark was lit! The hilarity passed and Elise invited Simon to come into the kitchen for some hot soup. He followed her. He sat down at the kitchen table rather awkwardly, in his unusual mode of dress, and he commented cheekily, "At last, I've found a way to stop you calling me 'Senor Guilder'."

He drank his soup, feeling it warming him and looked around to see his belongings on a clothes horse around the stove. She followed his eyes.

"They may take some time to dry, Simon, are you in a hurry to leave?" she enquired.

"No," he said glancing at his watch, "I have no further appointments today." Finishing his meal, he thanked her profusely and again apologised for his soggy entrance. She made a pot of tea and suggested they drink it in the lounge – it was still raining. He asked about Isabella and Elise explained the older lady's new working hours. Sitting opposite Elise in the lounge Simon asked where she had learned to speak English. She told him about her school and the nuns from different countries. He was impressed.

"So, you speak three languages?" he asked.

"Yes, although Spanish is the one I use most of the time. I have a French friend and when I am with her, we speak French all the time. I don't get many chances to speak English," she commented.

He smiled at her, mischievously. "Then I will have to visit you more often, Senorita, so you can practise your English."

Elise felt herself blushing, as a slow smile spread across Simon's face. He asked about her occupation. She told him she was a piano teacher, and he raised his eyebrows in surprise. "Will you play for me please?"

She looked hesitant at first, then went over to the piano and lifted the lid. She started to play – 'Fur Elise'. Simon was transfixed. Not only was this young Spanish senorita stunning, but she was talented as well – even if it was a tune that seemed to follow him around.

When she finished, he clapped and said, "Thank you. That was excellent," in Spanish.

"I see your Spanish is improving," she commented.

So, he spoke a few of his well-rehearsed phrases in Spanish and she replied in Spanish. They laughed. The tension between them released.

"So, what do you have for me belonging to my mother?" he asked.

She got up and returned with a large envelope. They spent the next hour looking at the photographs and documents, and as she reached across to point to various features in the photographs, he detected an alluring aroma of perfume.

Simon was amazed at his likeness to the photograph of his grandfather. Then he became very thoughtful when he saw the newspaper cutting and the invoices. "I wonder what it means. There's a house belonging to me in Barcelona – maybe I'd find someone there who may remember something." He looked at her. "Did my mother ever mention a house in Barcelona?"

Elise shook her head then remembered the sketch. She told him about it.

"May I see it?" he asked. "I visited the house a year ago – I intend to go back, it seems a waste to leave it shut up."

She led him upstairs to the bedroom where he had changed earlier and showed him the sketch.

"Yes, that's it," he replied. He sat down on the bed and rubbed his head. He felt a headache threatening and was very tired. He must leave. "I must get dressed. You don't want a Roman emperor hanging around all evening." He grinned.

"Your clothes are still damp, Simon. Would you like to rest for a while and stay for a meal? I have students later this afternoon, but we could eat afterwards?" she asked. It was such a kind offer, and he had no plans for that evening.

"That would be lovely. Thank you." He rubbed his eyes – his headache was getting worse. Elise watched him and then suggested he rested, while she prepared the meal. He took no persuasion. After she left the room, he lay down on the bed – it was only afternoon, but he didn't wake up until the next morning.

Simon had developed a fever – probably brought on by his escapade in the rain. He vaguely remembered feeling so hot, then shivering and hearing the piano. He was aware of someone lifting his head to get him to drink. His head throbbed...his body ached. He tossed and turned. He lost all sense of place and time. Eventually the fever passed and he slept.

He opened his eyes. Where was he? What time was it? What day was it? Slowly he began to remember. His throat was parched, he drank the glass of water on the bedside table. Memories of the previous day filtered into his consciousness. He looked down at his body...he was naked. Oh no, he thought – what happened? He climbed out of the bed and noticed his clothes neatly pressed lying on the chair. Quickly dressing, he descended the stairs and found Elise in the garden with the dog. Judging by the height of the sun and its warmth... it was late morning.

"Elise, I'm so sorry...what happened? All I remember is lying on the bed to rest. After that it's a blur. It's obviously a new day." He lifted his hands in puzzlement.

"Simon, don't worry," she answered. "I trust you're feeling better. I will make some refreshment. Come and sit in the summerhouse." He followed her into the sun-filled summerhouse and took off his jacket.

"I don't remember seeing this on my last visit," he commented.

"Well, it was here... but it was shut up and used as a storage room for years. I recently brought it back to life again," she replied then returned to the house. Within minutes she was back carrying a tray with a jug of lemonade and some bread and cheese. He was very hungry. When he finished, he lay back in the chair; it was so peaceful and restful, and they seemed to be so easy in each other's company.

"What happened to Friday?" he asked, not really expecting an answer.

"You must have caught a chill after your soggy adventure." She smiled then continued, "You had a fever during the night."

"I remember someone urging me to drink...was that you?" he asked.

"Of course," she replied, "I'm the only one here."

He looked at her and enquired, "The toga...what happened?"

She grinned mischievously.

"Well... I tried to help... as it was ravelled, and you fought me... but in the end... I won."

He felt himself blushing, he was so embarrassed and decided to change the topic of conversation.

"What time will I catch a train?" he asked.

She looked at him. "Simon, you are not well enough to return to Madrid. It's Saturday – I have no teaching commitments today. Please rest – I will make a meal. If you have no pressing engagements, stay another night. You'll feel better tomorrow."

She left him to attend to household matters and he suddenly realised she was right – he did not have the energy to contemplate catching a train. He closed his eyes. The warmth of the sun and the satisfaction of the snack lulled him into a gentle, healing sleep.

He was woken by Pepe, Elise's little dog, sniffing at his feet and wagging his tail. "Hello, boy," he said, bending down to pat him. He stood up and stretched. "That's better," he declared, feeling refreshed.

He walked over to the doorway and looked out across the town. Glancing down at the windowsill he noticed the little musical box. He remembered seeing it in the bedroom where he had stayed on his visit with Carlos. He opened it – it was empty, he turned the winder, and the tune 'Fur Elise' began to play. Suddenly, the penny dropped – 'Fur Elise' meant... for Elise. He closed the box, but as he did, he sensed a flashback to the 'toga moment', when Elise had started to giggle and said he looked like a Roman Emperor. Elise... Elise... he said to himself and as he looked at the box, a warm blanket of happiness and wellbeing wrapped itself around him. He turned and looked up at the house; she was walking down the path towards him. Once again, he noticed the short hairstyle, the fashionable dress, the dainty shoes ... and he felt something stirring inside him.

They spent a restful afternoon, sitting in the summerhouse after eating a substantial lunch. He asked to see the photographs and documents again. Simon was amazed at how relaxed he felt in her company. An idea formed in his mind...I wonder, he mused.

"I must visit the Barcelona house again," he commented, looking across at her...wondering if he dared to ask? "Elise...how would you feel about coming with me to Barcelona?"

She was silent for a few minutes...perhaps it was inappropriate, but he continued, "I mean as my interpreter – I struggle with the language. She was your aunt. You knew her...I didn't."

She smiled and looked directly at him, weighing up the implications of this proposal. Then she answered coyly, "Yes Senor, I'll accompany you... you will need help with your Spanish."

He pretended to give her an angry stare. "Please, Elise...stop calling me Senor – it makes me feel like an elderly gentleman."

They both started laughing. As he studied the photographs again, Simon realised he'd inherited physical features from his mother's side of the family – build, colouring, and eyes most definitely. His height was from both sides as Robert was also tall and his jawline was like his father's. He looked at the family groups.

"So, my mother was one of four children – looking at the ages I guess she was the oldest." He ran his fingers over the children's faces and looked thoughtful. "If my mother was forty-two when she died, then her two brothers and sister must only be in their late thirties now." He stopped and stared at Elise. "That means I must have an aunt, two uncles and lots of cousins, living here in Spain."

Elise thought about the newspaper cutting but did not comment. He asked her to keep the pack of photographs at Casa Galiana.

Later that evening they chatted freely over coffee in the lounge, sharing tales from their school days, journeys they'd made and even touching on politics. She possessed a sharp mind and a sense of humour. Simon Guilder really enjoyed the companionship of this young senorita.

The next morning, he returned to Madrid. As they parted, he kissed her lightly on the cheek and thanked her profusely for her kind hospitality and tending to his needs the previous night. He said he would be in touch about Barcelona, hopefully before he returned, but if not, then in the autumn.

Sadly, Simon was unable to arrange to visit Barcelona before he was due to return home. There was so much to attend to, as Alberto was very thorough in making sure Simon was fully apprised with all the facts, figures, and systems of the remaining companies. This group of companies was more complex. He was finding it tight to fit everything into four weeks. He decided he would add an extra two weeks to his autumn visit so he could visit Barcelona. He would treat it as a holiday.

He wrote to Elise to explain. He asked if she was still willing to accompany him, as he was hoping to visit Barcelona in mid-October and stay for two weeks. He added she could contact him via Alberto, who would forward her communication. Simon saw Carlos on the two remaining weekends of his visit. They renewed their friendship – enjoying trips out in his car, fine dining, and nightclubs. This time Simon resisted the temptation to drink too much and declined the invitations back to Carlos' apartment, choosing to walk by himself to his own apartment.

***

LOFTAM ENGLAND

2019

Grace was cleaning windows today. Only the insides – a chap with a ladder cleaned the outsides. She passed through the hallway to put her cleaning things away.

"Yes, Benson, I'm coming," she said to her son's little dog lying at the front door. Pleased to have finished the windows, she sighed to herself and opened the front door to take Benson for a walk. These last few days she had found herself thinking about her childhood home many times ...the Spanish House on Wood Lane. Windows, she thought. My mother had a hard job cleaning the windows in the Spanish House. They were all different sizes – tall and thin, wide, and panelled. Some were small and then there were the French windows. There was a French window in her bedroom leading onto a balcony. As a child she often wondered why a Spanish house... in England ...possessed French windows!

All the frames were metal and were painted in blue to match the blue shutters hanging at most of the windows. Benson stopped and refused to walk on. Oh, thought Grace...dachshunds – they have a stubborn streak. She bent down to encourage him. Their family pet had been a dachshund, when she'd lived in the Spanish house – different colour and smooth haired, she recalled, as she stroked Benson's long golden hair. When she was a child, her little dog usually accompanied her up to the summerhouse at the top of the garden.

I wonder if that Summerhouse is still there? She pondered. Once again, she remembered the little box she had found under the floorboard...who put it there? Why was it hidden? She wondered.

CHAPTER 12

1923

Two days of travelling gave Simon plenty of time to think and assess. This was his third visit to Spain, and he thought the business side of things was going well. He'd now attended a board meeting for each of his holdings. He'd assembled an overview of each company in his notebooks. He was grasping a few Spanish phrases and could understand polite conversation and respond accordingly. The property portfolio was managed well under the watchful eye of Alberto. His friendship with Carlos was good and provided him with a likeminded companion to while away his leisure time – his assistance in learning Spanish was invaluable and he really should think of some way to show his appreciation on his next visit. Having given all this about two hours' thought, he put his head back and promptly went to sleep.

After changing trains in Paris, he put his mind to the matter which was now uppermost in his thoughts... his bewildering problem. Some might say it was a good problem. The trouble was...he'd fallen for two women!

He knew there were many hours of travelling ahead of him to calm the waves of emotional turmoil taking place in his mind. How can I possibly love two women? He asked himself. How can I have a worthwhile relationship with a woman I only see twice a year? He'd known since 'toga moment' his feelings for Elise were strong, and so far, they'd only been in each other's company on two occasions. She was only just calling him by his first name... oh, he was letting his imagination run away with him, but he could not deny the feelings he held for Elise Dominguez. Loving Elise was just a figment of his imagination. It wasn't real...she could already be in a relationship with another man, for all he knew. But he also knew if the opportunity presented itself, he could not hold back the emotional force building inside him. He was attracted to her – but how could it possibly manifest itself...he was clueless. Since staying with the Spanish senorita, he'd been thinking about her constantly.

But... and it was a 'big but'... he knew he loved Livvy – sweet, gentle, kind, intelligent Livvy. She would go to the ends of the earth for him, he was sure. He only needed to write one letter asking her to marry him – they'd been special friends for many months. They shared a connection, a blending of heart and mind. Livvy was also in his thoughts... daily. Both families seemed to be expecting something to happen between them, but that was the stumbling block. He knew he had wounded her by asking for her patience and understanding as they waited on the station platform in York. Perhaps... he questioned himself, there are some women you can love physically and some you can only ever aspire to love in your dreams? He was right to be honest with Livvy – it was giving him time, but the much needed 'time' was presenting him with a bigger problem – now there was another woman in the equation. Was it love? He was young and inexperienced...were his feelings for Livvy and Elise just infatuation? He closed his eyes and slept again. The sea crossing woke him up and travelling on to London it dawned on him – just who was asking him to decide? Perhaps he could love both women for now. After all, life, he was sure, had a way of sorting these things.

***

Elise was reflecting on Simon's visit – it had turned out to be an interesting episode. She had originally thought the visit would last two hours at the most, but she prepared a pan of homemade soup in case he wanted a snack before returning to Madrid. However, what happened opened a whole area of her life she thought was firmly closed... attraction and desire. After losing Phillipe she had dismissed any thoughts of a romantic liaison in the future. She'd experienced the love of a man and given birth to his child – the fact that both were snatched away from her was just life...and life could be cruel. The night Simon took poorly came back to her. She had tended to his needs by instinct – she was no nurse, but her concern for his wellbeing was paramount in her mind. She recalled helping him to untangle himself from the toga; he was unaware of his actions. Earlier in the day the sight of him emerging from the bathroom clad only in a towel; seeing him standing in front of his mother's portrait wearing that ridiculous sheet, stirred feelings within her. The laughter that ensued, the easy manner with which they conversed, the way he looked at her and his smiles – all these things made her realise...yes, she could be open to love again. I wonder what Barcelona will be like, she mused?

***

YORK, ENGLAND

Olivia looked up from the design she was perusing. She looked at her surroundings. She was sitting in the work room of a ladies' millinery shop. For over two months she'd been learning to become a milliner. After her shock at hearing Simon asking for her patience, she engaged in a considerable amount of soul searching. She was stuck in a solitary occupation. She was not even qualified, more of a librarian's assistant. Yes, it was only a part-time position, she could swap her hours to suit whatever was happening, and it was enjoyable – but she wanted more out of her life. She was twenty-five years old and so far, the expected 'marriage route' was proving elusive. She admired her friend Serena. In the short time of their acquaintance, she'd become a successful store owner and businesswoman.

Millinery had always interested Olivia. As a child dressing up, she often wore a hat and sometimes she would add a decoration. A few days after Simon's devastating announcement, she was walking down a street in York and saw a notice in a hat shop saying, 'Assistant required – training given, apply within'. On impulse she entered the shop and two weeks later she had resigned from the library and started to learn the skills of millinery. The remuneration was poor, but that wasn't important – acquiring the skills were what counted. The position was full-time, so it was helping to keep her mind off Simon. Not that she could ever stop thinking about Simon. Their correspondence had ceased after receiving his general note of thanks for accommodating him that weekend in March.

Serena kept in touch, and Olivia was looking forward to visiting Loftam at the weekend. She was travelling to Newcastle on Friday straight after the shop closed. Saturday was her 'day off', so she would return on Sunday evening. She hoped Simon was still away – meeting him would be awkward.

***

LOFTAM

SUMMER 1923

The warmth of the June sunshine was bringing the ladies out to shop. Serena's new range of summer prints were proving popular, especially the blouses. Her friend Olivia was arriving today for the weekend. The pair were meeting in Newcastle later, then they would go to a restaurant for dinner before returning to The Gables later. She favoured this arrangement. It would give them plenty of time to catch up before meeting Father and Simon. Serena didn't know any details, but since Simon had visited Olivia's family three months ago, things seemed rather quiet. Easter passed and there were no visits. Then Simon was in Spain, returning only about three weeks ago. There had been no post for Simon from York as far as she knew, throughout that time.

Although the friendship between the two young women was fairly recent, there was a real bond between them. Serena went to York for a day's shopping with Olivia at the end of April. She was delighted to learn about Olivia's new job and was looking forward to hearing how it was progressing. After meeting Olivia in the station, they dined at a reputable restaurant in Newcastle and the two young women caught up on each other's news. Olivia talked at length about her training and how helpful her tutor, the shop owner, was being.

"She thinks I'm learning fast and will soon be ready for my first commission," Olivia remarked.

Serena soon realised her friend was blessed with an eye for design and was thrilled when she mentioned she'd brought a book of her own design sketches with her – she was keen to have Serena's opinion.

Olivia was nervous about meeting Simon. Serena had mentioned he was home again, but she was determined to overcome these feelings – it must not spoil her friendship with Serena. When they returned to The Gables, Robert informed Serena her brother was out...Olivia breathed a sigh of relief. The two friends enjoyed a cup of tea and looked through Olivia's designs. Serena made a few observations here and there and gave advice on colours and trends. She was impressed with her friend's creativity.

"Olivia, I think you've found your forte," Serena declared and gave her friend a hug as they went upstairs to bed.

***

Simon's passion to own a car soon became a reality. Having carried out extensive research, he was ready to make his purchase. He visited a motor car showroom in Newcastle the week after his return from Spain and placed his order. He bought a Wolseley... but kept his purchase a secret.

During the week, Serena told Simon about Olivia's impending visit – he received the news with a straight face. Oh dear, thought Simon – this is going to test my resolve. The only contact between them in three months was a general letter of thanks for the kind hospitality shown towards him for the weekend in March. In retrospect he realised he should have apologised for his abrupt comments that night at the station, but it was too late now. He could not face meeting her, so went into town after leaving the store on Friday. He ate alone and went on to the jazz club, which had opened a few months earlier. It was an enjoyable evening, but awkward. He was so used to being with Carlos. He encountered a couple of eager young ladies asking to keep him company, but Simon had become adept at handling these kinds of situations in Madrid and politely indicated he was waiting for someone ... it avoided a potentially tricky encounter.

The next morning when Simon went down for breakfast, he 'braced himself' for meeting Olivia 'face to face', but he was relieved to find the ladies were absent, having left earlier for Serena's shop. He'd already excused himself from the store today. It was proving a struggle to keep his interest at Guilder's, and they managed perfectly well without him when he was away, but for his father's sake he knew he must try harder.

Later that morning Simon became the proud owner of a Wolseley motor car. It was dark green with leather upholstery and a soft top in black. Simon was ecstatic – it was like being a boy again with a new toy. He drove around the city to get a feel for driving in traffic, then he made his way back to Loftam. He wanted to give his family a surprise, but no-one was at home, so he went for a spin by himself. He was just returning when he saw his father walking very slowly up the hill. He pulled up alongside him.

Robert stopped and stared at his youngest son and the bright, shiny motor car. "Simon, my boy, what's this?" he asked, looking at the car in amazement.

"Get in, Father, and I'll take you for a drive," Simon replied.

Robert climbed into the front seat beside Simon and off they went. Robert was overjoyed with the new motor, asking about the make, model and performance and where Simon had learned to drive.

"A friend in Spain taught me in his car," he replied.

Robert realised how little he knew about his son's life these days, especially the Spanish side.

Simon knew he could not delay meeting Olivia for much longer, so decided to surprise the ladies with a lift home, as they left Serena's shop. He went down to the end of the High Street to wait for them. He guessed at the time and did not have to wait too long. He watched them walking down the street through his mirror, then stepped out of the car onto the pavement, just in time to bow and say, "Ladies, your chauffeur awaits you."

He observed Olivia, but was distracted as his sister shrieked with delight.

"Simon, you dark horse," she said, walking around the car admiring the new motor. "When did you buy it?"

"I ordered it a couple of weeks ago, and went into town this morning to collect it," he replied, trying to keep his eyes off Olivia, who was wearing a new bobbed hairstyle, reminiscent of Elise. Their eyes met and his insides melted.

"Olivia," he greeted her. "So lovely to see you again." He lifted her hand, gently pressing it to his lips, then held onto it for perhaps a moment longer than was necessary. He wanted to pull her into his arms and embrace her... but resisted.

"Good to see you again, Simon," she responded with poise and dignity. He opened the door and the two young ladies climbed into the back seat. Serena was full of questions and begged Simon to take them for a drive. It was a lovely summer's evening and they drove through lots of country villages and up onto the moors. Eventually they returned to The Gables. Serena declared the whole experience as fabulous. The surprise car journey 'broke the ice' between Simon and Olivia and the evening meal was cheerful, full of laughter and cheeky banter... as if Olivia was part of the Guilder family.

After dinner Serena mentioned Olivia's new job. Simon sat back in his chair, crossed his legs and raised his eyebrows. "A new job, Olivia ...tell me more."

Olivia stiffened, acutely aware he was using her proper name. She straightened her back.

"I've been thinking about branching out into a new occupation for some time. Millinery has always intrigued me, so when I saw a job offer with training, I jumped at it," she explained. "I've almost finished my training and hope to take on my first commission soon." For unidentified reasons Olivia felt great satisfaction informing Simon Guilder of her changed circumstances. She felt his penetrating gaze and sensed his surprise.

"Why don't you show Simon your designs?" Serena interjected.

Olivia hesitated, then went upstairs to collect her sketch book. Serena looked at her brother. "What's gone wrong between you two?" she asked. "Do you still care for her?"

"Yes, of course I do... but it's a private matter, Serena," replied Simon. "And it's all a matter of timing," he added, giving her an empty smile.

"Well don't leave it too long, dear brother. I think our Olivia is set to go places, now she's entering the business world," Serena declared.

Simon stared at his sister intently, drumming his fingers on the dining table – he was deep in thought. A few minutes later Olivia re-entered the room. Simon was amazed at the sketches and the written detail. After looking carefully at them he commented, "Serena, I think you should commission Miss Brown to design an exclusive range for your shop."

Olivia was alarmed. "Oh, no, I haven't completed my first assignment yet... maybe in a few months when I've gained experience."

Simon looked directly at her, in a determined, almost superior way, unlike the way he used to look at her. "Don't underestimate yourself, Olivia," he remarked. His tone was business-like – were they strangers now?

Over the next twenty-four hours, Simon found being so close to Olivia challenging. He struggled to keep himself in check. There were several occasions when they brushed past each other – in the kitchen, in the dining room, in the hall. It would have been so natural to reach out and touch her. If he was trying to convince himself he could walk away from this attraction, then he was failing miserably. On Sunday, Serena suggested a drive into the country and a picnic lunch. Robert accompanied them. It was a beautiful summer's day. They found a perfect spot beside a river on a country road and enjoyed their picnic. Simon asked the ladies if they fancied a walk along the riverbank.

"You two go," suggested Serena, "I'll stay with Father."

Simon could have kicked his sister. He knew what she was trying to do. He stuck his hands firmly in his pockets. Simon and Olivia never lacked topics of conversation, so they walked and chatted like two old friends – well, that's what they were. Simon restrained himself – he longed to take her in his arms and kiss her. But he'd asked her for time and understanding and at least they were still friends. What was it about this new hairstyle? First Elise... now Livvy.

"I like your new hairstyle," he said, stopping and looking at her as they walked along. It was a personal comment and the chemistry between them was charged. For an instant Olivia thought he was going to touch her. She was trembling.

"Simon...I..." Olivia began, averting her eyes...but the moment passed. "I have to keep up with the fashions to suit my new hat designs."

His eyes seemed to pierce her. She felt uncomfortable. They turned and walked in silence. It was a test...but Simon wasn't ready.

All too soon the car and its occupants were returning home. It had been a delightful outing. Later Simon drove the ladies to Newcastle so Olivia could catch her train. They parted with hugs in general – just three friends.

"Hope to see you soon," they shouted and waved as Olivia boarded her train.

***

A few weeks after Olivia's visit, Simon was on the shop floor at Guilder's checking some new stock. Gwen, Robert's secretary, called over the balcony, "Mr Simon, your father needs you."

Simon detected the urgency in her voice – something was wrong. He dashed up the stairs, two at a time.

"What's wrong, Father?" he asked, looking at Robert's ashen face.

Robert rubbed his chest. "I've got pain."

Simon instructed Gwen to telephone Dr Morton. Within the hour, Simon was driving Robert home. The doctor ordered bed rest. He would also do some tests. The following week the doctor told Robert he was suffering from heart disease and must seriously think about retiring. It came as a blow – Guilder's Outfitters was his life. How could he just stay at home all day? Who was going to run the store when Simon was away so much?

William visited several times during Robert's period of convalescence. The two brothers started to converse meaningfully, much to Simon's surprise.

"Father needs to retire, Simon. What can you do to bring that about?" William asked.

Simon rubbed his chin thoughtfully. "I think we need to appoint a business manager. I'll draw up a list of the tasks Father performs and then look to organising some interviews."

Over the next few weeks, Simon assessed the tasks undertaken by his father, himself, Gwen, Mr Thorn and Barry, the young man who had stepped in for Simon on his first trip to Spain. Barry was now a valuable member of staff. He then consulted with Serena and William. The three Guilder siblings discussed the situation at length, and finally decided to appoint a new accounts manager, who would undertake tasks performed by Robert, Simon, and some of the others. Simon placed an advert in the newspaper and interviews were organised. Serena suggested the interviews be held in the dining room at The Gables so their father could be present. The new accounts manager was subsequently appointed, and Mr Thorn agreed to step in to cover for Simon, during his absences. As the weeks passed, Robert regained strength and begged the doctor to allow him to visit the store when he was having 'a good day'. The doctor agreed, but under strict instructions he took a taxi home to avoid walking up the hill.

Simon and Carlos continued their 'letter tutorials' during this time and Simon was pleased with his progress. He also wrote to Olivia a couple of times that summer, keeping her up to date with Robert's progress and asking about her new role as a milliner. Having 'broken the ice', he deemed it appropriate to keep in general contact. She'd completed her trial assignments and was well on her way to becoming a milliner in her own right. Their correspondence was friendly...but devoid of loving endearments.

As the autumn approached, Simon made plans to visit Spain. The accounts manager proved efficient, and he felt confident about taking the six weeks 'vacation' he had promised himself. He contacted Alberto to tell him his plans, asking him to make the necessary arrangements at the Barcelona house for himself and another guest. They would be staying for two weeks from mid-October and would need the services of a cook and housekeeper. He then included a separate letter marked 'Private' for Alberto to pass onto Senorita Dominguez. It was a formal letter – asking if she was still available to accompany him as his 'interpreter' for two weeks. If the arrangement was acceptable to her, he would meet her in the hotel foyer, on the morning of their departure; he gave the time.

As usual all this Spanish correspondence was handled by Mr Adams in Newcastle. Two weeks before his

Spanish visit he heard from Alberto who'd fulfilled the requests. Paulo, the caretaker at the Barcelona house, had arranged a cook and a housekeeper for two weeks. He included an equally formal letter from Elise agreeing to the arrangements. Finally, he penned a cheery note to Olivia informing her he would be out of the country until early December and wished her well with her new work. He also left Mr Adams' contact details with Serena, in case of any emergency.

'English Simon' was ready to become 'Spanish Simon' for the fourth time.

CHAPTER 13

SPAIN

AUTUMN 1923

S imon arrived in Madrid after two days of travelling and an overnight stay in London. He was quite used to this pattern now. It left him with a day to relax and do a few things before the journey to Barcelona. He called in to see Alberto and told him his visit to Barcelona was to assess the viability of the property, commenting that he may decide to sell it depending on this visit. He also made an appointment to speak with Eugenie's solicitor, Senor Perez, and needed Alberto to accompany him as an interpreter. He was interested to see if the solicitor could provide any background information on the Barcelona house. Senor Perez was unhelpful, other than to say the property belonged to Eugenie, not Juan. The first time Senor Perez heard about the house, was when Eugenie made her will, after Juan died. This confirmed what Simon had suspected ... the house in Barcelona was Eugenie's family home.

After leaving Alberto he went to find a jeweller's shop. He wanted to purchase two gifts – one for Elise and the other for Carlos as 'thank you' gifts – Elise for interpreting and Carlos for all the Spanish tuition. For Elise he chose a simple chain with a diamond drop – neat and dainty, unlike the heavy jewellery his mother used to wear. For Carlos he bought some armbands and cuff links. Presents bought and wrapped, he went back to his apartment to rest before meeting Carlos later for dinner.

The two friends enjoyed catching up – especially about Simon's new purchase – his car. He gave Carlos his gift and thanked him for all his help. He was feeling much more confident about conversing in Spanish during simple everyday conversations. They ate a delicious meal, but Simon left Carlos outside the restaurant; he wanted a good night's sleep before the Barcelona trip. He indicated he may see Carlos before he returned home... but was vague.

***

Elise was delighted to receive Simon's invitation to act as his interpreter on the visit to Barcelona. She knew he would struggle to make enquiries, with his limited Spanish. She was also curious to find out about this mystery house – Eugenie had never mentioned it. But it must have been significant for her, to have a sketch of it displayed on her bedroom wall.

Elise continued to add to her wardrobe over the summer months and kept regular appointments with the hairstylist. The morning of the Barcelona trip, she took extra care with her appearance, added a splash of her new perfume and included the bottle in her new suitcase, specially purchased for this trip. She set off, having left Pepe with Isabella. She'd cancelled her piano students for two weeks. How liberated she felt – setting off for a holiday with a man she hardly knew. Times were changing and a lot of preconceived notions were being challenged. Who was there to judge her? She was an independent young woman, with a mind of her own. She was looking forward to this holiday. She'd gained confidence since she returned from France just over a year ago.

***

Simon met Elise in the foyer of his hotel at 10 am that morning. He was sitting waiting for her and watched as the concierge greeted her like an old friend. Simon was perplexed. She was as beautiful as he remembered – so chic, so modern, so confident. He greeted her with a kiss on each cheek, detecting the delicate fragrance she wore.

"Elise, how delightful to see you again. Are you well?" he said in Spanish.

"Very well, thank you, Simon. How was your journey?"

"Rather long, as usual, but I arrived two days ago, so I feel rested now."

On the way to the station Elise explained how helpful the concierge had been during the weeks she had stayed at Eugenie's apartment when Eugenie was in hospital. Simon was unaware of this and realised how she must miss the use of the apartment now.

"Oh, I rarely stay in Madrid," she replied, when he suggested she use it when he was not there.

Simon decided to use the journey to find out more about his mother and about Elise, whom he barely knew and here they were going off on holiday for two weeks! This would never happen in England, he mused. An unmarried woman would have a companion or chaperone. He smiled to himself, and Elise noticed.

"What's amusing you, Senor?" she asked.

He gave her the 'angry look' at the use of the term 'senor'.

"Elise...I've told you..." he admonished, with a mischievous glint in his eyes. She pursed her lips.

"I promise not to say it again," she replied, looking sheepish.

He beamed at her...the ice was broken. "I was smiling because of our holiday...together, I mean in the same place at the same time. This would never happen in England. We are still Victorian, although the old girl's been dead twenty years."

She started to laugh.

"You must think me very forward, Mr Guilder."

"You don't know what I'm thinking, Senorita," replied Simon, raising his eyebrows. Their easy banter boded well for the vacation.

For the rest of the journey the mood was relaxed and so easy – they conversed as if they'd known each other for years. The teasing between them came so naturally. He asked about her aunt and uncle, and he was surprised to discover that until Juan's death, she didn't spend much time with Eugenie, being either at school or staying with her friend during vacations.

"You know, when the solicitor said you were my mother's companion, I pictured you as a spinster in her sixties, but I got that very wrong." He looked at her intently.

"I hope you weren't disappointed that I wasn't," she answered coyly.

He chuckled. "Well, I doubt if I would have asked a sixty-year-old companion to accompany me on this trip – would I?" He grinned mischievously.

He enquired about her parents, and she told him about their deaths just before the Great War, when she was away at school. Then he asked about his mother and Juan as a couple – what were they like? Did she know why they had no children?

She told him the little she knew. They made a handsome couple and were very loving towards each other. They entertained a wide circle of friends regularly. She also wondered why they remained childless, but Juan was twenty-five years older than Eugenie, so their age difference might have affected their decision. Elise commented that Eugenie would have made a wonderful mother, she was so caring and considerate. Simon swallowed... why would a young mother part with her new-born son?

"Do you know how long they lived at Casa Galiana?" Simon enquired.

"I don't know, but I can ask Isabella – she's been the housekeeper for years, so she might know."

Simon became silent...he was thinking again about his idea to build his Spanish House in Loftam... one day.

When they arrived in Barcelona, they took a taxi from the station to the address Elise provided for the driver. Simon was amazed at the size of the place. Although he'd visited with Carlos there was a great deal he had failed to notice on that occasion. When Elise saw the house, she was surprised. It was so different from Casa Galiana.

The sun was setting, and the air was starting to cool – so different from Simon's last visit, eighteen months previous in the spring. A burly man in his thirties answered the door. He remembered Simon and was introduced to Elise as Paulo. Elise was amazed at the way Simon conversed so easily – his language skills had improved every visit.

She elbowed him as they made their way from the front door to the kitchen. "I'm impressed with your Spanish," she commented quietly.

He turned and winked at her. "Senorita, I am full of surprises."

In the kitchen they met Paulo's wife, Violeta, who was to be the housekeeper. She explained to Elise that Paulo's mother would be their cook, but there was a cold meal left ready for tonight, as they were unsure of the time of arrival. Elise talked to Violeta in Spanish, and the speed at which they talked left Simon behind – he couldn't understand what they were talking about.

They were shown around the house. Fires were laid ready to be lit in both drawing rooms – one small, one large; a dining room with a table set ready for dinner. Upstairs were four large bedrooms and two bathrooms. As instructed only two were prepared – the others remaining under dust sheets.

They returned to the kitchen. Paulo asked if they required anything else from him – he was usually at the house each morning for about two hours. They indicated they were unsure about their plans and would speak to him each day but would see to their own breakfast to save Paulo's mother coming in early. This communication was made by Elise, as Simon had started to flounder with his Spanish phrases. Then Paulo and his wife left.

Simon and Elise picked up their bags and went upstairs.

"Which room do you want?" asked Simon. Both were large with a double bed.

"I don't mind...you choose," Elise answered, looking out of the window at the rear of the house.

"You have this one, I'll go and unpack," replied Simon, and leaving Elise, walked to the other bedroom.

A while later after unpacking, washing, and changing, Elise descended the large oak staircase and found Simon lighting the fire in the small drawing room. It was much cosier than the large room – more of a morning room with two comfortable chairs either side of the fireplace, a rug, two small tables with lamps, a bookcase and a dresser with colourful plates displayed.

Simon greeted her. "Thought we'd use this room, instead of the larger one. It should warm up quickly once the door is shut. Is everything alright with your bedroom?"

"Yes, thanks. This is a big house. Not as intimate as Casa Galiana," she observed, warming her hands beside the fire.

"No, it's quite different. I'm not sure I want to keep it, but I'll make my decision at the end of the holiday. Shall we go and eat? I'm starving."

She nodded and they went through to the kitchen to look for the prepared food. "Let's eat in here," suggested Elise. It was warm beside the stove, and the food was simple but welcome – fish salad and fresh fruit accompanied by a bottle of red wine. After tidying the dishes, they wandered into the small lounge to finish the bottle of wine. The room was cosy now the fire was lit. Elise felt drowsy – the effects of the journey, the food, and the wine.

"I can't remember when I last felt so relaxed," she remarked stifling a yawn.

Simon gazed at his companion... she was beautiful even when she was drowsy. If only he was brave enough to reach out and touch her – but was too much of a gentleman. They chatted generally. Elise stifled another yawn.

"Elise, go to bed...you're tired," he commented with a commanding tone.

Elise grimaced. "Senor Guilder... I think you are bossy!" she quipped, rising to her feet.

Simon pulled his angry face, then smiled. He checked the fire, and they walked up the stairs to their rooms and a good night's sleep.

Elise woke to an autumnal chill. "Brrr," she said to herself as she made her way to the bathroom. There was something about this house...it felt 'sad'. The strangeness of the holiday arrangement dawned on her as she dressed. How would she spend the next two weeks in the company of her landlord? It was a peculiar arrangement and, with hindsight, was she foolish to have committed to accompany him? The idea of visiting Barcelona appealed to her, but Senor Guilder was a stranger and a foreigner... had she made a rash decision? But joining Simon in the kitchen, she quickly dismissed her apprehension, as she immediately helped Simon understand what Paulo was saying. This, after all, was her role in being there!

After eating, Paulo offered to show them the exterior of the house. Elise's interpreting skills came in useful again as Paulo guided them around the grounds and outbuildings. Then they decided to explore Barcelona and taking instructions from Paulo went into the city. They were just two tourists taking in the sights, joining the crowds and admiring the architecture. The day was cool and overcast, but dry. They visited the Cathedral, Parc de Ciutadella, and wandered up and down La Rambla. They lunched in the Cafe de l'Òpera and walked some more before returning to Casa Mendoza, feeling exhausted.

As they walked into the hallway, they heard voices in the kitchen and stopped.

"Oh no," declared Simon, "high speed Spanish... here we go again." Simon pulled Elise's arm, and made a pretence of putting his hands together as if praying – "take over for me, Elise please..."

She grinned and walked into the kitchen to greet Violeta and Paulo's mother. Simon was a few steps behind Elise. The older woman stopped talking and stared at Simon. She looked shocked and turned pale. Violeta stared at her mother-in-law and gabbled something, then led her to a chair. The older lady was obviously shaken.

Then she pointed at Simon and declared, in Spanish, "Roberto Silvestre," then again louder, "Roberto Silvestre –a ghost, a ghost."

Simon was confused – what was the elderly lady saying? She seemed extremely upset about something and he was the cause of it.

Elise glanced at Simon then back to Violetta. She then introduced Simon to the older lady saying in Spanish, "This is Senor Guilder... he is the owner of this house. He is the son of Eugenie Silvestre and is from England. I am acting as his interpreter."

Sofia, the older lady, slowly calmed, realising her mistake and began to apologise.

Elise, understanding the confusion, commented to Sofia, "We think Simon resembles his grandfather...is that correct?"

The older lady nodded, saying he was so like him, when he was a young man, she thought she'd seen a ghost.

Elise turned to Simon. "I'll fetch the photographs... she may know the others," she added, going upstairs.

After Elise left the kitchen Simon pointed to himself and said, "caballero Inglis". The older lady nodded understanding.

Elise returned and showed the two ladies the photograph of Eugenie's father and one of the groupings when the family looked older. The two ladies looked at the group and Sofia pointed to each person saying a name. Elise retrieved a pencil from her bag. She quickly wrote down the names on the back of the photograph as Sofia identified them.

Then Sofia lifted her arms, a look of anguish spreading over her face. She cried out in Spanish, "Tragedy, tragedy," then pointing at Eugenie she shook her head and said something in a dialect Elise did not understand.

Paulo entered the kitchen at that point and Violeta explained to him what was happening. His mother started to speak in this strange dialect again. Paulo listened then asked her some questions.

Meanwhile Simon and Elise waited. Simon was struck by the fact these people were talking about his family, and he did not know what they were saying. Elise seemed to sense his bewilderment and quietly slipped her hand into his and gave it a gentle squeeze. He turned to her. She looked straight into his eyes with a look which seemed to say, 'I feel your pain'. He squeezed her hand and neither of them attempted to pull apart.

After a few minutes, Paulo turned to Simon and Elise, cleared his throat and said, "My mother says there was an accident in this house many years ago – a fire. Roberto Silvestre, his wife and three children were killed in the fire... but not the oldest girl – she was away at the time. I am sorry. My uncle knew the family better than she did. He might know more details."

Elise translated for Simon, who asked if they could speak to the uncle. After translating, Paulo said he would try to contact his uncle, but he was old now and lived in a village a few miles away. Elise asked if Paulo would let them know. He said it would take a few days, but he would try his best.

On impulse, Elise asked Sofia if she knew what had happened to Eugenie. She shook her head. Simon was a bit behind with all this translating going on, but when he caught up, he asked Elise to ask if the family were buried nearby. They shook their heads, but Violeta added that there were three possible cemeteries nearby, if they wanted to search.

Later that evening, they ate a Spanish casserole, courtesy of Sofia. This time they sat in the dining room as the table was set in readiness. Like the previous night they went to relax with a glass of wine in the small lounge. The fire was on, and the room was cosy. Over dinner, they tried to assess the information Sofia had given them. Simon was amazed at how much they had learned, all because of his likeness to his grandfather.

Over the next few days, Simon and Elise slipped into an easy, holiday mode of life. They breakfasted sometimes early, sometimes late. They read, they walked. They laughed, they talked. They were perfectly at ease in each other's company. They visited the cemeteries Violeta mentioned, but they could not identify his relatives' graves. The days were warm, and the nights were chilly, but they enjoyed sitting in the cosy, small lounge beside the fire, after dinner each evening.

One morning towards the end of their first week, Simon was woken by Paulo's truck crunching up the drive. He leaped out of bed and went downstairs. Paulo was standing in the hallway. He started to speak in Spanish. Simon was barely grasping what he was saying when Elise appeared and floated down the stairs wearing a long, flowing kimono in a very pale, delicate material. Simon felt a surge of desire rushing through his being. During the week there were moments when he wanted to put his arm around her or hold her hand, but something always held him back.

He was brought from his dreams when Elise stopped babbling away in Spanish and turned to Simon. "Are you awake or dreaming, Simon? Did you understand what Paulo said? We must be ready quickly and he will take us to see his uncle."

Simon gulped, dismissing his dreams. "Yes, I'll be ready in ten minutes," he replied and followed the 'floating senorita' upstairs.

An hour later, after a very bumpy ride in Paulo's truck, they arrived at a tumbledown old farmhouse. They were hot and dusty, thirsty and hungry. The old man, Paolo's uncle, smiled a toothless smile and offered them some wine. They accepted out of politeness, having missed breakfast. Simon and Elise were prepared with questions, but first they showed the old man the photographs. His eyesight was failing, but he held them close to his face. He began to speak in the strange local dialect Sofia used. The translation went from the uncle to Paulo, then to Elise and finally to Simon.

Eventually they grappled with some basic facts. Roberto Silvestre was a 'good man', a factory owner, he was fair to his workers and rewarded them well. The business climate of the day was highly competitive. Some bad men were paid to set fire to the house of a corrupt factory owner. But they made a mistake and chose the wrong house. He then shouted 'Tragedy, tragedy'. He shook his fists in the air. It was covered up, he said, they did not bring the bad men to justice. Five members of a family killed by mistake – he then shook his head and seemed to go into a daze.

After a while he stood up and patted Simon on the back and babbled in the dialect again. Paulo translated.

"He says you look like Roberto, and you must be a good man like your grandfather."

Eventually, after thanking him, they departed. Simon and Elise were lost in their own thoughts on the way back. Violeta provided some lunch – Simon and Elise were starving. Afterwards they went to their own rooms for a siesta – it had been a long morning.

When Elise woke up it was already dark. She walked to the top of the stairs... she could hear voices in the kitchen. She was unsure of the time, so floated down the stairs in her kimono, intending to dress once she'd established how long it would be until dinner. Simon was already in the kitchen conversing, as best he could, in his limited Spanish, to Violeta and Sofia.

He greeted her with a big smile. "Hello, sleepy head – you must have been tired."

She felt embarrassed. "What time is it?" she enquired.

No-one answered, but the evening meal was obviously ready, so they went straight to the dining room to eat, as Paulo, Violetta and Sofia left. As before they shared a bottle of wine, moving to the small cosy, lounge to finish it – after almost a week it was becoming a habit. Simon stretched out in his chair. At first, he was deep in thought, sipping his wine. Then he started to summarise their findings.

"So, now we know – the newspaper clipping Eugenie kept referred to a fire in this house. Judging by the appearance of this house...I'd say most of it was demolished and rebuilt. I noticed when we viewed the outbuildings they were constructed in different stone. What a tragedy, a case of mistaken identity. There must have been many corrupt factory owners at the time, but thankfully my grandfather was not one of them. The criminals were probably from outside the area and did not know they'd found the wrong house. Fortunately, my mother was not there. Perhaps she was in England giving birth to me?" he queried.

Simon became lost in his thoughts for a while. Elise was listening to Simon's summary. He continued, "I still can't understand how a mother can give away her new-born baby?" It was a rhetorical question; he wasn't expecting a response.

Suddenly, he became aware of a sniffling sound and looked over at Elise as tears started to trickle down her face. She began to sob quietly.

"Oh, Elise, don't cry, I lived a splendid life," he uttered. "Gertie was a wonderful mother to me. Whatever Eugenie's reasons were for parting with me...I didn't suffer in any way." He watched as Elise shook her head, continuing to sob. Then he realised the tears were not for him, but for Elise herself. He got out of his chair, went across and knelt in front of her. He gently lifted her chin.

"What's wrong, Elise – have I said something to hurt you?" he pleaded, searching her face for an answer.

The tears came in loud uncontrollable gasps. He pulled her into his arms and hugged her as she sobbed into his shoulder. Her body was heaving with the depth of her sadness. He was bewildered but held her tightly, as she unloaded her grief. Slowly, she calmed. Lifting her head, she looked into his eyes. He tenderly wiped the tear-drenched hair from her brow.

"I did the same," she gulped, "I gave my baby away just after he was born."

He stared at her, stunned, gradually taking in the enormity of her revelation. "Oh, Elise... I'm so sorry. You must have had good reasons. I'm not judging you."

He hugged her again then after a few minutes he took her hands, pulled her to her feet, and enveloped her in a loving embrace.

"Elise, you don't need to explain."

Elise shook her head and spoke softly. "I want to tell you, Simon."

They sat together on the floor, in front of the flickering fire and he cradled her in his arms. After days of longing just to hold her hand, here she was relaxing in the protection of his arms. Every sense in his body was heightened – he yearned for intimacy.

For a while, she was silent. He didn't rush her, sensing she was returning to a painful experience, opening a door to her past – a door that would awaken hurt and loss. Her voice sounded like broken glass. "He was called Phillipe; he was Francoise's brother and a serving soldier when we met," she gulped. "I was only fifteen, spending my school vacations at Francoise's home. We were attracted to each other and began a three-year friendship conducted mostly by letter. He talked of marriage, but his duties separated us. Those days were desperate. We were two young people in love who knew we might never see each other again. That last Easter, in 1918, he received his posting – we could resist no longer." She paused, struggling to speak. "He...he... he died in battle, never knowing he was to become a father. Our son was born two months after the war ended. I wanted my baby to be adopted...so Eugenie organised it." A fresh wave of tears engulfed her.

Simon was struck by the similarity in the tragedy of two young women – Eugenie and Elise. Who was he to ask why a mother could part with a new-born child? Circumstances at the time determined their decisions. For a while they sat in the glow of the warming fire, neither of them wanting to break the silence. He pulled her closer and looking down gently kissed her lips. Then he whispered in her ear, "Do you think you could love again, Elise?"

Her answer was to reach up and pull his face towards hers. Their lips met again and without words their actions did the talking. Slowly, and passionately Simon and Elise became one...urged on by the tragedies life brings.

Much later, as they lay on Simon's bed, in the cosiness of satisfied love, he looked down at her and caressed her face. "Do you remember 'toga moment'?" Elise nodded. "Well...I think something happened between us then," Simon added.

Elise reached up and touched his lips. "You looked so funny, Simon," she whispered softly. "But when you tried to remove that sheet in the height of your fever later that night," she remarked, "I knew I was falling for you."

He embraced her again.

"That sheet has a lot to answer for," he commented as they expressed their love for each other again.

***

During the remaining week of their holiday Simon and Elise lived in a dream – they wanted time to stand still. Their teasing and playfulness led them to love. A walk on a deserted beach led to love. They loved and laughed, they loved and walked, they loved and took in more sightseeing, they loved and talked. They were two young people madly in love and they did not care who knew.

She wanted to know about his life in England. So, he told her about his father, his sister, his nephew, his work at Guilder's, his car, his love of jazz music, his hope to be a better trumpet player, only mentioning his brother briefly in passing.

One evening Elise asked if there was a special love in his life. For a moment he almost shook his head in denial, but he did not want secrets with Elise. He was quiet for a while.

"Yes," he answered truthfully. "There was…there still is… I've asked her to give me time. So much has happened in my life since I found out about my mother. I need time to sort myself out."

He gazed into her eyes and kissed her. She sensed the strength of his love for this woman.

"Were you lovers?" she asked.

Simon shook his head. "No, Livvy is an English rose."

"What's she called?"

"Livvy. It's my pet name for her – her real name is Olivia."

Elise noticed the faraway look in his eyes as he said her name. He pulled away and was silent for a few minutes. There was a lot of soul searching going on and again, Elise could sense it. Then he looked up.

"I know this sounds crazy... but I love you, Elise," he declared taking her in his arms. "I love you so much... but...but I love Livvy as well. It's not right... I must decide and I can't."

They lost themselves in their love once more.

The holiday was over. They'd exhausted their enquiries, giving up finding a family grave after a few more attempts. There were still lots of questions regarding Eugenie – they would never know for sure why she married a much older man. After twenty years, it was probably as much as they would ever know.

The night before they left Barcelona, Simon gave Elise her gift – the diamond drop pendant. "It was meant to be a 'thank you' gift for being my interpreter, but you are so much more than an interpreter, Elise. This is a token of my love," he said, as he fastened it around her neck and kissed her. There was a sudden flashback of giving the pearls to Livvy.

"Simon, it's beautiful. When I wear it...I will always remember our love," she declared.

The next morning Simon took one final walk around the house and garden. They thanked Paulo and his family for all their help and departed for Madrid. On the train Simon put his arm around Elise.

"I've decided to sell the Barcelona house – it was a house of tragedy for my family. I am going to sell it and use the proceeds to build my Spanish House in England."

Elise snuggled up to him and smiled.

"I agree, Simon. There was something about it...a coldness...a sadness...as if the walls held a dark secret – I sensed it the night we arrived. Yet it became a haven of love for us, Simon. But I don't think you could ever be happy there, knowing its history."

He squeezed her. "I don't see myself visiting that house again. I've made my decision," Simon remarked.

During the next few weeks Simon stayed with Elise at Casa Galiana. They couldn't bear to be parted. Simon attended his meetings with Alberto, spending the minimum amount of time there. He met Carlos, for dinner, after one of his meetings. Simon's absences from his usual pattern did not go unnoticed.

Carlos was puzzled. He asked questions and received vague answers. He concluded ...it's a woman! There is only knowing the love of a good woman can put that kind of energy into your being – but he didn't find out who she was...

Alberto suspected. A two-week holiday in Barcelona with an interpreter... mmm, he'd seen the senorita – there was more than interpreting going on there.

Isabella knew. She'd been around the block too many times in her sixty-plus years, to not recognise two young lovers when she saw them. They tried to behave circumspectly when she was around doing her daily chores, but after a couple of days they gave up trying, and Isabella just smiled and thought 'young love'.

Simon asked Alberto to organise the sale of the Barcelona house. He also asked him to source an architect who could replicate the plans of Casa Galiana. Alberto was somewhat confused but agreed to his employer's wishes.

The night before Simon's return arrived, as they lay entwined, Elise spoke; she sounded so serious.

"Simon, this is our last night... you must go home and marry Livvy... you belong to her. I have only borrowed you for a little while. I think it is possible to love two people at the same time – one in a physical reality, the other in memory and dreams."

He failed to understand the implications of what she was saying. He knew he had told her he still loved Livvy, but he could still meet Elise...Livvy need never know.

"But I'll visit twice a year, Elise, spring and autumn when I'm here on business."

She pulled away from him and stared deeply into his eyes. Then she shook her head.

"Only as my landlord, Simon – you can visit whenever you want to view your house. If you marry Livvy, you must honour your vows."

Her words stung him – but he knew he must choose... and somehow, he sensed a decision was already made. She left the room and returned a few minutes later with the square musical box. He looked at her perplexed.

"Take this with you," she said. "Put the memories of our love in there, Simon. Our love was beautiful but transient, we both knew it would end."

He opened the box. She walked over to her dressing table and returned with her perfume bottle. She sprinkled the green baize interior with more than a few drops.

"Your mother gave this to me as a gift and now I'm giving it to you, in memory of our love...it plays 'Fur Elise'."

He already knew the tune from the day he'd picked it up in the summerhouse. Tears sprang from nowhere...he felt the finality as they made love for the last time.

The next day Simon left Spain.

CHAPTER 14

LOFTAM ENGLAND
WINTER 1923

The dark, damp, foggy days of December did nothing to lift Simon's mood. Daily life was humdrum. Robert was making an appearance at Guilder's when he felt up to it. Simon would work in the backroom of Serena's shop on those days as there was little room at the firm. Even his car was not much fun in those dark days. He seriously thought about moving to Spain permanently – it beckoned him... Elise's love, sunshine, business, nights out with Carlos. But he knew he could not do that. He would count the days until his next Spanish visit.

Christmas was a repeat of the previous year and every bit as enjoyable. Laughter frequently reverberated in the walls of The Gables, but Olivia detected Simon's underlying melancholy – there was something different about him. Her work as a milliner was progressing. With her training completed she was taking on commissions and developing her own clientele. She had started designing her own collection and was ready to put it into tangible form, but she felt she wanted 'ownership' of it. So, she began to order materials and have them delivered to her home.

But there was a problem – no-one in her family was blessed with a business mind to advise Olivia. Her father worked in local government and her brother was a schoolteacher. Neither of them had any idea about production and marketing. She decided to bounce her ideas off the Guilder family over the Christmas holiday.

The day before Olivia's return arrived and an opportunity to raise this discussion had not presented itself. She was resigned to forgetting about it, when over breakfast Simon said he was free that day and would take her to Newcastle for her train later. Serena was delighted to hear this – ever hopeful her brother and friend would overcome their differences. She invented some commitment at the store and Robert said he was having a quiet day in his room.

As they were carrying their dishes to the kitchen, Olivia decided to take the plunge...she was nervous about mentioning it.

"Simon, would you mind if I asked your opinion over a business matter?"

He looked at her with a stern face. Getting used to Simon in business mode was still strange.

"Certainly. Let's go into the dining room," he suggested.

They sat opposite each other, and he listened to her proposals for her own millinery business. She had drawn up a business plan, which she handed to him. Simon perused it, only making one or two minor changes. When he finished reading it, he looked up at her, but his facial expression remained unchanged. Where oh where was the young man who once kissed her so tenderly? Simon drummed his fingers on the table.

"I'm impressed, Olivia. You are enthusiastic and organised. Your plan is well thought out."

He sat rubbing his chin thoughtfully. She was so full of love for him, but at least he was treating this seriously.

"Olivia," he said, "give me a couple of hours to look at this." He glanced at his watch. "Serena said she might be free at lunchtime. So, we can go somewhere for lunch. We'll leave about 12.30." Then he left the room.

Her mind was in turmoil – he treated her like a sister. Her love for him was as strong as ever, but he did not return it. They were just 'good friends'.

At 12.30 she was waiting in the hallway with her small suitcase. He dashed down the stairs, donned his coat and hat and without a word opened the door. She sat in the back seat of his car, and they collected Serena from her store and went for lunch. Olivia brought Serena up to date with her ideas as they ate. Having spent the morning thinking through an idea, Simon sat back, crossed his legs, and stroked his chin. He lifted Olivia's business plan out of his coat pocket.

"Ladies... I think Olivia has a good business plan. What she needs now is some financial backing to give birth to this idea." He continued, "Olivia, you have the acquired skills, you're pulling together resources, but you need a work room and a display outlet."

The two women nodded. Then he looked directly at Olivia.

"Olivia, would you consider moving to Loftam?"

Olivia gasped. Simon's face remained solemn.

"I am offering to back your business venture, source you a property and loan you an amount of money – to be decided and legally arranged of course. This will give you time to manufacture your designs. Serena, I am sure could provide you with a display outlet in her store... ladies, I await your initial response."

He looked across at her and smiled, the first sign of emotion he'd shown all day. Her heart melted. Was she dreaming? Was this really happening?

Olivia was silent for a few minutes, then spoke. "That's a very generous offer, Simon and... I accept it. I would be willing to move to Loftam; however, I would need to find lodgings."

"Don't be ridiculous, Olivia," said Serena. "You can live with us – your room is already there."

"It might spoil our friendship, living in each other's pockets," warned Olivia.

Simon got up from the table.

"Personally, I think that is a side issue, the main decision is to get this business launched."

As she left them at the station. Olivia thanked Simon for his generous offer and indicated she would talk to her parents and let him know in a couple of days.

***

SPRING 1924

1924 was a turning point in Olivia Brown's life. During March she moved from York to live in Loftam at The Gables – one year after her 'relationship' with Simon had ended. Her parents held some initial reservations. They admired Simon, but he liked to 'splash the cash' and that concerned them. Olivia put their minds at rest saying he was left a legacy and was keen to invest in property and business ventures. They could see Olivia's devotion to him, so gave her their blessing.

Meanwhile Simon found some suitable premises off the High Street. A shop and workroom, although initially the shop would be curtained off to provide a light area for Olivia to create her designs. She was to spend six months putting together her first collection in time for the Autumn/Winter season. As agreed, the loan was attended to legally by a local solicitor. Simon was to seek no return on his investment for six months.

When Olivia arrived at The Gables it seemed strange at first, but within a few weeks the extended 'family' found a working rhythm and Robert watched with delight as his two children embraced the world of business.

***

SPAIN

Simon arrived in Madrid for his spring meetings. He was full of anticipation at the prospect of meeting Elise again. In the intervening months he regularly relived their moments of passion and longed to write expressing his love in written form... but hesitated to do so. He felt sure she would be there to welcome him when he arrived at Casa Galiana.

He met with Alberto and was disappointed there was no 'private' letter for him. After two days of business, he took the train to Toledo; with every mile his anticipation grew. Just to feel her, touch her and... There was certainly a spring in his step as he crunched up the driveway. Isabella answered the door and looked surprised to see him.

"Oh, Senor," she exclaimed. "The Senorita is on holiday in France staying with her friend. I have no idea when she is returning."

Simon was gutted and could not believe it. He'd been counting the days since he left in December. Elise knew his work pattern – there must be some logical explanation as to why she was away. He went into the lounge, found some writing materials and left her a note, placing it on the mantelpiece underneath his mother's portrait ...surely, she was on her way back from France.

The following week he returned. But she was still away. He wrote another note and left it beside the first one. By the end of his Spanish visit there were four notes on the mantelpiece, all dated and saying:

Darling Elise, where are you? Please contact me. I love you, dearly. Simon.

The last one added Mr Adams' address in Newcastle for her to contact him directly and not through Alberto.

Simon was like a ship without a rudder during that Spring visit. Two positive things did happen, however. Firstly, he sealed a deal on the Barcelona house, and was there in person to sign all the documents. Secondly, he took the architect with him on the final visit to the Toledo house. He made lots of sketches and took many measurements. Simon returned home at the beginning of May with a very heavy heart.

**

SUMMER 1924
ENGLAND

By June Olivia was working hard on her new collection. Her parents made a surprise visit to see her. She was overjoyed and showed them her work premises. They were delighted and impressed to see their daughter's handiwork with the neat little labels saying, 'Created by Olivia', sewn into them.

As the summer rolled along, Simon started to look for a suitable plot on which to build his Spanish House. He found one on the other side of Loftam to The Gables. It was really a country lane with a few detached houses at intervals. He viewed two plots and eventually decided on one. He made an offer and two weeks later it was accepted. Meanwhile he received the architects' detailed plans from Spain and put them in to the local council for approval.

Each week he visited Mr Adams in Newcastle – there was no 'private 'correspondence for him.

September arrived and Olivia's new collection was launched. It was a slow start, but the weather was still warm, and ladies were not thinking about winter hats.

"Give it time," encouraged Serena, who by now had learned to ride the ups and downs of the fashion world. As the days grew cooler sales in Olivia's Hats took off. She soon possessed an order book.

Throughout this time Simon and Olivia settled into a 'working relationship'. Simon visited Olivia's store on a weekly basis and kept abreast of the progress of his investment. He was often out on an evening and Olivia was unaware of how he spent his leisure time. Serena and Olivia settled for an occasional trip to the theatre – their working lives were too busy to be socialising.

One morning during October Olivia was surprised when Simon made an offer over the breakfast table.

"Ladies, I think you both deserve a treat to celebrate the success of your business ventures, so I've booked a table at a restaurant in town for Saturday evening. Will you be able to attend?"

Olivia and Serena were excited and responded positively.

Olivia paid extra attention to her outfit that evening. Recently she suspected seeing Simon all day and every day probably made her 'invisible' in his eyes, because he treated her like a sister. She wore the pearls he had given her for the first time in ages.

The evening arrived and the atmosphere was buoyant. The threesome chatted and laughed. Olivia observed how relaxed Simon appeared – she'd become accustomed to his 'stiffness'. Simon ordered champagne and raised a toast to the success of 'Serena's Fashions' and 'Olivia's Hats'. As they were drinking their champagne, Simon looked across at Olivia who was sitting opposite – their eyes met. He was struck by her beauty and vivaciousness. Gosh... I'm a fool, he thought to himself. She's a beautiful woman. Simon noticed she was wearing the pearls he had given her. His eyes watched her as she talked to Serena, she was confident and elegant. What was holding him back?

It dawned on him he'd been treating her like a sister – and he'd let it happen. She was so poised, a modern business-woman. She was wasted as a librarian. But he was the one who had closed the door on their romance. Maybe he should open that door again. He knew it would be easy to light the fire ... he felt sure the embers were still smouldering.

The Spanish autumn trip to Spain was looming. The next day he went into town to book his tickets. As usual he called in to see Mr Adams. They were chatting about his building plans when Mr Adams remembered there was a letter marked 'personal' for Simon; it had arrived the previous week.

Ten minutes later Simon was sitting in a tearoom and drinking a beverage. He looked down at the letter. He experienced a sense of foreboding, even before he opened it.

Dear Simon,

Sorry to have missed your visits to Casa Galiana.
I was on holiday staying with my friend in France.

*I am in good health, and all is well with your property.
I hope this letter finds you well too.*

Yours sincerely,

Elise Dominguez.

He froze. He stared in disbelief at the terminology. 'Yours
sincerely'... How could she? It was impossible! He cast his
mind back to their lovemaking. He thought of the long
nights of intimacy they had shared. The hours they had
spent holding each other, declaring their love for each
other, gazing into one another's eyes.

'Yours sincerely' ... It was unbelievable! Did their love
mean nothing to her? All the talk about meeting him as
her landlord – surely not. Oh Elise...Why? Why...What's
happened? He continued to sit and stare at the letter. We
could have met twice a year. Elise ...I still love you. He
was torturing himself. Eventually he made his way home
in a daze.

That night he took the little musical box out of his
drawer and opened it for the first time since arriving
home last December. The perfume fragrance was still
strong, arousing his senses... he wept... it was over ... he
sat staring at the box for ages. Slowly, he felt realisation
sink in. It must only have been a holiday romance for
Elise –a few weeks of enjoyment. He knew it meant far
more to him. He sat for ages struggling to accept it.

Finally, he stood and put the little box away in the
container Serena called his 'Boy's Junk'. Rubbish he could
not part with – it sat on the top of his wardrobe. He knew

what he must do... climbing into his bed he eventually fell asleep.

The next morning, spurred on by his decision, he left the house before the ladies came down for breakfast. He drove into town and walked around for about an hour. Then as the business day was beginning, he found a jewellery store. He was looking for a particular item and made a purchase. He then returned to Loftam. After parking the car, he made his way down the High Street into the side street where Olivia's Hats was situated.

He knocked and went straight in. There was nothing unusual about Simon visiting at any time of the day. Olivia looked up from her work.

"Hello, you must have been away early this morning. We missed you at breakfast," she remarked.

He did not respond. Olivia shook her head... I guess he's in a mood, she thought.

Simon was wandering around looking at the stock, touching this, feeling that, looking at sketches. He was backing this business, so was perfectly within his rights to do this. He didn't look at her, but just muttered, "I needed to do things in Newcastle, so I left early."

He smiled...an empty smile, one Olivia was used to seeing. He was acting strangely, she sighed... he would leave soon.

"Olivia," he asked in his pompous tone of voice, "could you spare me some time this afternoon?"

She stopped and looked up from her work. "Of course... is anything wrong?" she enquired tentatively. All sorts of possibilities were going through her mind.

"No, I'll pick you up at the end of the High Street at two o'clock, sharp," he pronounced, turned and left the shop.

She put her work down and gazed after him. He was acting in a very peculiar manner. He was abrupt and offhand – he didn't say hello or goodbye, he had delivered his message and left. Oh, Simon Guilder what is wrong with you now? Sometimes I think my patience with you will run out. Are you going to end our business arrangement? Are you going to move to Spain? On and on her mind ticked. She had three hours to wait to find out.

She couldn't concentrate, so she picked up her belongings and locked the shop. She went along to Serena's store – maybe she knew something. Serena was busy with a client. She waited a few minutes then decided to leave. She mouthed "See you tonight," to her friend and left.

She decided to walk back up to The Gables. She possessed her own key. She ran the risk of bumping into Simon but if she did...well, so be it. This was obviously something serious and she needed to calm herself. The house was empty. She paced the floor of her bedroom, then decided to have a bath and change clothes. If this was to be their 'finale' then she was going to look smart. It would also fill in some time. Two hours later she was back in her shop looking very smart – a trifle overdressed for her line of work.

She was waiting at the agreed place at the appointed time. When Simon arrived, she climbed into the front seat beside him. It was the first time she'd sat in the front – she was usually in the back with Serena. She felt nervous.

CHAPTER 14

He greeted her with a big grin on his face. My, she thought, you've changed your demeanour since this morning.

"Hello Livvy," he said. "You look amazing." He was playing games with her. She was annoyed. Why was he calling her Livvy? She was used to him using her full name. She bristled, turned and faced him.

"Simon, please tell me what's wrong, I'm concerned," she said honestly.

"Nothing's wrong, my dear," he answered and started the car. They sat in silence as he drove out of the town to a part of Loftam she didn't recognise. They turned into a leafy lane. It was flat with a 'country' feel to it. There were a few large detached houses with big gardens. There were also lots of empty spaces. He drove slowly then stopped the car in front of a plot. He climbed out of the car, came around and opened the door for her...very strange, unless he was trying to be funny, which by the look on his face he was not. He was looking serious again. He didn't wait for her to get out, just walked off and stood by the fence looking at the plot of grass...a small field.

She felt exasperated with him, but she got out and went over to stand beside him. He didn't speak and neither did she. Then he turned and looked at her.

"This, Livvy, is the place where I am going to build my Spanish House."

She was dumbfounded but said nothing – what did it have to do with her anyway? He spoke again.

"I'll rephrase that, this is the place where we are going to build our Spanish house, Livvy."

She just stared at him. "Simon, what on earth are you talking about?"

He turned and took hold of both of her hands.

"Livvy, darling. Will you marry me?"

She was speechless. That was not what she'd been expecting.

She began to shiver. "What did you say?" she asked, finding her voice.

"Don't look so terrified." He grinned mischievously. "I've just asked you to marry me, Livvy. Feel free to slap me across the face and tell me to shut up." He continued grinning.

The tensions of the last eighteen months rose to the surface. She pulled her hands away...she was angry.

"Simon Guilder, you are the most infuriating, self-opinionated person I've ever met. I have spent the last three hours imagining the worst. You strut into my shop, fail to greet me, and rudely summon me to meet you at an appointed time and place, then you drive me across town to look at a... field. To top it all you have the audacity to ask me to marry you." She could not believe what she was saying.

He grinned at her again – making her even more angry.

"Oh, I love you even more when you're feisty," he remarked, beaming.

That comment did it. She lifted her hand, removed her glove and slapped him across the face, with force. He winced. He could not believe it and it hurt. It was a quiet road, but there were some houses around, so pulling himself together, he said calmly, "Olivia, will you get back in the car please."

"Stop ordering me around," she retorted loudly... but obeyed.

He drove out of the road and turned towards the country. They travelled for a few minutes in silence until he parked the car in a gateway on a country road. He stopped the engine, turned to face her, and folded his arms.

"What are we doing here?" she asked with a frustrated edge to her voice. "Have you come to show me another field?"

He pulled a face of exasperation. "No, Olivia... but I thought you might like to continue this tirade somewhere more private... please continue."

She did not take a second bidding. "Simon, it's about time someone burst your bubble. Eighteen months ago, you asked me to give you time, then promptly walked out of my life. You traipse off to Spain twice a year doing 'dear knows what' – I gave up trying to find out what you do over there ages ago. You set Serena, and then me, up in business and expect to be treated like some little tin god. Then to add to the insults, I might as well be invisible, because you treat me like a sister." Then she stopped.

He raised his eyebrows and asked, "Finished?"

"No, I have not. The truth is I have loved you since I first saw you standing at your mother's graveside. I tried to forget you, oh... how I have tried; but I couldn't because you kept reappearing in my life with that stupid grin on your face, and the more I saw you, the more I loved you. But you take me for granted. I have become part of the fixtures and fittings...you care nothing for my feelings, and I have just about had enough, Simon. If you think I am sitting around waiting for you to snap your fingers ...expecting, I'll come running...then you're sadly mistaken. There, that's it."

"Anything else you want to throw at me while you're fired up?" he asked with a poker face.

She shook her head. He got out of the car, walked around to her door and opened it. Oh, dear she thought –is he going to make me walk back?

"Would you step out of the car please, Olivia," he said. His face was expressionless, except for the red blotch where she'd slapped him. He stood and looked at her for a moment. She was cold and trembling. He raised his hands in a sign of surrender.

"Olivia, I stand guilty as charged. I'm sorry you've found my behaviour in recent months difficult, and I apologise, wholeheartedly." He looked at his watch. "Just over an hour ago I asked you a question. I'm waiting for your answer please."

She sighed inwardly – he was still using that same supercilious tone of voice – what would it take to get through to him?

"Simon... please be normal. This is not a business transaction," she added, then reached out to touch the red blotch on his face. For a moment he thought she was going to strike him a second time, so he dodged, and she pulled her hand away.

"Does it hurt?" she asked with a straight face.

"It certainly does," he replied without showing any emotion.

"Good," she replied, "because I meant it and I'm not going to apologise... you deserve it. Neither am I going to give you an answer. You'll wait for my answer, Simon Guilder, and stop using that supercilious tone of voice with me. Take me back home. I'm freezing, standing in this field."

Then she got in the car and shut the door. She couldn't believe the way she'd just spoken to him.

He stared at her and shook his head. She was obviously going to make him wait.

They drove back to The Gables in silence – he knew his behaviour towards her was unacceptable, but he'd tried to be honest with her.

When they arrived at The Gables, she jumped out of the car and ran up to the front door, without waiting for him. She used her own key and shut the door. She took off her hat and coat and went into the morning room, where a cosy fire was burning. She stood in front of it, warming her hands.

Meanwhile, Simon sat in the car. He hadn't reckoned on that reaction – what a mess he'd made. In his eyes he had planned a 'romantic proposal' and all he had got for his effort was a hefty slap on the face and a boat load of harsh comments. Women, he thought... why do I bother?

He locked the car and went into the house, leaving his coat and hat in the hall, but putting the little box in his jacket pocket. When he entered the morning room, he shut the door and stood behind it. He looked over towards Olivia – she was silhouetted against the glow of the fire. She was so beautiful, and he knew he loved her deeply. One more attempt, he thought to himself.

He walked over to stand behind her and put his hands on her arms – she continued to stare into the fire. Slowly he turned her around to face him. He searched her face but could not read her reaction. He picked up her left hand and gently kissed it without taking his eyes off her.

"Livvy, my darling, please forgive me... please will you marry me ... with all my faults?"

She gazed at him then slowly a smile lifted her lips. She slid her arms around his neck gently. He responded, putting his hand on the back of her head, pulled her close and kissed her passionately. Pulling apart he hugged her.

"Is that a 'yes'?" he whispered in her ear. He still was unsure. He looked at her questioningly.

"What do you think?" She smiled and they kissed again.

He picked her up and spun her around. "My, you certainly made me work hard for that answer," he commented. He reached into his pocket and produced the little box.

"This is what I went into Newcastle for this morning." He opened the box and placed the ring on her finger – a tiny solitaire diamond ring in a gold setting. It was a perfect fit. She looked at the ring.

"It's beautiful, Simon, thank you and a perfect fit – how did you know the correct size?"

He looked at her intently with a straight face. "Olivia Brown, you've spent the last hour and a half telling me what a 'self-opinionated, big-headed, know it all' I am... so of course I knew what size to get!"

"I didn't say all that," she snapped at him, punching him in the chest.

He pretended it hurt and added, "You'll have me covered in bruises before long... I never thought proposing would be so painful...please can we call a truce?"

She stroked the red blotch on his face.

Simon wrapped her in his arms and kissed her lovingly and tenderly. "I quite like your feisty side," he whispered in her ear. He kissed her again. Mmm, he thought to himself, my English Rose has a thorny side to her... but I like it!

Afterwards he showed her the plans for the house. They were now approved by the local council and Simon was already organising a builder to commence work on the house in the next few weeks.

Later that evening Simon telephoned Olivia's father to officially ask him for his daughter's hand in marriage. Everyone was delighted, Father and Serena too. Simon even phoned William to tell him the good news. Serena brought out a bottle of champagne – Simon had no idea there was any in the house.

"It's been there a while... I was beginning to think you two were never going to get engaged!" she admitted.

When Robert and Serena retired for the night, Simon and Olivia were alone. He took her back into the morning room. He looked serious. He took her in his arms.

"I need to tell you what you've signed up for, Livvy." He then told her what he was involved with in Spain twice a year – the extent of his property portfolio and business holdings. He explained that it was a regular part of his business life and not a 'jaunt'. He did not, however, mention the tenant in the Toledo house.

Olivia was amazed at the extent of his wealth. She sat and listened and pondered for a while. Then commented, "Simon, please don't take me for granted again. I love you deeply but from now on I will give you a dose of 'home truths' whenever I think it is necessary."

He stroked his face, which was still a bit sore. "I guess I will probably need it... but not so hard next time, please." He pulled her into his arms and kissed her – relief flooded him...they would make a good partnership.

That autumn Simon went to Madrid. He attended to his business meetings, stayed in the apartment, met Carlos a few times for visits to the jazz club and told him he was engaged. He wrote to Olivia several times. He did not visit the Toledo house, neither was there any correspondence marked 'private'.

Chapter 15

ENGLAND 1925

The Christmas festivities of 1924 were attended by Olivia's family at The Gables. During the time of celebration, it was decided Simon and Olivia's wedding would take place the following July. Olivia wanted to be married at the Methodist church in Loftam and her parents were happy with the arrangement. They all went to view the Spanish House which was starting to take shape.

In January Simon suggested to Olivia she could use the front room of her workshop as the town's first millinery shop. It was only a suggestion – he made it clear he was only offering some 'business advice' – he was beginning to learn his lesson. So, Olivia mentioned it to Serena who thought the time was right. Early in the new year the shop opened. An assistant and a young girl to run errands were engaged. The business seemed to increase overnight, the shop was so popular.

One day Emily, William's wife, visited. She'd taken to visiting once a week to see the two ladies and enjoy lunch with them. Emily expressed an interest in learning to become a milliner. Olivia was thrilled. Simon was unsure. She was a sweet, gentle soul – he could never understand what she saw in his pompous brother – but he was interested to see what William would say about his wife working for her future sister-in-law.

Simon was surprised to hear William fully supported the idea. Felix was at boarding school now, so Emily found 'time on her hands'. She was to work four days a week, taking the train to Loftam from Newcastle after William left for the office and returning just before he got back, Olivia told Simon.

"Very convenient," he commented.

"Oh, Simon," she replied. "Why are you so negative about William...try to see the positives."

"Mmmmm," was her fiancé's reply.

By March, the wedding plans were well underway. A wedding dress maker had been recommended by Serena and there was a first glimpse at designs and materials. Serena and Mildred were to organise the wedding breakfast at The Gables, and they also set to, revamping the spare bedrooms which had been unused for years.

Simon and Olivia met with the Methodist minister – Simon knew him through Guilder's. He suggested the young couple might like to attend some services before their wedding. Olivia thought this was a good idea, but she only managed to persuade Simon to join her a couple of times. Gertie had been a 'big' Methodist all her life, attending lots of services. The older Guilder children attended Sunday School until William went to boarding school, but not Simon.

Simon took a wedding invitation for Carlos when he made his Spring visit to Spain. He was delighted and said he hoped to be there, as it was in his vacation time, and he hoped to spend another holiday in London. The time in Madrid passed much as usual apart from one weekend when Carlos and Simon went out for a drive. Before he realised it, they were driving into Toledo. Simon always journeyed there by train, so the roads were not familiar.

"Do you want to call in at your property as we are passing through anyway?" Carlos asked.

Simon was taken off guard for a moment and hesitated briefly, but quickly came to his senses.

"No thanks, Carlos. I don't mix business with pleasure," he replied, so Carlos drove through the town and back out onto the open road.

The experience proved something to Simon. It revisited the special place in his heart he still held for Elise. But it made him realise it was in the past. It was an enjoyable part of his life he would never, ever forget... but there were no regrets whatsoever. It was over... she would always be special, but she was just a memory... a cherished memory. And he was going home to reality! Simon was soon on his way back to England, with only two months to go until his wedding.

The house was nearing completion when he returned. The builders were putting the finishing touches to the interior. After that... it was over to Olivia. Simon insisted Olivia was responsible for the décor and furnishings and she set about ordering furniture, fittings and drapes. Simon gave his approval, but it was her choice as she was the one with a keen eye for design.

Simon spent a night in Paris on his way back from Madrid, for a special reason. He wanted to find a lovely hotel within easy walking distance of the main sights. He was going to take his bride to Paris for their honeymoon. He asked the reception team at his own hotel if they could recommend any Paris hotels and arrived with a list of three establishments to inspect. He stayed in one of them; dined in the second one and took a drink in the bar of the third. He made his decision and booked the honeymoon suite for one week – no expense spared.

The next few weeks were a frenzy of activity in the Guilder household and Simon let it all wash over him.

"Do you want to discuss the details of the ceremony and the reception?" Olivia asked Simon as they shared a quiet time together late one night. He pulled her onto his knee.

"Livvy, you are a stickler for detail, and I trust your decisions implicitly. Leave the bigger stuff to me," he declared then smothered her in kisses.

The builders finished and Simon went to see the completed house. He was thrilled with the result – it was 'Casa Galiana a la Loftam'. From the outside it was the Spanish House he had dreamed of building since first visiting Toledo – whitewashed walls, two balconies, windows in various shapes and sizes with metal frames and blue shutters. There were French windows onto the balcony from the main bedroom and French windows leading out of the lounge onto the rear garden.

The garden was yet to be landscaped but Simon was already consulting with a local gardener and preliminary plans were drawn up. An area at the top of the garden, beside a stream, was earmarked for a summerhouse – just like the Toledo house but without the view.

He took Olivia to see the house the next day. She was amazed – the plans did not do it justice. It was so compact compared to The Gables and her home in York. They were to have a daily help. Simon hoped they could find a 'Mildred', but this was a task for Olivia to sort – he did not want a 'home truths' episode again – he stroked the side of his face, where she had slapped him that day. Several times over the intervening weeks he almost ventured into the danger zone, but Olivia reached out and stroked his cheek – it was enough to remind him.

"Where did you get your ideas from?" Olivia asked. Amazingly this question was never asked until now.

"Oh, one of my Spanish properties is identical – my mother used to live there, it's leased to a tenant now. An architect took measurements and did sketches."

As he said the word 'tenant', he saw a vision of Elise and his heart thumped.

***

The day before the wedding Simon went into Newcastle to collect Carlos. The two friends enjoyed lunch together then Simon took Carlos to see the Spanish House. By now a team of cleaners had been in and the furniture and fittings and drapes were in place. Olivia's taste was impeccable – Simon knew she would be a great homemaker. Carlos brought his wedding present. It was an artist's painting of Casa Galiana. Carlos had commissioned an artist to go to the house and make sketches by standing on the opposite side of the road. The finished painting made Simon's stomach flip – he could almost see Elise standing at the front door.

"I'll leave it for Olivia to decide where to put it," he told Carlos. Simon did not want to have such a vivid reminder staring at him from a prominent position – he would have to be very tactful over its positioning.

The night before the wedding Carlos and Simon were to stay with William and Emily in Newcastle. William owned a car now. He was very affable these days and extended the hand of friendship to his brother's friend. After enjoying a splendid meal cooked by Emily, Simon left Carlos at his brother's as he wanted to see Olivia one last time before the wedding.

The Gables was in a buzz. There seemed to be people everywhere. All Olivia's family were staying there.

Simon managed to extract Olivia from the guests, and they went off into the morning room. He wanted to give her a gift...a pair of tiny pearl earrings to match her pearl necklace. She was delighted and flung her arms around his neck.

"Oh, Simon they're perfect – so neat and dainty," she declared.

"Just like you, my darling," he said taking her in his arms and kissing her passionately. "Only one more night, Livvy...then we will be together," he whispered in her ear.

While Simon was away William had been busy. He was an excellent host, with an ulterior motive. William was curious about Simon's Spanish inheritance. He was in no doubt it was substantial, judging by the amount of money he'd spent over the last few years. William did not have any money problems – his wife owned a house and had significant savings when he married her. He earned a good salary and was now a partner in his firm of solicitors. But he wanted to know about Simon's wealth and this young man might just be able to give him that information.

So, he kept replenishing his guest's drink and asking carefully crafted questions which were well rehearsed. Poor Carlos fell into the trap and gradually 'spilled the beans'. Well... well...well.... thought William to himself when he turned the subject around to other matters. He'd extracted what he wanted to know. William was even more jealous of his young brother now, and that was before he thought about the beautiful young woman Simon was to take as his bride the next day.

***

The wedding day dawned bright and beautiful. The sun shone on the whole of the proceedings. Olivia arrived at the church with her attendants – Serena as maid of honour and Ann, Olivia's niece, was bridesmaid. William was best-man and a smart young Felix completed the wedding party.

Simon gazed adoringly at his gorgeous bride. Her ivory dress was in the fashionable shorter length with a scalloped hemline. It was embroidered with rose scrolls and tiny pearls. The neckline was scooped, and Olivia wore Simon's two gifts – the single string of pearls and the new dainty earrings. Her headdress was a foundation hat, embellished with tiny flowers and a full-length trailing veil. She wore dainty, satin, mid-heeled shoes with a strap.

She was so beautiful...he felt blessed.

The church was packed with guests and onlookers, and many of their customers and staff were outside waiting to greet the happy couple. The photographs were taken in the park over the road from the church. The wedding breakfast was served back at The Gables – having been prepared in advance by Mildred, Serena and Freda, Olivia's mother, who had arrived three days before. The three ladies provided an excellent buffet meal. Emily played her part too – she loved arranging flowers and had made the bride's and attendants' bouquets. She also decorated the church and house tastefully.

Olivia met Carlos for the first time and found him charming. Some of Olivia's extended family and family friends travelled up for the day from York. Speeches were made, including one from Robert, who mentioned how sad it was his beloved Gertie did not live to see her youngest son on his wedding day. The comment brought a tear to Simon's eye.

All too soon it was time for the happy couple to depart for their honeymoon. Olivia changed into a low-waisted, long sleeved short dress in a delicate shade of green. Her cloche hat, specially crafted by Emily, was decorated with interwoven ribbons which matched the contrasting scarf and satin collar of the dress. Goodbyes were said then William drove the happy couple to their hotel in Newcastle, close to the station, where they would take a train to London the following day. After an overnight stay in London, Simon and Olivia were to travel on to Paris for a week.

Simon and William shook hands when they got out of the car at the hotel. William put his hand on Olivia's arm and asked, "May I kiss the bride?" He gave her a gentle kiss on the cheek.

"It's been a splendid day," he said, then added, "you made a beautiful bride, my dear."

As William drove away Simon thought the relationship with his brother had certainly 'turned a corner' in recent times.

It was a spectacular day. Simon only thought about Elise on two very brief occasions. The first was during the pledges in the church service. When the minister said, 'forsaking all others keep yourself only unto her', Simon answered with a definite "I do". Secondly, was when he beheld the beauty of his new bride – a brief memory of his first time with Elise...but the thought soon vapourised... as he embraced the reality of making Livvy his wife.

The honeymoon in Paris was all Simon hoped it would be ...the sights, the sounds, the experiences of the iconic city mingled with the delights and pleasure of their love.

Back at The Gables, two days later, Serena was exhausted as she finally waved goodbye to the last of the guests. One more task to complete and then she would relax. William offered to help her transport the wedding presents over to The Spanish House – Simon had left her a key. It was the first time William saw the inside of the house. Simon had showed him the outside soon after the builders had finished. As he walked from room to room, he made admiring comments, but that visit to the house did little to assuage the wave of jealousy forming inside William Guilder.

***

CHRISTMAS 1925

Christmas 1925 was a 'full house' at The Gables. Serena employed her organisational skills and all of Olivia's family were invited for a five-day celebration. Accommodation was no problem, the bedrooms having been revamped for the wedding, earlier in the year. Freda and Tom, Olivia's parents, stayed at the Spanish house along with their two spaniels.

The food, as always was excellent – all the ladies helped with the preparations. William, Emily, and Felix came over each day – there was lots of hilarity, games, carols, and music, and of course the trumpet made an appearance – everyone admitted he was improving.

Robert was so happy to see the extended family unit and wished Gertie had been spared to witness it all – she loved entertaining. Serena was certainly following in her mother's footsteps.

However, during all this activity, Robert started to feel unwell. He didn't want to make any fuss, so just excused himself to go for a 'lie down' each afternoon and retire early at night. No-one noticed. The day after the guests departed, Serena wondered why her father was so late coming down for breakfast. When she went to investigate, she found Robert had died peacefully in his sleep – his heart disease finally taking him. The doctor said he'd been dead for many hours and indicated it was sudden.

Serena was distraught. She blamed herself for allowing such a crowd of people to be in the house, when Father was used to peace and quiet. But everyone remarked how engaged Robert was and the festivities probably helped to take his mind off his health issues.

At the end of the first week in January 1926, a large gathering attended the funeral of Robert Guilder – a much loved businessman of Loftam. Another crowd was entertained at The Gables, but this time in sombre circumstances. Serena was left to live in a large house by herself, and Simon knew the mantle was truly on his shoulders as he became the Manager of Guilder's Men's Outfitters.

***

TWO YEARS LATER
LOFTAM ENGLAND
1928

It was a bright Spring morning as Olivia was walking home from church. She enjoyed the Sunday morning service. It was almost three years since her wedding in the Methodist church and she was now a regular attender. Serena often joined her, but not Simon. He usually took Fritz, their little black and tan dachshund, for a walk instead. But today that task would fall to her, as Simon was away in Spain. Later, about four o'clock, William would come over to collect

Serena, Olivia and the two dogs and take them over to Newcastle for a late Sunday lunch.

Serena was coping well on her own now – thanks to Maisie, the mother of Fritz. The two little dogs were a joy to watch playing. After Robert died, six months after their wedding, Serena got her dog, Maisie, to keep her company in the rambling house. Last summer, two-year-old Maisie had given birth to pups. As soon as she saw them Olivia knew she wanted one. Simon wasn't averse to having a dog but preferred spaniels. However, Olivia knew from her own family's pets, spaniels needed a lot of exercise, and she reminded Simon she would have to do the exercising when he was away in Spain. So little Fritz came to live in the Spanish House. They didn't call it The Spanish House – it was just 25, Wood Lane – they couldn't agree on a name, so left it.

I wonder what Simon is up today, she thought, as she meandered her way to the outskirts of the town. He often asked her to accompany him on his visits.

"Come with me, Livvy, please...discover Spain," he would say. She knew accommodation would have been no problem – he'd told her about his apartment. But somehow, she avoided accompanying him.

"I can't leave Emily to manage the shop for that length of time," was her usual excuse.

Only one more week and he will be home, she mused. Oh...she missed him so much when he was away. She could feel herself yearning for him. The physical side to their marriage was an unexpected joy. She'd been brought up, in the wake of Victorian thinking, to expect the activity of the bedroom as something to be tolerated by the wife, under a cloak of darkness. Well... that was certainly not the case in her experience. Simon was an amorous lover. When he returned from his Spanish trip, he was even more energised in that regard. She often teased him about it.

"It's all the Spanish sun and thinking about being with you again, my darling," he would chirp and kiss her. She smiled, feeling a warm glow enveloping her.

Their marriage was wonderful...even more after she dispelled the 'nagging doubt' present in those early days. She smiled as she remembered Simon's Spanish Secret, as she thought of it. She always sensed Simon kept something secret in Spain, even after the ground levelling of 'the proposal' when she delivered some home truths.

Firstly, there was the picture of his mother's house in Spain which Carlos had commissioned and given to them as a wedding present. It was a beautiful painting worthy of prominent display, yet Simon insisted it was placed on a wall in a corner of the spare bedroom next to the wardrobe. Strange, she always thought...why build an exact replica in England and 'hide' an excellent painting of the original?

Secondly ...the musical box. It was about a year after Robert died and Serena was doing some sorting. She brought a wooden storage box from Simon's old room at The Gables.

"The boy's memorabilia," Serena commented. "Get him to sort it, Olivia – it's just junk but he won't part with it."

But Simon didn't part with it, and it ended up on top of their wardrobe. So, when Simon was away the next autumn, Olivia brought it down to see what was in it. Serena was correct. It contained old car magazines; half built models; a bag of marbles; a catapult – why does a grown man keep a catapult? She grinned to herself.

Then she found the musical box. She opened it and was alerted to a smell...a fragrance...a woman's perfume.

The tune it played was vaguely familiar, but she could not recall its name. Why has Simon kept this? She wondered. She left it out on the top of the drawers. The next week, when Simon returned on a Sunday afternoon, he followed his usual pattern. He went upstairs to take a bath and unpack. She went upstairs about half an hour later and he was lounging on the bed, a towel around his waist. He was holding the little musical box.

"Where did you find this?" he asked, looking thoughtful.

"Oh, it was in that box of junk Serena brought over from The Gables months ago," she replied. "I was curious what you kept in it."

He opened it and wound the handle – the tune played...'Fur Elise'.

"Serena used to play that," he commented.

"Why did you keep it?" she enquired.

"It belonged to my mother," he replied.

Olivia was puzzled and sensed there was more to it.

"Simon...what is she called?" she asked in her 'home truths' voice.

"My mother was called Eugenie," he responded and looked up at her. She sat down on the bed beside him.

"No, Simon... please tell me the name of the woman who gave you the box and wore that perfume."

He looked deeply into her eyes and the significance of the moment was tangible. After a few minutes he reached out and pulled her beside him on the bed. She could tell he was struggling to form the right words. She snuggled into his arms, and he sighed.

"Her name was Elise...hence the tune 'Fur Elise'. We had a brief ...relationship, but it was over long before I proposed to you, Livvy. She gave me the box because my mother, her aunt through marriage, gave it to her."

The revelation put things into perspective for Olivia. The night of their separation at the station in York, when he had asked her to give him some time, she sensed another woman was involved. He was always so vague when Spain was mentioned. He was a handsome man, and it was only natural he would have 'encounters' in Spain, possibly more than one and probably where he'd learned his amorous ways. But why did he keep this musical box? This Elise person must have meant a great deal to him. She asked one more question.

"The painting, Simon, the present from Carlos...did she live in that house?" She remembered the silence – it spoke volumes... he was lost in his memories.

"Yes," he replied truthfully. "Still does, as far as I know... but I have never seen her again."

She just looked at him. He seemed to anticipate her next question.

"I don't know why I kept this box... it means nothing to me now." As he spoke, he wrenched the little winder from inside the box and threw it across the floor, then threw the box after it.

"Olivia," he said – he always used her full name when he wanted to say something important. "It's you I married. You are my real, true love. I love you so much Livvy ...and I'm going to show you how much I love you, right now." He pulled her close and the intensity and passion of their lovemaking that afternoon, remained in Olivia's mind. An hour later she slipped off the bed, pulled on her robe and retrieved the little box and discarded winder from where he had thrown it. She placed them in the bin. She never saw the box again.

**

Simon's role at Guilder's continued to be very relaxed. After his father died, he thought he would have to be more 'hands on', but it appeared Robert only attended the firm to keep himself busy – he was manager in name only, he did not really 'do' anything much. The accounts manager did an excellent job and young Felix was all set to join the firm when he left school. Like Simon he had no desire to go to university. He was following in Simon's footsteps.

The terms of Robert's will were tricky. He had bequeathed the store, The Gables, and savings to his three children to be shared equally. The savings were easily shared, but The Gables was Serena's home and William had no interest in the firm. Eventually, it was decided that the firm would be owned jointly by William, Serena, and Simon. Simon remained Manager, but only as an overseer, taking little income – his day-to-day involvement was tenuous. He knew he would have no trouble relinquishing his connection with Guilder's when the time came. He intended to hand over to Felix in the fullness of time.

The house was to be owned jointly by the three of them on the understanding if Serena were to marry or die, it must be sold, and the money divided. All this sorting was quite upsetting for Serena. Her business was flourishing, so financially she was in a good position, but carving up the family assets seemed rather brutal. Anyway, she reflected – I shall probably die in my bed upstairs an old spinster, so I will not be around to see what happens.

**

LOFTAM

2019

Grace was sitting in the summerhouse. She was tired, having just returned from her walk and was enjoying a cup of coffee. She'd walked down Wood Lane again today. Someone will think I am 'casing the joint' or whatever it is called when you are sizing a place up to do a robbery.... as if!

Since she had heard that little tune 'Fur Elise', she could not get the Spanish House out of her mind.

Today, she'd been remembering something her mother told her. The Spanish House must have been built around the middle of the 1920s. Her mother would have been about ten years old at the time. Wood Lane was a new area of building in Loftam – quite select. There were a few detached properties scattered at intervals along the road.

The Spanish House was built by a local man. He travelled frequently to Spain on business. It was quite a talking point at the time. The style of architecture was unusual. Its whitewashed walls, balconies and blue shutters were so unlike any other properties in the town. Local people would take a walk down the lane just to look at the house...and her mother was one of them, along with her older sisters.

She recalled her mam saying, "We often took a walk down Wood Lane on a summer Sunday evening after chapel, just to gaze at the house and imagine what it looked like inside. I longed to live in a house like that with its balconies and blue shutters. It was a childhood dream."

Grace did a quick calculation...my mam was about forty when we moved into that house in 1955. Her dream had come true. My mam and dad gave it a name ...they called it... 'Blue Shutters'. But there's no name plaque now, just a number.

CHAPTER 16

LOFTAM ENGLAND

1930

The azure blue of the clear sky, and the pleasant warmth of the July sunshine, caused Olivia to sigh with peaceful contentment. Today they were hosting their fifth anniversary garden party. Five years since she became Mrs Olivia Guilder. Five very happy years. She had a devoted husband, a beautiful house, and a thriving business – Olivia's Hats. Only one small addition would complete her happiness …a baby. For some reason it had not happened. There had been a few false alarms, but her doctor could see no medical cause, so they kept on trying and hoping.

She looked around at the gathering. Felix, at fourteen, was chasing the two dogs, Maisie and Fritz, around the lawn. His parents William and Emily were watching on. Emily was such a good friend and a skilled milliner. She worked full time at the shop with production, which left Olivia more time for designing. William seemed more relaxed these days. At first, she had found him a surly, intense person – she knew Simon cared little for his brother but speak as you find... she always found him a real gentleman and very polite.

Her eyes drifted to Serena, and Fred her brother. Poor Fred – a year ago today his wife Betty was here –she had looked so well, but two months later she had died suddenly from ovarian cancer. Fred and his daughter Ann were devastated. They were like lost souls bobbing in a deep dark sea, searching for an anchor. Her parents Freda and Tom were so helpful, but she could sense her mother's weariness.

Serena and Fred looked so relaxed, chatting away. They would make a lovely couple, she thought. Fred needs to find a wife – he struggles to be both mother and father to Ann and keep his job as a schoolteacher. At thirteen Ann needs a mother figure. Suddenly, she was grabbed from behind. It was Simon.

"Penny for them darling?" he asked and bent over to kiss her.

"You look funny from that angle," she commented when he stood up. She watched as he wandered off to ask if anyone wanted another drink.

Simon – she followed his movements; he was so tall and handsome and becoming more so with maturity. She remembered back to the tall, thin young man who had captured her heart the day of Gertie's funeral. He was not quite as slim these days – filling out a bit. He was not as 'full of himself' either. Back then he thought he knew it all, and with his wealth he was unstoppable. She hoped she'd helped to keep his feet on the ground. He had certainly ceased ordering her around after she gave him a few 'home truths'. She smiled – loveable, likeable Simon...may you always keep those traits, my darling.

***

Simon sat on the rug and played with Fritz – he was a cute little dog, but he was most definitely Olivia's dog. He threw the ball and both dogs chased after it. Maisie got there first, but Fritz kept on running, heading for the stream at the top of the garden. Simon leapt into action – they did not want a soggy, muddy dog running around.

"Catch him, Simon," yelled Serena.

Simon disappeared behind the bushes in search of Fritz and found him sniffing around the summerhouse door. "What are you after, Mr Fritz?" he asked and opened the summerhouse door. The dog jumped over the step and Simon followed.

This was his retreat. Olivia did not come up here. He sat down. It contained his stuff – a nice comfy chair from The Gables when Serena was sorting out. 'I'll have it,' he said, but Olivia objected as it didn't match the other furniture. So, he said it could go in the summerhouse. He liked to come in here to sit and think, make models, read magazines and books and play his trumpet. It was peaceful – not that their house was noisy – he wished it were. They longed for a child – it wasn't for lack of trying, he mused.

He sat and looked around. Fritz sat at his feet and sighed. There was one item in here that he hadn't looked at in ages. Over there in the corner, under a short piece of floorboard – a little square musical box with no winder.

He smiled and reminisced...he remembered the day Elise had given it to him. 'The memories of our love are in that box Simon,' she said. He didn't really understand what she meant at the time... but she did mean it. He'd never seen her again, and these days he only thought about her when Casa Galiana was mentioned at a property review. In her wisdom she sent him back to marry Livvy, saying she had only 'borrowed' him for a while. She left him with a box of memories.

He also remembered the day Livvy found the box... that was the day Spanish Simon and English Simon became one. The day he told Livvy about Elise. Until then it was his Spanish secret – but his darling Livvy knew there was something to tell. The perfume was the giveaway. Why keep it secret? Olivia was his wife. But it was important to tell her it had ended before he asked her to be his wife. He could never have sustained a relationship with Elise and Olivia at the same time – even if it would have been an ideal arrangement – meet twice a year and have a month of fun together.

No... Elise in her wisdom had sent him home to marry his Livvy and he would be forever grateful to her for doing that. Olivia was his reality. But he couldn't bring himself to throw the box away. Olivia had put it in the bin, but he had retrieved it and hid it. Why? Somethings in life are too precious to be thrown away. Voices in the distance pulled him from his reverie.

He jumped up and so did Fritz. He left the summerhouse and joined his guests, attending to their drinks. He took his own drink and walked up to the top of the garden. He turned around and looked at the house. This house was never about Elise. He had built it in memory of his mother. He raised his glass to the house and said softly, "To you, Eugenie, and to your future grandchild who may one day live in this house."

"Who are you talking to?" asked his wife, sneaking up beside him.

"Oh, just toasting my mother. After all, this house was built in her memory," he replied, placing his arm around Olivia. "I think she would have approved of my Spanish House," he added, squeezing Olivia's shoulder. He looked around and admired the happy family scene on this anniversary day. He prayed next year there would be a new baby Guilder to celebrate.

***

Next year there was a celebration at the garden party, but it was not a baby.

Fred and Serena were married at Easter in 1931 – much to everyone's delight. Serena moved to live in York where Fred worked as a schoolteacher. She retained a staff at Serena's Fashions and remained the buyer, but spent time travelling around to exhibitions. Ann was thrilled to have a new mother and Serena was equally thrilled to have a daughter.

In line with the agreement drawn up regarding The Gables – it was sold, and the new buyers, much to everyone's amazement... were William and Emily. They sold their house in Newcastle and moved to live at The Gables in June 1931. Serena and Simon received a cash settlement in lieu of their share of the inheritance.

CHAPTER 17

NOVEMBER 1932

Olivia woke up to the sound of barking. It was dark and it took a few minutes to rouse herself – she was so tired. She felt disorientated as she swung her legs out of the bed and put on her robe, remembering Simon was in Spain. She went downstairs to see to the dog. Thankfully, little Fritz did not want to linger outside, so was soon back in the kitchen.

She poured herself a glass of water. She was feeling light-headed again. She wandered back upstairs. It was Sunday, she recollected, but did not feel well enough to go to church this morning. She climbed back into bed. She snuggled under the blankets...only one more week and Simon will be home, she thought. She still hated their partings – twice a year – but at least he was only away for three weeks these days.

She smiled to herself as she thought back to their telephone conversation last night. 'Are you doing this, are you doing that? Be careful with this, be careful with that.' She shouldn't have told him; he was such a fusspot.

But two weeks ago, the night before he set off for Spain, she had taken his hand and placed it on her stomach.

"There might be some good news when you get back, Simon."

He understood instantly and hugged her tight. "Maybe I should cancel my trip," he suggested.

But Olivia shook her head. "No, Simon... I won't visit the doctor's for another two weeks. You may as well see to your business commitments; we've been here before – it might be another false alarm. So, don't build your hopes up too much... but I feel different this time."

Her appointment with the doctor was tomorrow and she was feeling different. She rubbed her hand over her stomach and prayed, then turned over and went back to sleep.

She woke to a rattling sound. It was the window in the spare room. Simon must get it seen to when he gets back. It only happened when the wind was in a certain direction and a few months ago it had blown the window catch open. She listened to the wind building outside and snuggled up again. No need to get up just yet, she thought.

Eventually she left the cosiness of her bed, took a bath and dressed. I must eat something, she thought. She was going to The Gables for a late Sunday lunch. Emily told her yesterday that William would pick her up as usual at four o'clock. They were such good friends and she relied on them for company when Simon was away. She went downstairs and made some toast then took Fritz for a walk... not a long walk – it was too windy. At four o'clock William collected Olivia and Fritz. The Sunday lunches when Simon was abroad continued after Serena had married and moved to York.

"That wind's getting stronger," observed William as they drove out of Wood Lane.

"Yes," replied Olivia, "I must remember to check the catch on the window in the spare room when I get back – the handle works loose in the wind."

"Remind me when I bring you home and I'll secure it," he added. "Otherwise, it might blow open and smash the glass."

"Oh, thanks that would be helpful," she remarked.

The late lunch passed pleasantly. Emily was an excellent hostess. She was gradually making changes to the decor at The Gables and each week there was something new to share. Gone were the heavy drapes and dark floral wallcoverings which adorned the house when she had first visited The Gables ten years ago. These days the walls were plain, and light, and the curtains striped. Emily insisted it was called the lounge now...not the drawing room. A roaring log fire crackled in the grate and Olivia was struggling to keep her eyes open.

William, who was reading, looked up and said, "Just say when you want to go home, Olivia."

Olivia stifled a yawn. "Actually, if you don't mind, I think I'll go now. Judging by the sound of that wind, I will need to 'batten down the hatches' tonight."

So, William and Olivia left The Gables. Olivia reminded Emily she was working on designs at home tomorrow, so would see her on Tuesday. She did not want anyone to know she was visiting the doctor.

It was certainly blowing a gale and raining. It took five minutes to reach The Spanish House. Olivia ran up to the front door urging Fritz to hurry up.

William followed saying, "I'll check that window for you – which one is it?"

Olivia stepped out of her shoes, took off her damp coat and started to climb the stairs.

"It's the room on the left," she answered.

"I'll leave my shoes here; they might be muddy," called William from the hallway, taking off his coat.

Olivia went into the spare bedroom, switching on the lamp. The window was already off the latch and William closed it very thoroughly. Oliva went over to the window at the side of the bed to close the curtains. She did not see it coming. The next thing she knew William's hand was over her mouth and he was pushing her towards the bed.

"Now, now, Olivia, just relax... I only want a little taste of what my young brother has been enjoying all these years."

She tried to fight him and kick him...but he was too powerful. With his free hand he tore away at her clothing, exposing her flesh. She was thrashing from side to side and could hardly breathe. His hand moved from her mouth, and she started to cry out as he groped at her.

"Shhh, Olivia...no-one can hear you," he said in such a calm voice.

His weight was crushing her now, pinning her to the bed... she tried to bite him but to no avail, there was nothing she could do, but endure the ordeal...

When he had taken his enjoyment, he stood up. She was paralysed with fear, dreading his next move. He looked down at her and in an equally calm voice said, "If you tell anyone, my dear... I will be back for more. Now off you go to bed, I'll see myself out."

A few minutes later she heard the front door close.

She lay there ...frozen...unable to move. What just happened? Surely it was a dream? He was always such a gentleman. Then she started to shake. She pulled the bed cover over herself and sobbed. She felt so dirty and degraded. How could she tell anyone? Who would believe her? He was a pillar of society in the town. Serena would believe her, but she couldn't tell Simon – he would kill him. She lay for an age shaking and sobbing.

Eventually she got off the bed and looked down at her ripped clothing ... the monster – he is an absolute monster, and I am helpless to do anything. Her skin started to crawl at the remembrance of his brutality. She went to the bathroom and ran a bath. She soaked for ages, then scrubbed herself to try to remove the memory of his body touching her skin. She could hear poor little Fritz crying in the kitchen. She realised he must have shut the dog in there before climbing the stairs... she shuddered... did he intend that outcome all along? Oh, how foolish she was to have put herself in that position...all because of a stupid window catch.

Fritz slept on her bed that night and every night for the next week. Next morning, she rang to rearrange her doctor's appointment. When Molly, the daily help, came, she feigned illness and asked her not to come back until Friday. She lay in bed all day for days on end – only letting Fritz out into the garden, instead of walking him.

She rang the shop on Tuesday to say she was unwell and would be taking a few days off. On Tuesday night Simon telephoned. He detected something was wrong.

"I'm not feeling too good. I think I might be coming down with something," she lied.

On Wednesday Emily arrived at the door. She answered... she did not need to say she felt wretched – she looked wretched. She wouldn't let her come in – "It might be something contagious," she warned, then thanked her for calling and for holding the fort at the shop.

On Thursday Simon rang again. "One more meeting to attend, my darling, then I'm leaving early on Saturday morning, so should be home on Sunday afternoon," he informed her.

She tried to sound chatty, talking about anything she could think about.

On Friday, the daily came again. Olivia gave her a shopping list. When Molly returned Olivia was back in bed. She felt beaten, desperate and oh... so...so lonely. She still could not erase from her mind the loathing she felt for William Guilder – by his cruel actions, he'd turned something she thought of as beautiful, into something sordid.

By Saturday she knew she must eat – for her baby's sake – it was the one glimmer of hope in the middle of this nightmare; she was convinced she was pregnant. She forced herself to eat and it did make her feel better. On Saturday night Simon thought she sounded more like her old self. I must eradicate this hatred from my mind, she thought –it will harm the baby as well as me.

"Yes, darling," she said trying to sound normal. "I think I've managed to throw this wretched thing off. I've eaten today and I'm so looking forward to seeing you tomorrow, Simon."

"So am I," he replied. "Take care, my darling, see you tomorrow. I love you, Livvy."

On Sunday morning she knew she must attend to her appearance. She changed the bed linen, washed, and styled her hair. She laid out some new underwear, she'd bought on a trip into Newcastle. Then she selected a dress Simon always admired and put it on the bed. Finally, she lifted her pearl earrings and string of pearls out of the drawer and laid them beside her dress. She went downstairs and the telephone rang – it was Simon... he was leaving London. After a quick chat, she cooked a boiled egg and ate it with some toast. Then she shut Fritz in the kitchen to stop him jumping on her clothes. She checked the time – a nice bath and a bit of pamper she thought, feeling so much better.

She went upstairs and ran a bath, adding some new bath oil she'd bought recently. Now, she thought, I must forget my ordeal and concentrate on the future...she placed her hand on her stomach. She stepped into the bath... her head felt light... she turned dizzy...she slipped... into oblivion.

***

Two hours later the front door opened.

"Livvy, I'm home," called Simon, "Livvy, Livvy."

There was no sign of her... he went into the lounge, dining room, kitchen - the dog greeted him – the back door was locked. He ran up the stairs, calling her name ...panic was rising. He looked in the bedroom and saw all the clothes laid out. He ran to the bathroom, pushed open the door...ah there she was...was she asleep?

He reached into the lukewarm bath and lifted her out – but he knew...he picked her up; she was so small, so light; he ran with her to the bed. What could he do? He tried breathing his breath into her to no avail. Help, I need help. He flew down the stairs, picked up the telephone yelled 'emergency' at the telephonist and ran back to her side.

Later as he sat in the lounge with the doctor and the police – he just stared blankly, as if he was in a trance.

"Mr Guilder, is there someone we can call for you?" asked the policeman. He did not seem to hear them. The doctor, who had replaced old Dr Morton, said there was a brother. A short time later William arrived. He was shocked. He put his arms around Simon and hugged him. He asked the doctor what had happened.

"That will be for the inquest, sir, but I think it's possibly been an accident – she must have fainted when getting into the bath." William thought of the beautiful creature he'd defiled, one week ago, and he started to cry.

***

The following weeks passed in a haze, for Simon. He was like a robot. He went where he was told, sat down for meals, but hardly touched them. The post-mortem report stated that Olivia had fractured her skull, her lungs were filled with water and there were no other obvious injuries. It also revealed she was in the first trimester of pregnancy. At the inquest it was ruled as misadventure – she probably fainted and slipped when stepping into the bath, fracturing her skull and subsequently drowning – an oily residue was found in the bathwater which may have caused her to slip.

Simon stayed at The Gables until after the funeral – Serena came from York to be with her brother. The Methodist church in Loftam was packed – she was a much-loved member of the congregation. All the Guilder-related shops were closed for the day as a mark of respect. Many people could not get into the building, so stood outside. It was as if the townsfolk of Loftam were bereaved, as well as the Guilder family.

Simon went to York to stay with Serena and Fred after the funeral. He dreaded returning to the Spanish house, but eventually he did. He stayed alone, going through all of Olivia's belongings – it took him days. He remembered the clothes which were laid out on the bed – someone had folded them neatly and put them on the chair. He laid them out again – some of the items he'd never seen before...she was dressing up for me, he thought. Holding the new underwear items, he pressed them to his face and started to sob. It was the first time he'd cried since he had found her. He cried and cried – it was like an under-water spring gushing out. But it found release and ultimately Simon found peace.

He went back to York for Christmas – a very subdued time. Simon went through the motions and hardly spoke. He lost over a stone in weight, and it was beginning to show in his face.

In the new year he went back to Guilder's – young Felix was working there now – Mr Thorn was delighted with him – "He reminds me of what you were like, Mr Simon, he's a chip off your block." Slowly, very slowly, Simon started to come through his grief – he visited Olivia's grave every Sunday and in a strange way it helped. He started to give Felix driving tuition and it helped take his mind off things

Spring 1933 saw Simon travelling back to Spain. At first, he did not want to go; however, it turned out to be just the tonic he needed. There were no memories of Livvy in Spain. He met Carlos and his new bride Maria – they had been married just before Christmas. He could not believe his old friend had finally settled down. Maria was a bubbly character... Carlos was besotted with her. Simon spent most of his leisure time with them.

"Shall we visit the jazz club?" Carlos asked halfway through Simon's visit, but he refused.

"It feels frivolous, Carlos. How can I go out and enjoy myself knowing my Livvy is dead?"

"Simon...it wasn't your fault; it was an accident. You are still a young man. Olivia wouldn't want you to become a recluse."

The last night before his return he visited the jazz club and lost himself in the music. On the journey home he kept thinking there were no memories of Livvy in Spain. An idea was slowly starting to form in his mind.

***

LOFTAM

2019

Grace closed the front door and headed up the road. A chilly October morning. Guess the days are nearly over for sitting in the summerhouse now, she thought. She passed a man hammering in a 'For Sale' board in a garden

– someone on the move. Houses are selling well, she observed, not staying on the market for long. Unlike the sale of the Spanish House.

She was back to her reminiscences again. Her parents had noticed the 'For Sale' board at the Spanish House, but the asking price was too much. However, the house did not sell. Probably too unique and too pricey for Loftam in the early 1950s. After it stayed on the market for several years, her dad made an appointment to view.

Grace remembered her mother telling her, it was everything she dreamed it would be inside. Her mother loved it. So, her dad put in a 'cheeky offer' to the selling agent in Newcastle. It was rejected, of course, but he told the agent to keep his offer on the table.

Apparently, there was a reason why the house was not selling. Local rumour had spread – the wife of the businessman who had built the house, had committed suicide in the bath in the Spanish House. The owner went to live abroad, and the house was 'shut up' for many years. Was the rumour true? Her parents took no notice, but the gossip mongers said the house was 'jinxed'.

That, however, made no difference to my parents' thinking, pondered Grace. They waited...and waited. Then five years after the house went up for sale – my dad's 'cheeky' offer was accepted and we moved in...my childhood home – 25, Wood Lane. But my parents called it 'Blue Shutters'.

CHAPTER 18

1933

The summer after Olivia died, Simon invited Serena and Fred to stay with him for two weeks when Ann was on holiday with a friend. Fred and Simon always got on well and it was good to have Serena fussing around him again – a taste of old times. Fred and Simon had a lot in common...they had both lost a wife at an early age... and their love of motor cars. Fred had bought a car before Betty, his first wife, died. The two men spent hours walking the dogs – Maisie and Fritz. They sat talking in the garden at the Spanish House, enjoying the warming sun of an English summer. Simon used this time to share his decision with Serena and Fred.

"I have something to tell you," he told his sister and brother-in-law, as Serena brought tea and scones into the garden.

The couple stared at Simon, unsure what he was about to disclose.

"I've decided to stay in Spain this next winter. There are no memories of Livvy in Spain," he commented. "I am torturing myself staying here, especially when the dark, damp days arrive. I miss her so much." Tears threatened and Serena could hear the constriction in Simon's voice, as he tried to speak. "So, I intend to spend the autumn and winter months in Spain. I will go as normal to attend to my November business, but I'll stay on until May, then return here for the summer."

Serena and Fred were silent for a few minutes then Fred spoke.

"I think that's a good idea, Simon. You are like a lost soul. We'll miss you, old chap, but you need to start to live again and if you can do that in Spain... we will adjust."

They all missed Olivia so much...a husband...a sister... and a friend.

Serena, always the practical one, asked, "But what about the house...the business...the dog?"

"I was hoping you would take Fritz. Felix is a competent young man, and he does an excellent job at the store when I'm away. The house... well with your help, Serena – I will 'mothball' it. I've got until November to sort things and I'll be back in May."

So, Simon made his plans. He sorted the Guilder's side of things – they were used to his absences, so it was easy. Next, he started to sort out Livvy's belongings; he kept her wedding and engagement rings, also her pearl necklace and earrings. He packed up the rest and took it down to York for Freda, Olivia's mother, and Serena to keep or dispose of as they wished.

He returned from his weekend in York and purchased a trunk. He spent a few days packing up his belongings then arranged to send the trunk to his apartment in

Madrid. He handed the keys of his beloved car to his nephew Felix – he may as well use it while he was away.

Finally, Serena and Fred arrived to help him 'mothball' the Spanish House. The night before he left, they all stayed at The Gables. It was a tearful departure, especially for Emily.

"Look after Livvy's shop Emily," said Simon. She was already the manageress. She hugged him and sobbed.

"Oh, Simon, we'll miss you," she cried.

"I'll be back next spring," he shouted as he waved goodbye at the station and headed off to become Spanish Simon but this time ...he might just stay that way.

***

SPAIN

1933-1934

In the beginning, it was just like any autumn business trip. He attended the same meetings and made inspections and read reports. However, after the time passed when he would have normally returned home, he tried to make new routines. The first anniversary of Livvy's passing was hard, but at least he was not spending it in The Spanish House. Again, he was tormented by the knowledge his dear wife had been alone. He knew she hated being on her own. If only he'd been there to protect her. Time and time again he revisited the accident in his mind – how had such a normal daily routine as taking a bath, ended in such tragedy?

The nights were the worst. He kept himself occupied during the daytime hours – Livvy was never with him in Spain. But oh, the nights...he missed her so much. A lonely bed was the same whichever country he was in. He missed her physical presence, her lively conversation, and the unique way they anticipated each other's words before they were spoken. He missed the way she kept his 'feet on the ground' – he dreaded to think how insufferable he would have been without her regular dose of 'home truths'.

He was a widower at thirty-three – what did life have in store for him? He was so thankful for Carlos and Maria, who by now were expecting twins. He spent many nights at their home, especially over the Christmas season – they were so hospitable. Maria often invited one of her many friends, to join them for a meal – he knew she was trying to 'match-make'. Some of these ladies were attractive and good company, but Simon was not ready to develop a friendship with a particular lady and was happy to be part of a group. He also joined in some festive fun at the hotel.

He visited the jazz club, where he used to go with Carlos, and befriended the trumpeter who was also the band leader. He was an older man called Miguel. Simon told him about his hilarious attempts at trying to play along to the recorded band music. He offered to give him some tuition. Simon had packed his trumpet in the trunk. Soon, he was going along to practice sessions at the jazz club and Miguel gave him some lessons. It provided Simon with a hobby, and he loved it.

He spent a lot of time perfecting his Spanish. The Carlos tutorials via letter had ceased years ago, but every trip he practised the language and by now he was almost fluent. He found reading a Spanish newspaper was a good exercise, so another daily routine he adopted was taking a morning coffee at an outside cafe in the Plaza. He became a regular and even had his own table reserved for him. He would sit for about two hours reading the paper, people watching and drinking his coffee. Anyone who looked at him, and listened to him conversing with waiters, would never have guessed he was an Englishman. It was slowly dawning on him, that he would be happier making Spain his permanent home, with an annual summer break in England. To that end, he needed to buy a house – living in the apartment had its limitations, and so he began to look around for a place he might be able to make his home.

One morning in early March, as he was whiling away his time reading his paper and drinking his coffee, he looked up from reading. It was pleasantly warm, and crowds were already walking around the Plaza. Suddenly, he saw her...Elise. He was not sure at first. She was with a young boy – probably one of her piano students in Madrid for an exam. She was pointing out various buildings and statues. He just sat and gazed at her for about ten minutes – yes, there was no mistaking her... it was Elise. Once, she was within calling distance, but he stayed silent. She looked the same, except perhaps there was a fuller, curvier look to her figure, but it enhanced her. She was still a classy dresser, and her hair was short and neat. She wandered away and he gazed after her. He'd not thought about her for a very long time. Oh, Elise, he said to himself...he knew the embers of his love for her were not dead, they were still smouldering and could be easily fanned into flame. Was she married? Did she still live in Casa Galiana? He pondered.

On impulse, he got up, paid for his coffee, and went to see Alberto, who was not quite used to seeing so much of his employer. He asked him about the Toledo house – does the same tenant live there? Alberto looked out the relevant file.

"Yes, Senorita Dominguez still resides there – rent free with a two-year renewable contract." He raised his eyebrows at this.

Simon was thoughtful... she's still called Senorita Dominguez.

Alberto continued, "The property is well maintained and there are invoices for some alterations and decoration. The only other change is the housekeeper, she's new, the previous one died a few years ago."

Simon listened, rubbed his chin, then said, "Alberto, can you arrange for the Senorita to attend a meeting here at the end of the week. Say it is a matter to do with the lease. Please don't make any mention of me."

Alberto was perplexed but said he would attend to it.

Two days later, Alberto informed Simon the Senorita would attend a meeting at 11 am on Friday morning.

Simon thanked him and added, "I'll attend to that appointment in person." Then he left the office.

Simon paid particular attention to his appearance on Friday morning. He was always a smart dresser, but since coming to Spain his moustache was small and he now wore a trimmed, short beard. He visited the barber that morning. It made him look older, but, Simon hoped, more mature. He'd regained his weight loss and was 'filling out' a bit.

He was like 'a cat on hot bricks' as he waited in the entrance hall to the office block. He was there early and was looking at some information posted on the wall, when he heard the door open. Out of the corner of his eye he saw her as she walked over to the stairs. He turned around and greeted her warmly in Spanish.

"Good morning, Senorita Dominguez, how are you?" He reached out to shake her hand. She was completely taken aback.

"Simon," she declared. "What a surprise! You look... different. How are you? What are you doing here?"

"I'm well, thank you. I live here now."

They stepped to one side as some people entered the building.

He looked down at her, gazing directly into her blue eyes, and asked, "Are you free to have lunch with me, Elise?"

She looked flustered. "I have an appointment at Silvestre Holdings...but afterwards I'm free. I am unsure how long my appointment will last," she added.

He smiled at her.

"I am your appointment, Elise. So shall we go to lunch?"

She was confused, glancing up the stairwell.

"Well, in that case, I will have lunch with you, Simon. Thank you."

He opened the door for her, and they walked silently across the road, to a stylish restaurant, where Simon had made a reservation earlier. He was a regular customer, and they were shown to a corner table, beside the window. As they were early, he ordered coffees. They sat down and were given the menus. They sipped their coffee and perused the menu. There was an awkwardness between them.

Having made their choices, Simon ordered a bottle of wine, then sat back and looked her directly in the eye.

"I confess it was I who arranged this meeting, Elise... it was nothing to do with Alberto or the tenancy. I saw you in the Plaza last Monday."

She looked puzzled, so he went on to explain he was having his morning coffee when he saw her with a young boy, who he assumed was a piano student. She made no comment.

"What are you doing here in March?" she then asked. "I thought you only came to Madrid in April and November."

So... she remembered, he mused.

"As I said, I'm living here now – at least most of the time. I'll probably go back for a couple of months in the summer, then return."

Elise looked startled. "But what about your wife – you did marry Livvy –didn't you?" she asked, a worried look clouding her visage.

A sad expression came over Simon's face and she guessed something had happened.

He continued, "Livvy died sixteen months ago. It was a tragic accident. We were married for seven blissful years."

She reached her hand across the table and placed it on top of his – her touch felt warm.

"Oh Simon, I'm so sorry. I know you loved her dearly."

They were silent for a few minutes, as the waiter brought their starters. He cleared his throat and went on to tell her the details of Olivia's death – although they had never met, Elise felt she 'knew' Livvy. She asked about their life and were there any children. That brought the sad expression to his face again.

"She was three months pregnant... we wanted a child so much," he explained.

She asked about his 'Spanish House' – did he build it? What happened to the Barcelona house? The conversation flowed. They finished their meal and continued catching up like the two 'old friends' they were. Then she looked at her watch and explained she needed to go as she was expecting piano students later. Simon sat back. He was reluctant to end their meeting. He wanted to know about her life.

"I've rather monopolised the conversation, haven't I? I've not asked what you have been doing all these years... how long has it been – ten, eleven years? Did you marry? Have children?" he asked.

She looked sheepish, but replied, "Oh, nothing much, I still teach piano and I'm looking after your property, Senor... I didn't marry."

He smiled at the reference to their old joke. The phrase evoked a pang of nostalgia. He knew he desperately wanted to see her again, so thought this was a good opportunity to suggest it.

"I guess I look more like a senor these days," he said, stroking his small beard, and smiling at her. "I understand you have made alterations to the house – may I come and view them sometime?"

"Senor," she replied, "you are my landlord, you may view your property whenever you wish." She smiled coyly – the banter was still there between them.

He rose from the table, having settled the bill, and escorted her out of the restaurant. He stood looking down at her, ever the gentleman, and asked, "Would Monday morning be convenient to visit you, Elise?"

She agreed.

He lifted her hand and pressed it gently to his lips. "Until Monday, Senorita."

As they parted, he watched until she was out of sight... something was stirring within him.

***

As he travelled to Toledo on Monday, he wanted to find out if there was anyone special in her life – if there was, he would leave and that would be the end of it. If not, then he would have to think how he could arrange another meeting. He could certainly feel the embers of their love were warming.

When he arrived, she greeted him and suggested they took coffee before viewing the house. They chatted – his mother's portrait was still hanging over the fireplace, but the decor was lighter and brighter. She showed him the changes she'd made to the kitchen – a range cooker and new tiled floor, also the cupboards were painted and new drapes at the windows. He asked about upstairs but apart from a new bathroom floor – that was it. He needed the bathroom so went to see. As he was returning, he noticed her bedroom door ajar and could not resist a peep. Apart from new drapes and bedcover it was the same. He looked at the bed – it stirred happy memories.

When he arrived back in the kitchen she asked if he would like to stay for lunch. He agreed, saying he was free for the remainder the day. Then he indicated he would have a look down the garden. He wandered down the path to the summerhouse. It was open so he went inside, sat down, and looked around. He noticed something shiny under a cupboard in the corner and went to investigate – it was a marble. Strange, he thought, picking it up and putting it in his pocket. After sitting for about five minutes, he left the summerhouse and stood outside, admiring the view. He looked around the garden and spotted a football under a bush. By now, he was curious – piano students? He doubted it. Perhaps a visiting friend's child...possible. His mind started to go into overdrive...rounded hips, fuller breasts...did she have another child?

He meandered up the garden to the back door which was open. She didn't notice him, so he stood and watched her.

Yes, he thought, appraising her figure...I might be right. All morning there'd been a feeling there was something she was withholding from him. Well, if there was a man in her life, better to find out before he made any move. Then she spotted him.

"Oh, Simon, you gave me a start," she said in English. Up to now they'd conversed in Spanish.

"Have a seat. Lunch will be ready soon."

He took off his jacket and put it on the chair and then took his tie off – he was warm. He sat at the table watching her.

"Shall we eat in the dining room?" she asked.

"Elise, please stop being so formal, we'll eat in the kitchen, but first will you sit down, I want to ask you a question."

She wiped her hands and sat down. He put his arms back on the kitchen chair.

"Is there a man in your life, Elise?"

She was shocked at the directness of the question, then shook her head.

"Then is there something you are not telling me?" He pulled the marble from his pocket and put it on the table. She stared at it.

"I also found a football," he commented, watching her carefully.

She blushed, looked sheepish and said, "I thought I'd hidden everything, I forgot about the summerhouse."

She got up to serve the food, realising she'd avoided answering his question. She passed him his plate of food; it smelt delicious –she was always an excellent cook. They began to eat in silence – neither wanting to start up the conversation again. As they ate, she was conscious he was staring at her – she felt uneasy. Eventually they finished eating. He thanked her for the food and picked up his jacket.

"Leave the dishes, Elise...we need to talk," he said, in the commanding tone of voice, which always annoyed her. He walked off into the lounge and she followed. They sat facing each other.

"Well," he said, "are you going to tell me?" He sat with his elbows on the arms of the chair and his hands pointing upwards as if in prayer, he gently tapped his fingers together. It was a pose which had characterised him for years and usually had the desired effect – it made the other party talk.

"Yes, Simon, you guessed correctly. I have a son." She coughed. "We have a son."

His eyes nearly popped out of his head – he was not expecting that. He was silent, slowly absorbing what she had announced. It was his turn to cough. He shuffled in his chair.

"Barcelona?" he queried, and she nodded. He should have guessed.

"Roberto will be ten in July," she continued.

Simon stiffened; his face was solemn.

"Why didn't you tell me? I had a right to know." He spoke in a stern manner.

She felt nervous ...he was intimidating, but she continued, "When I realised I was carrying your child, I knew I needed to be away when you visited in the spring. So, I went to stay with Francoise in France. I intended to return after you went home, but Francoise and Pierre were so kind, they persuaded me to stay until after the baby was born. I received excellent care and returned when Roberto was two months old – that's when I found your letters."

Simon was seething. How could she do this to him? "You wrote the blandest of letters to me and signed it 'Yours sincerely'... that really hurt me, Elise." He almost exploded.

"I can't remember how many attempts I made writing that letter – so many of them were wet, with tears."

"You still could have told me," he said, without a flicker of expression on his face. He was a father...he was struggling to absorb the news. His eyes pierced her, she felt uncomfortable.

"Am I named on the birth certificate?" he asked, and she nodded.

"He is named Roberto Guilder Dominguez."

Simon sighed. "Well, I suppose that's something to be thankful for," he said, almost sneering.

She just stared at him. Never did she think he would react like this... if he found out.

"Simon, I'm sorry. I admit you had a right to know... you are making me feel bad about this."

He stood up and walked over to the open French windows. He stared out at the garden.

"You should feel bad about it...you denied me the chance to see my only child grow up. I could have supported you financially." His manner was so severe, so angry, yet controlled.

"I thought you'd be married by then and it would make things difficult for you. Roberto has never wanted for anything...except a father's love."

He turned around and glowered at her. "I would have thought of some explanation. It was your duty to inform me," he replied.

She was fed up with him talking in such a superior way, as if it was all her fault. She stood up and faced him, inwardly trembling.

"Simon, we knew what we were doing. We knew there was a risk. Roberto is the product of our love." Her voice started to crack.

Quite frankly, he could not remember having those thoughts at the time… he'd just been enjoying himself. "I want a relationship with my son," he retorted, placing his hands in his pockets.

Elise dropped her gaze…she could not allow him to intimidate her in this fashion. She lifted her eyes and stood straight. "Even if you have nothing but disdain for his mother?" she shouted at him, anger rising – he was insufferable.

"I think you better leave, Simon. Come back to see Roberto when you are prepared to meet me in a civil manner as his mother. I suggest you visit on Saturday, that will give me a chance to prepare him and you a chance to improve your attitude towards me. I'll show you out."

Fifteen minutes later Simon was journeying on a train back to Madrid.

***

All the way back, Simon was so frustrated with himself. What made him behave in that way? On discovering his son's existence, he should have taken his son's mother in his arms and embraced her; instead he had reacted in a supercilious, self-righteous manner. Olivia would have slapped him across the face and given him a few 'home truths' for displaying such selfish behaviour.

However, Elise retaliated in her way, making it clear he could only have a relationship with his son, if he treated her with respect. Simon stood to be the loser if he did not get down off his 'high horse'.

When he got back to his apartment, he sat down to write a letter of apology. After numerous attempts he wrote,

Dear Elise,

Please forgive my despicable behaviour this afternoon. I am extremely sorry if I caused you offence. I admit we went into this very much together with our eyes open, and you should not have been left to carry the demands of raising a child and the stigma of being a single mother, without my support physically or financially. I beg you to give me another chance. I long for a relationship with my son and dare I suggest a friendly relationship with you. Please can we start again, with a 'clean slate', when we next meet on Saturday.

I sign this and truly mean it.

With my deepest love, Simon.

When Elise received the letter two days later, she welcomed his apology. As her anger abated, she hoped the re-emergence of Simon in their lives would end the years of shame and secrecy. For too long she had ignored the disdainful looks and unspoken comments. In public her manner and appearance were always stiff and unyielding. She was amazed her occupation remained steady. As the years advanced it became easier, but her son often questioned the whereabouts of his father. 'He lives in England,' seemed to satisfy him but that night she told Roberto his father was visiting from England and was coming to visit them on Saturday.

"You mean I've got a real papa?" he asked with excitement. "I can't wait to tell my friends."

She smiled – her son had missed so much growing up. Now was the time to build bridges and not dig ditches.

CHAPTER 19

SPAIN

On Saturday morning Elise opened the door. She looked the picture of radiance – her short, plain blue dress brought out the sparkle in her blue eyes. She was wearing the diamond drop Simon had given to her all those years ago.

He spoke in Spanish. "Good morning, Elise." He greeted her with a peck on both cheeks, now used to the continental style of greeting. She responded. He noticed a figure lurking behind her.

"And who have we here?" he asked.

Elise stepped back to let Simon enter and the figure moved with her, still hiding. Simon popped his head around Elise's back. It was the same boy he'd seen in the Plaza, that day in Madrid.

"Ah ha," he said and quick as a flash Roberto scrambled into the archway under the stairs. Simon winked at Elise and darted around to the other side of the archway beside the kitchen door and bending down looked at Roberto. The little boy was surprised.

"How did you know where I'd gone?"

"Well, I've been here before. I always thought this archway would make a great hiding place, but I think I'm too big to use it."

Simon started to walk back along towards the lounge, but Roberto called to him.

"Papa, I think you could hide in here, come back and I'll show you."

Simon turned and walked back.

Roberto proceeded to demonstrate, while Simon took off his jacket and shoes and rolled up his shirt sleeves.

"Papa, if you slide in like me, turn on your side and then curl up." Roberto emerged from the archway and Simon followed his son's instructions – it worked... just!

Elise passed by on her way to the kitchen and laughed, saying, "I'll make a drink." Simon and Roberto followed and sat down at the kitchen table. Elise served a drink and some freshly baked biscuits.

"Mmm...these are yummy," announced Simon.

Roberto nodded his head in agreement. "Definitely! My mama makes the best biscuits in Spain. Can I have a second one please?" Roberto asked as Simon smiled...his son, what a joy.

"What are your favourite things, Roberto?" asked Simon, having tried to prepare a few questions in advance.

"Well, I've got lots," he said munching his second biscuit, "but my real favourites are cars and football."

"Oh," replied Simon, "I've got a car back in England."

Roberto stared in amazement at Simon. "What – a real one?" he asked eagerly. Simon went on to describe his car – the make, model, colour, style, speed. The little boy listened intently, his eyes widening at the description. Roberto knew a great deal about cars but did not know anyone who owned one.

Elise watched and listened, realising how much her son had missed by not having a father – there was a great deal to do to make up for lost time.

"Have you got a football?" asked Simon, winking at Elise.

"Yes, Papa, it's in the garden, but Mama says I mustn't kick it too hard, or I might break something," he answered.

"I think you should take Papa and the ball to the park, while I prepare some lunch," Elise suggested.

An hour later, an exhausted Simon and an exhilarated Roberto returned.

After lunch, Roberto wanted to show Simon his room. It was the room he'd stayed in when he took ill –but it was transformed. It was most definitely a boy's room. Roberto showed Simon the models he'd made; it reminded him of the ones he used to make with Felix. They sat down at his desk and together they were soon lost in a modelling project.

"Roberto, we need to go to collect Pepe," Elise called up the stairs later.

"Pepe?" queried Simon.

"Our dog," answered Roberto, "he's at Carlotta's house."

Five minutes later they were trundling along the narrow streets to Carlotta's house. Simon learned that Carlotta was the daily help and often took Pepe back to her house after exercising him. Elise was walking in front and Simon bent forward and remarked in English, "Pepe must be a pensioner by now."

She wafted him away and replied, without turning around, "Don't be silly, it's a different dog."

Simon lifted his hand in salute behind Elise's back and said with a big grin, "I stand corrected."

Roberto burst out laughing at Simon's gesture. Elise stopped, and turned, Simon bumped into her.

"Am I missing something?" she retorted in a stern manner.

Simon displayed a face of innocence, which sent Roberto into more peals of laughter, saying to Simon, "You're funny – you make me laugh."

Simon thought how hard it must have been for Elise to raise Roberto on her own. They waited on the corner while Elise went to fetch the dog who greeted Simon like a long-lost friend. Roberto explained the dog was called Pepe II because they could not think of a different name, when the other dog, Pepe I, had died.

"How is he so friendly with you?" asked Roberto.

"Oh," replied Simon, "I just have that effect on people and animals." He looked at Elise and asked, "Don't I?"

She pulled a grumpy face, and they walked down into the town.

In the town Simon bought some car magazines and gave them to Roberto. While Elise prepared their evening meal, Simon and Roberto became absorbed in the magazines, full of chat. After eating and tidying up, Simon got ready to leave.

"It's been fun to meet you, Roberto...I hope we can meet again soon," Simon remarked, putting on his jacket.

"When will that be, Papa – are you coming tomorrow?"

Simon looked at Elise, trying to judge her reaction. Elise nodded.

"Yes, Roberto, I'll see you tomorrow," he added, giving his son a hug.

Roberto went back to his magazines. Elise followed Simon to the front door.

"He's a grand boy, Elise. You've raised him well. Thank you for allowing me to see him." He bent over and gave her a gentle kiss on the cheek.

She stood stiffly, but looked up and said, "Thanks for visiting, Simon, and thank you for your letter...your apology is accepted."

He smiled and waved as he went for his train.

***

Over the next few weekends Simon spent time bonding with his son and they added to their list of shared interests. They enjoyed playing chess – very competitively. Simon discovered how well Roberto could play the piano, not surprising given his mother's occupation. One weekend Simon brought his trumpet and introduced Roberto to the genre of jazz music. He picked up the style very quickly and was soon making a good attempt to accompany Simon on his trumpet. They had great fun. Within a short time, father and son became great friends. However, the relationship between Simon and Elise remained cordial and polite, but cool. The iceberg which surfaced between them when he found out about his son, was taking a long time to melt. As a family, they shared lots of fun and Roberto picked up on his father's sense of humour. Poor Elise was often the butt of their jokes, but she did not mind and turned a 'blind eye' to the comical gestures the pair often made behind her back. Laughter would often grace their mealtimes, but when Roberto left the room, the ice returned. No matter how hard Simon tried – bringing her flowers, visiting the ice cream parlour, taking them out for lunch...the coolness remained. But as the weeks went by, the iceberg gradually shrunk to the size of an ice cube.

It was Roberto who finally brought an end to this freezing situation. One Saturday evening, about two months after Simon started visiting, they were just finishing their meal. Simon usually left after they tidied up.

Roberto remarked, "Why can't papa stay here tonight, instead of going back to Madrid, that way he would be here in the morning?"

Elise answered, "Your papa and I are not married, Roberto. So, he needs to go back to his home."

But Roberto continued, addressing Simon, "My friend Ricardo says you can't be my papa, because you don't sleep in the same bed as my mama."

Simon nearly choked on his food and tried hard to stifle a laugh.

Elise remained 'poker faced' and replied, "That's for 'grown ups' to decide, not little boys, Roberto."

However, the young boy was not going to let the subject drop and continued, "Well, I think Papa should stay tonight." Then he got up and ran out into the garden to play football.

Roberto's words seemed to hang in the air. Simon looked across at Elise who tried to avoid his eyes – she was so beautiful. He was in no doubt the love they'd shared all those years ago was still there...at least it was on his behalf. If only he could break into this wall of resistance she'd built between them. She stood and carried a dish to the sink and started washing up. Simon continued to watch her, saying nothing, but marvelling at the wisdom of a young boy in bringing two stubborn adults to this point.

After a few minutes Elise spoke. "You can stay... if you want to, Simon." She continued to concentrate on her task.

He got up from the table and walked over to stand behind her. He put his arms around her waist and snuggled his face into the back of her neck, her perfume filling his senses ...she felt so good.

"I will... if you'll answer a question for me," he said, then whispered in her ear, "Elise, I love you."

She froze, her hands still submerged in soapy water.

"Would you consider marrying me?"

She lifted her hands out of the soapy water and turned around, staring deeply into his eyes. With a straight face she placed some soap on his nose, then reaching up she slid her arms around his neck. "If you promise to stop being 'a pompous, intimidating know-it-all', then I will consider it."

He looked down at her as the soap suds slid off his nose and they both stared to laugh.

"Please forgive me, Elise...I promise I will never treat you in that way again."

She looked thoughtful for a few moments. His eyes rested on her lips...he bent over and gave her a whisper of a kiss.

"Yes, Simon, I will...I will marry you," she replied.

He picked her up, twirled her around. Then he kissed her again... passionately.

Roberto didn't comment when Simon continued to sit in the lounge after their meal.

"Goodnight, Mama," he said, kissing Elise. "See you tomorrow, Papa," he added, giving Simon a hug.

Later Simon followed Elise upstairs – he sat down on the bed and watched as she drew the curtains. Then she turned around.

"This feels a bit awkward," he said.

She walked over towards him grinning and commented playfully,

"Well, I could put on my kimono, and we could go down to the lounge in front of the fireplace, like that first night in Barcelona."

"What!" he exclaimed. "And have my mother's portrait presiding over the proceedings... I don't think so."

"Well... will this help?" She reached up and unfastened her dress...it dropped to the floor. He gasped at her womanhood...her beauty ...the young girl he'd known in Barcelona had blossomed into a curvaceous, mature woman. He reached out to her, and the embers of their love were soon fanned into flame.

They were woken at seven o'clock the next morning, by a boisterous Roberto, who jumped in between them and snuggled up. He shouted, as if he were making an announcement, "Now you really are my mama and papa!"

Simon and Elise burst out laughing at the innocence of their son.

***

Three months after seeing her in the Plaza in Madrid, Simon married Elise in a simple, civil ceremony. Simon placed Olivia's wedding ring on her finger – a perfect fit, it accompanied Olivia's engagement ring – Elise said she would be honoured to wear them. Carlos and Francoise were their witnesses. Francoise had no hesitation in coming to be with her friend on her wedding day, even with the short notice. The 'good feel' she sensed all those years ago, about this English gentleman, when Elise first mentioned him, finally manifested itself.

They all enjoyed a first-class celebration meal in a private room in Simon's hotel. There were only a few guests, but Miguel and his jazz band were among them, and after the meal they entertained the wedding party well into the night. The music was vibrant, and Roberto was given a chance to join in and amazed everyone with his skill. The guests stayed in Simon's hotel that night.

In July, Simon, Elise and Roberto travelled to Loftam, England, for another wedding celebration. This one was small and was provided by Serena and Emily. Serena had nearly jumped on top of the breakfast table when she'd opened the letter a few weeks earlier...she'd been waiting to hear from her brother concerning the date of his arrival for weeks.

"Fred, Fred, come quickly. This is fantastic news," she shouted to her husband who was in the hallway about to go to work.

"That dark horse of a brother of mine, has got himself married in Spain – would you believe it? Oh, I'm so thrilled for him." She continued reading down the letter. "His wife and her son are coming with him to stay for six weeks in July."

She couldn't wait to telephone Emily and William, who had also received a letter the same morning. The sisters-in-law started to make the celebration plans. One week before Simon and his family were due to arrive, Serena travelled to Loftam. Emily helped her 'open up' the Spanish House and make advance preparations.

Meanwhile, Simon, Elise and Roberto stayed for two nights in Paris and two nights in London, in lieu of a honeymoon. Roberto was fascinated on the Channel crossing, never having seen the sea before.

They arrived by taxi at The Spanish House. They had prearranged not to meet the family until the next day, as they expected to be tired. When Roberto got out of the taxi, he was so excited at the sight of the house.

"Papa, Papa it's the same as Casa Galiana."

Simon put his hand on his son's shoulder. "Yes, it was built to be identical," he informed his son and quietly to himself he said, 'Eugenie, I promised to bring your grandchild to see your house...and here he is'. Elise put her arm through her husband's, sensing what he was thinking.

"It's beautiful, Simon, Eugenie would have been so proud of you."

He squeezed her tightly.

After a good night's sleep and a quiet morning, the rest of the family arrived, laden with food and presents for the happy couple and birthday presents for Roberto, who was to be ten the next day.

A round of introductions were made. Felix at eighteen introduced his girlfriend, Sarah. Roberto was in his element playing with the dogs, Maisie and Fritz.

Simon had made the decision to remain 'quiet' about Roberto being his son – he reckoned it was none of their business, but he had overlooked something rather important... Roberto had inherited the 'Silvestre eyes,' and his family were an observant bunch. Simon found it quite amusing as one after the other at various intervals during the afternoon each sought him out quietly.

Fred was first: "You're never going to hide him, old chap, he's got your eyes!"

Simon smiled in acknowledgement but passed no comment.

A short while later William collared him, whispering in his ear, "If we were in parliament the response to the vote would be 'The ayes have it, the eyes have it' ...if, you'll pardon the pun."

Simon smirked and thought – why does he have to use strange terminology?

Emily was next. "Oh Simon, your son he's lovely, so like you," she said and gave him a hug.

Finally, it was Serena: "Simon Guilder, you little monkey, you kept him quiet. I always suspected you kept a little secret in Spain – there's no doubt whose son he is."

Simon grabbed his sister's arm. "Yes, Serena...Elise was my secret, but she knew I loved Livvy and ended things between us, long before I proposed to Olivia. I knew nothing of Roberto's existence until a few months ago."

Serena hugged him. "Simon, explanations aren't necessary. I know you loved Olivia...and I know you love Elise. I pray you will have years of happiness together."

Simon embraced his big sister, so thankful for the tight family bond. So, without making a big announcement, they all guessed, and Simon always did like to have a Spanish secret.

The English holiday was to become a feature for Simon and his family each summer until the civil and political unrest in Europe made it too difficult to travel.

CHAPTER 20

1935-1950

Roberto was delighted when his papa bought a motor car in the spring of 1935. Carlos was helpful in pointing him in the right direction regarding a good deal. It opened a new avenue of adventure and the family travelled miles that year. They often met with Carlos, Maria, and their twin boys – the two families were great friends. Simon had planned to buy a holiday home in Barcelona, but the civil climate was unstable, so those plans went on hold.

One morning in Autumn 1936 Elise came into the kitchen, having been into the town. Simon was doing the newspaper crossword in Spanish – his daily challenge he called it. He was struggling with the clue for 'six down' when Elise started speaking, so he was not really listening.

"What was that, darling?" he asked, putting his pencil down and turning around. She looked so radiant, and he could tell she was excited.

"I knew you weren't listening," she responded, looking directly at him.

He pulled her onto his knee and kissed her gently on the cheek. "There... you have my full attention." He grinned.

"I said, Simon, ...how would you feel about a new addition to the family?"

"Another dog?" he chirped.

She playfully elbowed him.

"No, Simon, I mean a baby." She beamed.

He looked at her in amazement. "Really? Seriously? Is it confirmed? When is it due? Do you feel alright?" On and on he went – he was thrilled. He picked Elise up and spun her round and took her to the lounge and put her on the settee and told her to stay there.

"Simon I'm not ill, I've carried two babies before, just relax."

But he treated her like a china doll over the next few months. Roberto at twelve years old took the news in his stride, not quite as excited as Simon thought he would be.

"I guess he knows about 'these sort of things now'," said Elise, "So it's a bit embarrassing for him."

Simon remembered how informed he was at that age and agreed.

But they could not hide their joy and Simon wrote to the family in England to let them know.

"I feel so privileged, Elise...I missed Roberto's formative years and Livvy's baby died with her." He also found pleasure in the fact the baby must have been conceived, when they were in England, staying at the Spanish House.

But their joy was short lived.

Elise went into labour at seven months. Simon took her to hospital, but the baby was stillborn – a little girl... they named her Eugenie, in honour of his mother. They were understandably upset, but Simon was so relieved when Elise recovered. The doctors were concerned for her well-being as she underwent an emergency hysterectomy.

Soon after the baby was buried, Simon was standing in the lounge one morning, looking at his mother's portrait, when Roberto entered the room.

"That's my Abuela," he said.

"Yes, I know," replied Simon. "She was my mother." Roberto looked at him astonished, he'd obviously never made the connection.

"So that's why you named my sister Eugenie," he said thoughtfully. "What was she like, Papa?"

"I don't know, Roberto, I never knew her. I was raised by my father in England."

Roberto, who was obviously understanding a lot more as his teenage years beckoned, answered, "Isn't it strange... you didn't know your mother... and I didn't know my father, until two years ago."

Simon put his arm around his son and said, "Roberto, you are learning quickly life rarely goes to plan – all I can say from my experience is, be prepared for the challenges and sadness life will throw at you, but always cherish your family. Our little girl was taken from us before she could breathe, but we have each other so we need to make the most of our times together."

Simon often remembered that conversation for two reasons. First ...it was a bit of fatherly advice he gave to his son. Secondly, it seemed to mark Roberto's stepping into manhood.

Elise struggled to recover both mentally and physically. The loss hit her hard. Simon often found her sitting, gazing into the distance, lost in some time warp. They spent hours just sitting in silence, holding hands.

One day she asked, "I wonder where my firstborn lives?" She then told Simon how she had found a letter when she was sorting Eugenie's belongings...a letter of thanks for the gift of the baby.

"He was named Andreas. He might live in this town, Simon. He will be a young man now. I might have seen him as I shopped." Pain was etched on her face. Simon could feel her anguish. He suggested she could make enquiries – she knew a name and a birth date. But Elise was resolute in her decision to leave that door of her life, firmly closed.

Those were difficult days. For about six months Elise just 'existed'. She ceased conversing. He bathed her, dressed her, fed her, and would only leave her side when Carlotta, the daily help, was around. He would walk the dog for miles knowing she was in safe hands; it became his 'escape valve'. Roberto played the piano for her every day – but she did not respond.

Simon sought medical advice – various doctors and clinics were suggested and he could afford the best, but Simon could not bear to let her out of his sight and her own doctor agreed that, in time, with Simon's love and care, she would pull through. He suspected she was like this after Eugenie died, when she had stayed in France with Francoise.

Simon learned how to be patient in those months. He was gripped with how fragile life can be... he lost his darling Livvy when she was thirty-five and he had come close to losing his darling Elise at a similar age. It became a turning point for Simon... his values seemed to change...but with love and understanding, he navigated the life hurdles.

One morning about a year after the baby had died, he was woken by her hand stroking his face. He opened his eyes. She smiled at him and said 'Simon'. It was a small step ...but a turning point and gradually she found her way back... to life... to Simon... to Roberto. Once again, she became a wife, a mother, and a piano teacher.

***

The next time Simon saw his English family the world had suffered another war. Thankfully, all were kept safe.

In 1946 Simon and Elise eventually bought their holiday home in Barcelona. It was situated near the coast and became a popular destination for them. They cherished the memories of Barcelona – the place their child was conceived. By then Roberto was twenty-two and studying engineering at university – the same age as when Simon had first visited Spain. Simon wanted Roberto to take an interest in Silvestre Holdings, but at that stage he was enjoying his studies and much to his father's amusement, he was enjoying the girls.

"Give him time, Simon," Elise advised, "let him be a young man – don't burden him with responsibility."

"I just hope he watches what he's doing with all those female companions," he commented, looking serious.

"Oh, Simon Guilder, I can't believe your comments... you didn't watch what you were doing at that age. As I recall, you made the most of every opportunity," she quipped. "I think it must be in the Silvestre blood!" She smiled and elbowed him.

Yes, he thought, perhaps she is right ... my mother visited London and I was the result... I visited Spain and Roberto was the result...so watch out, Roberto!

***

SUMMER 1950

ENGLAND

Simon lay back in the deck chair, stretched and sighed... an English summer's day – what a treat. The sky was cloudless, and the sun was warm. He was used to heat but there was something so perfect about an English summer. A cacophony of sounds penetrated his ears – birds singing, dogs barking, children playing. None of it concerned him. He could feel his eyes becoming heavy...

"Wake up, sleepy head."

He jolted... it was Elise. He'd promised to go for a walk.

"No... just leave me, I want to sleep," he pleaded.

She started to tickle him – she knew just the spot.

"Right ...you asked for it," he said, jumping up –she ran off but with his big strides he caught her and administered some revenge tickling which produced lots of shrieks and laughter and ultimately lots of embracing. It was a frequent occurrence in their sixteen-year marriage.

They set off on their walk, Simon with his arm around Elise's shoulders. They wandered dreamily down the road. It was a Sunday and people were out in their gardens. They said hello to a few people they passed; they didn't know their neighbours – they were only here for six weeks a year. But people seemed to know who they were.

They walked down Wood Lane and along the main road to Loftam cemetery; it was a route they'd taken many times before. They meandered along the avenues until they came to Livvy's grave. Elise always stood back and remained silent, until he spoke – she sensed his pain. She knew he blamed himself because Olivia was on her own when the accident occurred. He told her about the clothing laid out, ready to wear after her bath. Frequently, she heard him say 'she was dressing up for my homecoming'. He tortured himself with the memories. Over the years she had tried to soothe his pain. Now it only happened when he visited her grave.

After buying their holiday home in Barcelona, Simon gave serious consideration to parting with the Spanish House. He first mentioned it to Elise during last year's visit.

"Don't make a hasty decision, Simon," she warned. "You built it in memory of your mother, remember? Your marriage to Olivia was spent here. It holds happy memories, as well as sad ones. It's also a base to stay when we visit."

Elise watched him go over to the headstone and touch the lettering of Olivia's name. Her heart ached for him. Perhaps it would be better if he did sell...then he would avoid this every year. He picked up some bits of rubbish and some dead flowers and returned to stand by her.

"I wonder who left those?" he said, not expecting an answer. "I've seen flowers here before."

"Maybe one of her old customers?" suggested Elise, taking the rubbish and walking over to the bin. On her return she asked, "Did Olivia know about us, Simon?"

He nodded. Strangely she'd never asked before.

"She found the musical box... remember the one that played 'Fur Elise'? I said it belonged to my mother, but she asked me about the perfume." He stopped and cupped Elise's face in his hands. "You, my darling, poured a large glug of that seductive perfume into that box...it was a definite giveaway!" He kissed her passionately while standing in the middle of the cemetery. Then he hugged her and continued, "I saw no reason to be devious, so I told her we had had a brief relationship, but it ended, and I came back to marry her. I also said we didn't meet again."

They turned to leave. On the way back Simon commented, "I've made my mind up about the house – I'll get an agent from Newcastle to come and value it."

Elise turned to face Simon. "Oh, Simon...it was always your dream to build it, are you sure?" she asked. "It's not as if you need the money."

That was true – he was blessed with more than enough funds and properties, but he was becoming restless lately. His values were changing. He desired to do something useful with the rest of his life.

"I'm handing Guilder's and Olivia's Hats to Felix at the end of the month. He will become Manager... I won't be needed anymore."

The two companies, although always separate stores, were merged after Livvy's death, and Simon was handing the baton on to the next generation. Felix at nearly thirty-five was more than capable.

"Oh, I only wish Roberto would show an interest in Silvestre Holdings. It would be the obvious thing to do to hand over to him eventually, but he's not bothered about it." He sighed.

This conversation took place every few weeks and Elise would always say to 'give him time'. Roberto was to marry his girlfriend Gabriela next spring, and Simon thought it would be ideal if he became involved in his Spanish company at the same time.

"I want to do something different, Elise," he said. "I've got an idea but I'm not sure if it will work out."

"What?" she asked, stopping again and looking directly at him.

"I want to be a teacher," he announced.

She just stared at him in disbelief.

"Where did that idea come from?"

He shrugged his shoulders, and they continued their walk.

"I'll be fifty at the end of September and I want to draw the line under my English connections. I'm Spanish now. The house needs a family to live in it and enjoy it. It's selfish of me to keep it locked up most of the year. When we visit, we can stay at The Gables and visit Serena and Fred in York. We won't need to spend six weeks here if I have no business connections."

Later that week he arranged for the house to be marketed with a Newcastle estate agent.

Over the next few weeks, they began to sort the personal belongings they kept in the house and a firm was employed to pack and ship them to Spain. That only left the furniture, which was surplus to requirements, so the agent suggested leaving it to aid the viewings. It could then be disposed of when the house sold. He was a bit nostalgic when he emptied the summerhouse...most of the 'stuff' went in the bin.

"Livvy and Serena would be so proud of me parting with this," he commented to Elise.

As he closed the summerhouse door – he looked over into the corner where the musical box was hidden under the floorboard. He decided to leave it hidden; he did not need the memory, because... he lived with the reality!

At the end of August, he officially handed over the businesses to his nephew, Felix.

Simon shut the door on his Spanish House... twenty-five years after he had built it. He hoped a new owner would enjoy it – it needs to be 'lived in', he thought.

They returned home. Spain was Simon's home now. There were no reasons to return to England, unless there was a family event.

***

A couple of weeks after their return Simon came into the kitchen – he'd been out and Pepe IV was anxious for his walk. Simon walked miles every day, but usually with their little dog.

"Where have you been?" Elise asked, agitated. "The poor dog's desperate." She looked him up and down – he was dressed as if he'd been to one of his business meetings. She was perplexed – there were no appointments she could recall. She was busy baking – they were entertaining Carlos and Maria at the weekend and her hands were covered in flour.

He did not reply, but when she turned around, he was standing with his thumbs in his braces – he looked so funny.

"Meet the new English teacher at the local school. No qualifications, other than I speak English and Spanish fluently."

She promptly went over to him and placed her floury hands on his face – then laughed at him, saying, "Senor Guilder".

He scowled at her. "I guess I am an elderly gentleman now, so I'll let you call me Senor."

They laughed at their old joke.

"I didn't think you meant it," she said, wiping him down. "I am so proud of you. How will you manage to be serious?"

He folded his arms and with a mischievous grin proclaimed, "I once told you, Mrs Guilder, I was full of surprises, and this is one of them." And he meant it.

Simon became a teacher for the next ten years, until he turned sixty. He loved it, he found it a rewarding late career. It certainly surprised Elise. He also spent many nights at the local jazz club, where Roberto was the resident pianist in the jazz band. Simon frequently took his trumpet and on occasions father and son enjoyed playing together. Roberto eventually joined the board of Silvestre Holdings but retained his job as an engineer.

In 1953 Simon and Elise became grandparents. Gabriela gave birth to a daughter – who was named Eugenie, in honour of her great-grandmother. Elise and Simon were overjoyed. Elise was a very 'hands on' Abuela and gave up teaching piano to spend more time with the family.

Unfortunately, the Spanish House did not sell. The agent suggested lowering the price. Letters from England were a regular event now Simon and Elise did not visit.

One morning Simon was reading a letter from Emily who wrote a newsy 'epistle' every month.

"Listen to this, Elise," he shouted, as he was multi-tasking, getting his breakfast and preparing for school. "Emily writes...last week I overheard two ladies talking in the shop. I did not know them. One said, 'This was the shop Simon Guilder's wife owned – you remember the one who committed suicide in the bath in the foreign house on Wood Lane'. Simon, I was horrified. I confronted them and said, 'my dear sister-in-law did not commit suicide – it was a tragic accident.' They were extremely embarrassed."

Elise took the letter from Simon and read it for herself.

"Maybe you should lower the price, Simon," she suggested.

"Local gossip, I bet that's what's affecting the sale of the house," Simon retorted.

A few months later, after another price reduction, the Newcastle agent contacted Simon to say he'd received a 'cheeky offer' for the house. Simon told the agent to give it more time. It was 1955 before the Spanish House sold – when he finally accepted the 'cheeky offer'. It was on the market for a total of five years.

When the proceeds for the sale came through, Simon set up a Trust Fund for Eugenie and her new baby brother Marco, who had inherited the 'Silvestre eyes'. The legacy of the Spanish House lived on.

***

EIGHT YEARS LATER
1958

One Saturday morning Simon and Elise were just finishing their breakfast when the back door opened, and Roberto and Marco came in. Roberto and his family lived a short walk away from Simon and Elise.

"Yayo, Yayo – plane, plane," shouted three-year old Marco. The boisterous little boy ran up to his grandfather and tried to pull him.

"Papa, you shouldn't have started that game, he'll wear you out," laughed Roberto as he watched his father pick Marco up and put him on his shoulders. The pair went out into the garden and Simon proceeded to zoom around the garden with little Marco holding out his arms pretending to be an aeroplane.

Elise watched on with joy saying, "Oh, he's just a big kid himself, Roberto – he's enjoying every minute of it." She turned to Roberto, who was playing with Pepe IV, and asked what Gabriela and Eugenie were doing.

"Ballet lessons this morning," Roberto replied. At five years old Eugenie loved to dance.

An exhausted Simon and lively Marco zoomed back into the kitchen.

"And the aeroplane's coming down to land NOW," declared Simon sitting down with a bump and pulling his grandson onto his knee. Simon's face was red with all the activity.

Elise was wiping the sink and said, "Simon, get Roberto to help you put the portrait on the wall before he goes."

Simon gave his mock salute, then little Marco tried to copy him. Roberto and Simon burst out laughing at his attempts.

"Like this, Marco," demonstrated Roberto. The little boy copied his father.

"What's going on?" asked Elise, turning around to look at them... what a sight.! Her boys... three generations, all saluting her with the same eyes! She beamed at them.

"You speak and I obey, darling," said Simon, exiting the kitchen, closely followed by a flying dishcloth.

Roberto stood and shook his head at his parents' playfulness and grinned. 'When will those two grow up!' he thought.

They'd been decorating in the lounge, and everything was back in place apart from Eugenie's portrait, which still needed to be hung above the fireplace.

"I'll keep Marco busy," added Elise, as father and son went to hang the picture.

A few minutes later there was a loud thud.

"What's happened?" shouted Elise, whisking Marco up into her arms and dashing through to the lounge. Simon and Roberto were holding the portrait... but it was in two pieces – the backing had come away, when Simon accidently dropped it.

Simon gazed down at the portrait; thankfully it was undamaged, but the backing was cracked.

"It must have been hanging there for fifty years," mused Simon. "It'll repair."

"There's something in there," observed Elise.

Simon looked to where his wife was pointing and noticed some sheets of writing paper stuck to the inside of the backing. Roberto gently peeled them off and handed them to Simon.

Simon opened them. It was dated 1903 and was a letter from Juan to Eugenie asking if she would marry him. Juan explained how he'd loved her since she was a little girl, and his love grew as she became a beautiful young woman. It referred to the great loss they had both suffered – Eugenie's family and his dear friend Roberto. Juan asked if she would make an old man happy by becoming his wife. He finished by saying he would build her a new Spanish House. Tears started to stream down Elise's face – it felt so poignant.

"I guess that confirms what we puzzled about all those years ago, Elise," said Simon, putting his arm around his wife.

Elise nodded, adding, "Eugenie was blessed... two Spanish houses were built for her – one by her husband and one by her son."

"What a strange place to put such a personal letter," remarked Roberto.

Simon and Elise looked at each other and said in unison, "The sketch."

Simon dashed off to the dining room and returned with the sketch of the Barcelona house and a sharp knife. Roberto watched, puzzled – that sketch had adorned the dining room walls for as long as he could remember.

"Papa, what are you doing?" questioned Roberto, as Simon carefully opened the backing on the sketch.

As Simon and Elise suspected, there was something stuck to the inside of the backing. It was a faded, yellowed newspaper account, referring to the fire at a house called Casa Mendoza near Barcelona, two days before. The fire had claimed the lives of Roberto Silvestre aged 45 years; his wife Cristina aged 40 years; daughter Lucia aged 16 years; and sons Pablo and Mario aged 14 and 11 years. The fire was being investigated as a deliberate act of arson.

Simon looked at the date on the newspaper...29th September 1900. Two days after his birth date.

Elise followed his eyes and verbalised what Simon was realising.

"Oh Simon, they must have died as you were being born."

They reached out and hugged each other. They were both crying.

"Would someone like to tell me what's going on?" asked their bewildered son.

Roberto knew nothing about the Barcelona house, so they sat down, and Simon explained the family history of the Barcelona house and Eugenie's London visit, to his son. By the time he had finished, little Marco was sound asleep.

CHAPTER 21

1962

E lise woke with a start...where was she? It was dark...
she'd lost Simon. She sat up shouting, "Simon,
Simon... why did you go? Why have you left me?"

Two arms enveloped her. "Calm down, Elise,
I'm here."

Slowly realisation dawned on her. Simon...oh, relief....
it was a dream. A very vivid dream. He rolled over and
tucked her under his arm. She could still feel the panic of
her dream. She was shaking. He cuddled her.

"Sssh... it's alright, my darling, I'm here – I haven't
gone anywhere," he reassured her.

"Oh, Simon I was dreaming. It was so real. Our life
together never happened. I was back to those days when
I told you to go to Livvy. I wanted you to come back to
me... but I sent you away. Then I found out about the
baby, and I knew I couldn't tell you, because you'd be
married to Livvy by then, and I could never hurt her. You
belonged to her not me."

Her words were tumbling out like a train running on a track, getting faster and faster. She was working herself into a frenzy. He sat up and switched the light on and took hold of her.

"Elise," he said, cupping her face in his hands, "I did come back – we've been married nearly thirty years; feel me, I'm real."

She rubbed her hand across his bare, hairy chest and gently kissed it... she could feel his heart beating. He put out the light and they settled down to sleep again.

The next time Elise awoke she felt calmer. It was still dark, but she sensed it was a good while later.

What day is it? She pondered. Oh yes... Simon's taking a flight to London today. It's November. He is going to a funeral. She felt herself getting sleepy again...

Elise opened her eyes and blinked ... it was breaking daylight...she felt exhausted. Why? Then she recalled her nocturnal ramblings. What had caused them? She reached out and touched a very real Simon – all six foot of him – still fit and attractive for his sixty-two years. She stroked his chest, twirling her fingers in the hairs.

"Mmmm...you're awake early," said a sleepy voice.

"Simon, what time is it?" she asked in a panic again, remembering his timetable for the day. She tried to sit up, but he pulled her back and started to caress her.

"Elise...will you stop panicking... there's loads of time." He began to smother her with kisses –she still didn't know the time, but it didn't matter, she clung to him ...her husband for nearly three decades. Yes ...she gave him away, but he came back. His lips found her mouth and she stopped her panicking and let him love her.

***

Later that day Simon took a plane from Madrid to London then an onward train to Newcastle. He was met at the station by Felix and his two teenage daughters – they were babies the last time he'd met them. Simon was introduced to the two girls – Kathleen and Joyce – he felt he knew them from their grandmother's letters. They drove back to The Gables.

Simon had received the telephone call the previous week. William had passed away. He was seventy-four. He had been terminally ill for about six months. The funeral was tomorrow. Simon had wanted Elise to accompany him... he hated being separated from her – but he suspected she was afraid of flying.

He longed to fulfil his lifelong ambition to travel. Now he'd retired from his teaching role, air travel would make it so much easier to visit places. Elise made an excuse about looking after the grandchildren; also they'd recently acquired a new puppy – Pepe V. Simon thought flying was a marvellous mode of transport. When he thought back to the length of his journey to Spain forty years ago...there was no comparison...days of travel now shrunk into hours.

It was twelve years since Simon had visited Loftam and he saw lots of changes. Emily was in a bit of a state. She'd nursed William at home until the end – but the sweet soul she was, said William was a splendid patient... Simon doubted that. William had fallen on his feet the day he met Emily –she didn't deserve him.

His 'twice over' brother-in-law Fred was looking old; he came up to Simon and slapped him on the back.

"How are you, Simon, old chap? How's Elise and Roberto? What kind of motor are you running these days?" He asked this, all in one breath and did not even wait to hear any answers, walking on to greet someone else.

"Simon, my little brother, how are you?" His big sis gave him a hug. Serena also wrote lengthy letters to Spain.

"Oh, Serena it's so good to see you 'in the flesh' again. I miss your hugs, but thanks for your letters – they mean a lot to us both."

Simon had not seen any of them for twelve years – nobody did foreign travel in his family. He would need to speak English for the next couple of days, while staying at The Gables. It was a happy family reunion but tinged with sadness, mostly because they were all so much older.

Surprisingly, the Methodist church was full – family respect, I guess, thought Simon. But in his eulogy the minister talked about a loving husband, a devoted father to his son and daughter-in-law and a loving grandad. Simon thought he was at the wrong funeral, and he gave Serena a nudge. The minister continued: "This dear man...a much-loved member of our congregation...a man with a pastoral heart....one of our sick visitors." He nudged Serena again.

"Stop it, I'll be black and blue," she admonished him, under her breath.

He whispered ... "Are we at the right funeral?"

Simon was perplexed. This was not the William he remembered. He just shook his head and queried 'can a leopard change its spots'?

In the cemetery, when the interment was over, Serena linked arms with Fred on one side and Simon on the other and led them along a few avenues until they were standing at Olivia's grave. No-one spoke, they were all silent in their own grief...a husband...a brother...a friend. She was a wife...a sister...a sister-in-law, to these three relatives.

Living in Spain permanently had certainly helped Simon – returning each year to The Spanish House reopened the wounds each time – taking a bath in the Spanish House was a nightmare... but he'd persevered. He looked up at the grey November skies and tried to fight back the tears, but they refused to be stemmed and trickled down his face. Again, he asked himself that question – how could I love two women so much? He could never compare them. They were both the 'love of his life' and it would never make sense, but then he was always English Simon and Spanish Simon. The threesome left the grave – Simon doubted he would ever return. He looked up as he wiped his eyes...Fred and Serena were doing the same.

After the refreshments, during the time when the solicitor summoned the immediate family into the dining room to read the will, Simon excused himself, to go for a walk. It was early afternoon, and the light would soon be fading on the chilling November day. He made his way down into the town, astonished at some of the changes, but he avoided the High Street – Felix was taking him to see the new store tomorrow on his way to the station. He meandered his way to Wood Lane and stood on the opposite side of the road to The Spanish House. Mature trees and hedges surrounded it, but otherwise it was the same – a few more coats of 'Snowcem' no doubt, and maybe a slightly darker shade of blue on the shutters. Simon could just make out a name plate on the gate. It said 'Blue Shutters' – good name, he thought.

He was distracted by the front door opening. A girl aged about twelve years old, with her hair pulled back in a pony-tail, came out shouting, "Trudie, Trudie, where are you?"

She opened the gate and looked up and down the road. She noticed him and he lifted his trilby hat in greeting but did not speak. Then a rotund, black and tan dachshund waddled around from the side of the house and came up to her.

Simon shook his head and said, "Well, I never!" as he experienced flashbacks of Fritz – their little dachshund. He turned to walk back to The Gables.

***

The following morning, after some very tearful farewells, the family left The Gables. Serena and Fred driving to York and Simon to catch a train from Newcastle to London then on to the airport. Simon begged all the family to come to Spain for a holiday – he doubted he would ever be back – but only Felix and family showed any interest.

Emily hugged Simon, tears streaming down her face. "Give my love to Elise and the family, Simon. I'll keep sending my 'epistles'."

Guilder's was in the same position on the High Street, but under the careful management of Felix it had been transformed into a modern clothing department store. The shops either side of the original shop had been purchased as they became vacant, and some interior work done to allow the buildings to become one large store.

The old mezzanine level now housed a 'ladies' hat department' and 'lingerie department'. Downstairs to the left was the Ladies' Fashion department, incorporating 'Serena's Fashions' --this was managed by Sarah, Felix's wife. To the right of the store was the Men's department, under the watchful eye of Barry who greeted Simon warmly, remembering the day when he had stepped in to work at Guilder's when Simon first went to Spain, forty years ago.

The ladies' shops – Serena's and Olivia's – had been sold to finance the department store. Serena handed over the baton and her share in the business to Sarah.

Simon was thrilled – a new store for a new generation and all under the banner of a more modern name ...Guilder's.

As Felix dropped his Uncle Simon at the station, he handed him a typewritten envelope.

"This is for you, Uncle Simon. The solicitor was very definite it was only to be opened when you left the country. There was a one for Aunt Serena also – only to be opened when she returned to York. The letters are from Father and were kept with his will."

Curious – thought Simon – how typical of William to have words from 'beyond the grave'. He put the letter in his jacket pocket and hugged his nephew.

"See you next summer in Spain, Felix," he shouted as he dashed to catch his train. "Thanks for the lift."

***

Having stored his bag, overcoat and hat in the overhead locker, Simon fastened his seat belt and sat back. Not long now until he saw his beloved Elise – three days away from her and he missed her so much. The plane took off and the pilot gave some flight information. A nice snooze, he thought and closed his eyes. Suddenly, he remembered the envelope Felix had given to him. He rummaged in his pocket and found it. He opened the envelope, wondering if Serena's letter was the same.

Dear Simon,

I write this knowing I will soon be leaving this earth to meet my maker. I have asked His forgiveness and I have made my peace with God. However, I cannot go until I have confessed to you, dear brother, and I beg for your forgiveness.

I resented you from the moment Mother brought you home. I 'suffered' you as a child...please forgive me.

I confess I resented your inheritance... I know not why, as I have always been blessed with ample finances... please forgive me.

I confess I defiled and raped your beautiful wife, one week before her tragic death, because I wanted what you had... PLEASE, PLEASE forgive me.

I have lived the last thirty years since her death, deeply regretting what I did to her, tending her grave as my penance.

I will never know if you choose to forgive me, but I pray that the God in whom I trust will give you the grace to forgive.

My confession is over, and I die in peace.

Your loving brother, William.

If the aeroplane had fallen from the sky at that moment, Simon would have understood, such was his grief, his pain for his Livvy. He put his head in his hands and entered a deep, dark tunnel of grief and remorse...the agony...the humiliation...the degradation she must have endured. She never gave a hint ...yes, she was unwell, but he had put it down to the pregnancy. That last telephone call she seemed so much better.

She would never have told him – she knew what he would do. But that would have been revenge.

Can I forgive him? At that moment... Simon did not think he could.

For the next two hours he sobbed; his face was red and swollen with the tears. At one point the man sitting next to him – a total stranger – placed a hand on his arm but said nothing. It seemed to reassure him that people do care and can sense another's pain.

Simon prayed for help.

Eventually, he lifted his head. He was still holding the letter. Who am I to withhold forgiveness? He asked himself. I have been greatly blessed in my sixty-two years. I have known the love of two wonderful women; the love of a father, mother, sister, son, grandchildren and wider family. I have been blessed with more financial resources than I could ever use.

He was at a crossroad and needed to make a choice – the path of unforgiveness and bitterness... or the path of forgiveness and peace of mind. He could never change what had happened, but he could change how to handle it.

He started to tear the letter into the smallest of pieces – each tear seemed to lift his pain. When they would go no smaller, he put them in the envelope and folded it over. The lights in the cabin were dimmed for landing, but strangely it seemed a lot brighter to Simon.

The aeroplane slowly descended into Madrid airport. He felt the thud as they hit the runway.

"Welcome to Madrid," said the pilot, "where the local time is 9pm. We trust you have enjoyed your flight and look forward to seeing you soon."

Simon retrieved his belongings and exited the plane. He entered the airport building, passing through the control desks, then he stopped at the first bin he saw, and took the envelope containing the torn letter from his pocket. As he dropped the envelope into the bin, he said out aloud, "Yes, William, I forgive you. Life is too short, too fragile, and too precious to carry unforgiveness."

Then, he put on his Crombie overcoat and his Trilby hat. Simon Guilder lifted his head, straightened his back, and walked boldly through the Arrivals Hall into the arms of his darling Elise.

***

LOFTAM

2019

Grace, finished reading the last page of her novel, put her book down on the coffee table and bent down to stroke her son's little dachshund. She shivered and spoke to the dog as if he understood.

"Oh Benson, I think this is the last time in the summerhouse for this year. I'll pack the cushions away today. One last stretch, then it'll be back to that 24 hours news I feel compelled to watch."

A sound drifted to her ears...it was 'Fur Elise' again. The pianist had certainly improved over the last few weeks. That tune had awakened her childhood memories and she'd enjoyed her reminiscences. As usual the tune took her back to the Spanish House - her childhood home, with its blue shutters and balconies - she had lived there for fifteen years. Benson was getting restless. She watched him hop over the step and off into the garden to explore and sniff.

Her mind drifted to her own tubby black and tan dachshund and a memory flashed through her mind.

She would be about twelve years old. She was calling for Trudie, her dog. She had gone to the gate to search for her. There was a very smart, older man dressed in a heavy overcoat and a Trilby hat, standing on the other side of the road staring at her. The man smiled and lifted his hat in greeting... such an old-fashioned gesture. Trudie appeared, sniffing around the lamp post, so she went back into the house.

But now Grace mused...

Perhaps he was the man who had built the Spanish House?

Perhaps he was the man whose wife had died in the bathroom, in Spanish House?

Perhaps he was the one who had hidden the little box she found in the summerhouse?

Grace's dad said it must have been a musical box and pointed to the hole where the winder used to fit. Grace sighed at the memory...

I wonder what tune it played before it was broken.

Somehow, she knew... it would have been 'Fur Elise' by Beethoven.

Acknowledgements

Memories spark the imagination... I wonder if?
I wonder why? I wonder who?

And so the recipe for the plot of Spanish
House Secrets began to take shape.

Many thanks to my husband for his longsuffering,
patience and support as I tackled my 'lockdown project'.

Also to Ruth for her cover painting. To the
dear friends and family members who read
the early drafts and gave their opinions – a big
'thank you'...all were much appreciated!

I am grateful to UK Book Publishing for
bringing this book to fruition.

BV - #0079 - 090323 - C0 - 198/129/19 - PB - 9781915338877 - Matt Lamination

Printed in Great Britain
by Amazon

42993586R00104